John—
thanks for
everything
Dave

HILLARY
& The Crash That Killed Me

HILLARY
& The Crash That Killed Me

A TRUE STORY BY ED FIKTUS
AS TOLD TO DAVE PUMPHREY

Copyright © 2022 by Ed Fiktus and Dave Pumphrey.

Library of Congress Control Number:	2022908324
ISBN: Hardcover	978-1-6698-2366-7
Softcover	978-1-6698-2365-0
eBook	978-1-6698-2364-3

All rights reserved. No part of this book may be reproduced or transmitted in any form or by any means, electronic or mechanical, including photocopying, recording, or by any information storage and retrieval system, without permission in writing from the copyright owner.

Any people depicted in stock imagery provided by Getty Images are models, and such images are being used for illustrative purposes only.
Certain stock imagery © Getty Images.

Print information available on the last page.

Rev. date: 05/10/2022

To order additional copies of this book, contact:
Xlibris
844-714-8691
www.Xlibris.com
Orders@Xlibris.com
836359

Dedication

This book is dedicated to all the hardworking men and women building, selling and applying machine tools to keep America at the forefront of manufacturing technology. Our time has passed. The future is yours. Keep up the good work.

Ed & Dave

Death is not an event in life: we do not live to experience death. If we take eternity to mean not infinite temporal duration but timelessness, then eternal life belongs to those who live in the present. Our life has no end in just the way in which our visual field has no limits.

—Ludwig Wittgenstein, Tractatus Logico-philosophicus

CONTENTS

Chapter 1   Death Does Not Come Quietly 1
It was a bad day . . . Just my luck, Hillary Clinton was there.

Chapter 2   I Feel Wonderful! 11
*Everything was strangely silent . . . the calm
after the storm, when even the air is different.*

Chapter 3   I Heard a Voice 19
"YOU CAN SURVIVE THIS IF YOU WANT TO."

Chapter 4   Klaus, Is That You? 29
He gave me the opportunity to lead the life I love. Now what?

Chapter 5   What Is That Voice? 37
Who is it? Where's it coming from?

Chapter 6   Going Nowhere Fast 47
Take it from me . . . you can slam into a brick wall . . . or a mountain.

Chapter 7   Am I Dreaming? 59
"YOU CAN SURVIVE THIS IS IF YOU WANT TO . . ." The voice was strong.

Chapter 8   Am I Dead, and Don't Know It? 75
But they were all dead. And I was there. What's going on? Am I dead?

Chapter 9   Our Business Was Ready to Take Off 91
Then Hillary Clinton showed up, and my life took a sharp left turn.

Chapter 10   I Think, and Then I Remember I Was Dead. 107
*But I didn't feel dead. I felt wonderful . . .
And who the heck was My Friend?*

Chapter 11   My Mom was an Angel. 113
My Mom . . . She died years ago. How could she be here with me?

Chapter 12 I'm Back 125
EEEEYYYYAAAAHHH! What the hell? Why do I hurt so much?

Chapter 13 The Burgundy Bed 141
*When I woke up, I was rocking back and forth . . . What the F**k?*

Chapter 14 Bye, Bye, Burgundy Bed 147
*She drove my van to the land with me in a
cast . . . Had no drugs; didn't think I could last.*

Chapter 15 The Stuff of Dreams... 155
*I had nightmares all the time. Really, really
vivid . . . I'm trapped in the darkness.*

Chapter 16 Home Sweet Home.. 163
My new reality. The reality I have to live . . . Not what I hoped it would be.

Chapter 17 Two Years in Hell 169
Misery. One word that can describe more than two years of my life.

Chapter 18 End of the Beginning... 179
There was a big storm brewing ahead . . .

Chapter 19 Dad Again. 185
Being a bedbound Dad was no way to live . . . It was the best I could do.

Chapter 20 Bye, Bye, Love. Hello, Happiness!...................... 195
I begged Nancy not to get a divorce. I didn't want a divorce.

Chapter 21 Hillary Makes a Comeback 201
*I told the FAA our plane crashed because we had to
use a different runway to make way for Hillary's big
jet. Then I tried applying for Social Security disability.*

Resources... 209

Photos and illustrations

Valley News, December 3, 1993, front page
SOCATA Trinidad, the type of plane that crashed (two pages)
FAA Inspector examining the crash
Ed's Dad's high school graduation photo
Ed's Mom in her wedding dress
Ed's Mom and Dad on a date
Ed's Mom and Dad years later
Ed's Dad getting off work
Ed's Mom with her new Maytag washer
Motch single spindle machine tool (vertical lathe)
Motch double spindle machine tool
Conomatic six spindle automatic lathe (horizontal)
Blanchard rotary surface grinder (vertical)
Rutland Herald (Vermont) December 4, 1993, front page
The Union Leader (Manchester, New Hampshire) December 4, 1993, front page
Diagram of fatal small plane crash, Valley News, December 4, 1993, front page
Ed's Mom and sister Lori with Santa
Ed and his new little sister, Lori
Ed takes Lori out trick or treating
Lori and Ed today
Spinal hardware removed from Ed's back

Chapter 1

Death Does Not Come Quietly

It was a bad day . . . shitty . . . overcast . . . sleety . . . snowy . . . cold . . . dark . . . Lebanon airport, New Hampshire at 5:00 pm on Thursday, December 2, 1993. Just my luck, Hillary Clinton was there . . .

After a full day of meetings, I was going to take my van and make the 12-hour drive back to Cleveland, but my boss, Klaus Eberius, talked me into taking a ride on the company plane—a fast little four-seater . . . a little over a four-hour trip. OK, I'd save eight hours. Why not?

The Lebanon airport was a small two-runway country airport designed primarily for small private planes. The runways were angled—from one, you would take off heading northeast; the other, you'd take off heading south southeast. There's not a lot of flat land in New Hampshire, and the airport looked like it was cut into the mountains next to the Connecticut River.

You can imagine the excitement when the First Lady's plane landed there. It dwarfed all the other planes. It was big. I thought it was a Boeing 737, but I found out later it was a Boeing C-40, the government version of the 737.

Anyway, the whole town and everywhere around was abuzz. Hillary Clinton flew into the Lebanon airport that day to visit Dartmouth College and the Dartmouth-Hitchcock Medical Center in Hanover,

New Hampshire, about five miles from the airport. She was there to promote the Clinton administration's healthcare reform bill. She made front-page news. Unfortunately, so did we.

At the end of the day, we all wanted to leave Lebanon at the same time. Obviously, her plane had to go first. Except we were already on the way when we were told to get out of her way. What? We were actually on the taxiway, ready to go! We had to turn around and go to a different runway. She had to take off from the main runway—the one we always used—because it was the longest runway they had. The extra few hundred feet were needed for that big plane of hers to take off. That made sense. But if we were going after her, anyway, why did we have to use a different runway? That made no sense.

Anyway, we got delayed and had to change runways to get out of her way. That was more complicated than you might imagine.

Klaus, who was 53, had been flying for about three years, but he always had Harry with him. Harry Frankford was Klaus's friend, flight instructor, and copilot. Our plane was a fast, little low wing speedster with a back seat—a French-made turbocharged SOCATA Trinidad TB-21. This little blue and white beauty had 250 horsepower, 25% more powerful than the standard model and the latest avionics on board. Programming the navigation was complicated—it was 1993—the Stone Age compared to now. Today's phones are way easier to use—and way more powerful—than that plane's computer. Yet it was state of the art back then.

Harry was 70 and retired. He would fly Klaus up to Lebanon from Cleveland, take the plane back to Cleveland, then come back to take

Klaus home. Harry dropped Klaus off on November 21st, and was back on this day, December 2nd, to take him home.

Klaus and I worked for a company in Windsor, Vermont, Cone-Blanchard Machine. Klaus was the CEO, and I was his right-hand man, Ed Fiktus, executive VP. Being a VP sounds good, but my real job was selling machines to keep the company's doors open and our employees paid. The Cleveland to Vermont connection is a little complicated. Both of us came from Motch Corp. in Cleveland, but from different directions. I started out as a part-time draftsman—a contract employee—and Klaus started as senior vice president.

Motch was the manufacturing arm of Motch & Merryweather, a major machine tool distributor based in Clevleand. The company started in 1904 when Stanley and Edwin Motch teamed up with George Merryweather. Over the years, Motch grew from six employees to nearly 1,500, becoming a manufacturer of specialized machines and one of the nation's largest machine tool distributors, doing more than $200 million a year in sales.

During the Depression, Motch, as a distributor, was owed money by several machine tool companies who could not afford to pay. To settle the debt, Motch took over the product lines. That's how they acquired Conomatic multispindle screw machines and Blanchard rotary surface grinders, which they consolidated into Cone-Blanchard Machine in Windsor, Vermont. Both were famous names in their day. Motch also picked up Springfield Grinders the same way. All of our machines were used to make various parts for cars, construction, and mining equipment, trucks, railroad machinery, oil drilling, and aerospace. Caterpillar, John Deere, GE, Hughes Tool, and Ford were customers, to name a few.

The idea was to become a dominant force in machine tools. We were a company on the move. Back in 1968, Motch & Merryweather became publicly owned. Basically, that move poked Motch's head up on the international machine tool market.

Many, if not most, U.S. machine tool companies were family businesses, started out by genius problem-solving engineers and continued on as best they could. The challenge was keeping them going after the original spark faded.

With rapidly changing technologies and the introduction of computer-controlled machines, the 70s became a time of mergers and acquisitions. A bigger company was a stronger company. In Motch's 75th year, 1979, Eddie Motch, the third-generation head of the company, got an offer he couldn't refuse.

Oerlikon-Buehrle, a Swiss conglomerate, saw Motch's rapid growth and wanted a piece of the action. Oerlikon, which was famous for making antiaircraft guns in World War 2, bought Motch to get access to North American customers for their European-made machine tools. The 50+ American manufacturers Motch & Merryweather represented in distribution recoiled at the conflict of interest and tried to get out as fast as they could. While we were losing American lines we could sell, nobody was buying the European machines we were trying to sell.

After about 10 years, Oerlikon gave up and sold what was left of Motch (the distributor side closed which left the machine tool building side with about $20 million a year in sales) to Pittler, a German maker of vertical turning machines; a direct competitor of Motch. They thought they could take all of Motch's customers and replace Motch machines with Pittlers to gain a profitable foothold in the U.S. Pittler didn't want Cone-Blanchard, so Oerlikon spun the company off, giving Klaus ownership control. He was then CEO of both Motch and Cone-Blanchard.

In the meantime, I worked my way up to becoming a full-time employee. I was outspoken in engineering. I had ideas—big rock-the-boat ideas—so they wanted to give me more opportunity, and get me out of engineering. This included moving me to marketing, then sales. I liked selling Motch machines. I was good at it, and I became the top salesman in the company—I had the gift of gab. I wasn't going to sell Pittler machines because I didn't believe in them—there were just too many problems. It was a lot easier to sell Motch.

All the deals I brought in during the first couple years under Pittler were for Motch machines, which kept the doors open for Klaus but drove Pittler crazy. The last big deal I did kept the doors open for a year but ended my career at Motch. Because Klaus let me sell the Motch machines, he was on the way out too. During his transition to full-time at Cone, he asked me to take over for him and run the place. That's the short version of the Cleveland to Vermont to Lebanon airport connection.

Our meeting at Cone that day was to set new ground rules and pave the way for new opportunities, which involved taking the Motch line off Pittler's hands and making the Motch machines at the Cone plant in Windsor, Vermont, across the river from the Lebanon airport. Wrapping up that part of the deal was why we had to get back to Cleveland. We were going to get the Motch machine blueprints and the rights to build them. Besides, it was December—holiday season.

In getting ready for the flight home, Klaus and Harry were used to doing the same thing the same way for years. Now, all of a sudden, because Hillary's plane was using our regular runway, they had to create different programming so we could take off safely from a runway heading in a different direction. Klaus was the pilot, so he sat in the driver's seat, with Harry next to him.

We were next in line after the First Lady, so the pressure was on to get the new programming done as soon as possible. Each waypoint on the flight path had to be entered separately. There was a lot of confusion, arguing, and even some hand slapping back and forth while they tried to get the new program put in the flight computer. After about 15 or 20 minutes, they thought they had it figured out.

Then we got clearance to take off. I was sitting in the back seat, behind Harry. Klaus had the flight manual stuffed behind his seat, so there was no room there for my 42-year-old, six-foot-four frame. Getting in the back seat through the plane's fashionable gull-wing doors required a level of flexibility I no longer have. Klaus and I were still in our business suits, and Harry was casual. The plane had a sort of a bubble top which made the cockpit a little roomier than most. I had a really nice winter overcoat, and I took that and my suit coat off to give me even more elbow room in the back.

SOCATA Trinidad similar to the plane that crashed, with me in the back seat.

As a student pilot myself, Harry's student, I had my headphones plugged in. When we usually take off, we would see the lights of Lebanon and turn left and head over the river.

We took off, retracted the landing gear, and Klaus, maybe still feeling rushed, asked Harry if he should engage the autopilot shortly after we were airborne. Harry said "Sure," putting the earlier conflict behind him. We were in the air probably less than a minute. We might have been up just a couple hundred feet or so.

When taking off from Lebanon, planes were supposed to reach 1,500 feet before making any turns to make sure they were in the clear. That was in the airport flight manual. As soon as Klaus put the plane on auto, he and Harry both leaned back in their seats, crossed their arms, and let the plane fly itself.

There were no city lights below us as there usually were, yet the autopilot had us turn left way too sharply. We turned too soon, too low, and too far. We were heading for trouble and didn't know it. We went the wrong way, but it was so dark out we couldn't tell.

It was pitch-black. No moon or stars to guide us. No ground lights for reference. We were flying blind. We had no clue as to what lay ahead. And we were still climbing.

My headphones crackled. The control tower radioed, "Do you see that hill?" Klaus said, "Say again?"

We didn't see that hill. We couldn't see it. It was so dark. A second later . . . clop, clop, clop . . . treetops hitting the belly of the plane. No time to react. The wings! The trees grabbed hold. *BAM! BAM! BAM!*

This poor airplane screamed in agony. You have never heard nor have I ever heard or ever want to hear again . . . the sound of that airplane being hammered by tree after tree . . . a 150-mile-an-hour rapid-fire beating.

You could hear the wings being ripped off. Everything shattered. The metal actually shrieked bloody murder. It was an incredible noise. That's what I remember most . . . I'm sure there were other noises, too, because all the plexiglass, all the glass just disintegrated. Everything just blew out.

But what I remember the most was hearing the spars and the wings. The metal just . . . it actually screamed like a woman. Incredible noise. Deafening. I don't even remember hearing the engine or anything like that. I remember hearing the airplane wailing—terrifying, awful.

The trees tore her open, clawed through her skin, crushed her bones, ripped her wings apart, and skinned her alive. The plane howled as it was shredded. Thunderous screeching. A horrible slaughter.

I was tossed around like a rag doll—up, down, sideways—so hard, I actually yanked the seat belt anchors right out of the plane's floor. My ribs snapped, my chest caved, my guts . . . *oh God, make it stop!* A voice boomed from the chaos, "*YOU CAN SURVIVE THIS IF YOU WANT TO!*"

Huh? I pissed and shit my pants. I was slammed senseless. Everything just blew out. What I remember most was the plane's screams, metal screaming—just screaming—as she was hacked to pieces. Louder and louder, she screamed. The brutal beatdown ended as she collapsed, twisted, to the forest floor; a crumpled, horribly disfigured wreck.

Then, silence. Dead silence. *Damn!*

A safety inspector with the Federal Aviation Administration examines the crash site. Valley News, photo by Geoff Hansen.

Hillary and Ed made the front page of the Valley News.

Chapter 2

I Feel Wonderful!

Everything was strangely silent. It was like the calm after the storm when even the air is different. Quiet. Peaceful. Wonderful. Klaus and Harry seemed miles away. A different world. I had no idea where I was. All I knew was that I felt great. No pain. Complete peace.

Where was I? And how in God's name did I get here?

This was supposed to be a night of celebration. Klaus and I were on the brink of closing the biggest deal of our lives, making me a part owner of Cone, and putting me in line to own a controlling interest in the company down the road. What an opportunity!

Pretty good for a guy who was first hired as a "rent-a-pencil" through an employment agency. My humble beginnings in the machine tool business carried on a family tradition—my Dad, Ed Fiktus Sr., had more than 40 years in at Warner & Swasey, the nation's second largest machine tool builder at the time.

At first, I think my entry into this "family business" was a bit of a disappointment to him. He wanted me to be a doctor. When I got my first job as a contract draftsman, I was a college dropout with no discernable future. He paid for my good times at Ohio State until enough was enough.

If you look at my family, I come from parents whose backgrounds and ideas were nothing alike. That's not a bad thing; it was actually a good thing, I think.

Both sets of my grandparents came from an area in Europe that's now Poland. Back then it was part Germany, part Russia, and part Austria. There was really no Poland when they came here. Both my Mom's and Dad's parents came here in the early 1900s. Most of my relatives are Austrian German—typical Aryan people.

My Dad was . . . hard to say exactly. I think the family background was Krakow, in Poland. At one time that was Austria; at one time that was Germany. My Dad had strawberry blond hair and blue eyes. I don't mean normal blue eyes. I mean *ice blue* eyes—the kind that glow in the dark. A lot of people have blue eyes, but these were ice blue eyes. Everybody in my family on my father's side had these blue eyes that almost light up at night.

My father's family was basically what you would call autocratic. In other words, they believed in discipline, almost like the military. My father was a disciplinarian. He believed in education, and he had our futures planned out almost from the day we were born.

My Mom's family was Lithuanian, and she was dark—black hair, deep brown eyes, olive skin. She had a ready smile, a quick laugh, a real people person. She was a true joy to be around. Everybody in both families spoke Polish, so that became the common language. Although my Dad, his mom, Julia (we called her Bobcia—bob-cha—Polish for grandma), and other people on his side of the family spoke German too.

My Mom was a very beautiful woman—movie star beautiful. If you saw a picture of her when she was young, you'd swear it was Loretta Young.

My Mom's family was the complete opposite of my Dad's. They were galoots—heavy drinkers and borderline criminals; rough undisciplined people. My Mom had a free-spirited personality. She never met a person she didn't like. So I had a straitlaced, stiff-backed father, and a very gregarious, widely loved and admired mother.

My Mom was a charmer. She was able to get away with anything and everything. She wrapped my Dad around her little finger. It was fun to watch him give in. Like when it was time to buy a color TV, my Dad said, "No we don't need it. It's too expensive." And she said, "I'm going to the store to buy a color TV, do you want to come?" And he would go along to make sure she didn't spend too much money.

I inherited my mother's hair, my mother's skin, and my mother's eyes. I am the only one in my family with cow eyes—big, brown cow eyes. In the summer when I go sailing, I would get really tanned—very dark, so dark my daughter, Taylor, used to always tell her friends, "My dad is black." Because I'd get mahogany colored, like my Mom.

I thought I got gypped. I wish I had blue eyes. I didn't care about the blond hair because I still have my hair. Everybody else on my father's side lost their blond hair.

So growing up there was always this internal battle. My personality is definitely from my Mom. My intelligence and ability to learn or do something is from my Dad. So I've got a combination of the two—the best of both worlds.

I inherited my Mom's outgoing personality, her friendliness, and her ability to talk to anybody. My mother could talk to a bum and have a nice conversation, where my father would just walk right by him and not give him the time of day. My Mom would always get something out of that conversation. She wasn't judgmental, where my father was very judgmental.

If you didn't dress right, if you didn't speak right, if you didn't do well in school, you were a terrible person. Where my Mom was like "Eh, you'll live just as long, and you'll be just as happy." So that's kind of how I grew up.

My Dad was our family's commander-in-chief—stiff-backed, detached, disciplined, unrelenting (except to my Mom), but with a strategic plan for the whole family. My older sister was going to be a teacher, I was going to be a doctor, and my little brother was going to be a lawyer.

Well, my older sister did become a teacher. My brother did become a lawyer. They became very straight and narrow people, in my opinion. I could never accept it. I couldn't be a doctor. It just wasn't for me. So I became me, for what it's worth.

I have my Mom to thank for that.

My Mom and my Dad, I couldn't imagine two more diametrically opposed people on the planet. They were that different. Mom was happy and outgoing, and Dad was stern, unmoving.

So these two people from completely different families and backgrounds got together to build a new family.

Because both sides of my family spoke Polish, we were brought up believing we were Polish Americans, with Polish traditions and customs, and a love of German beer. Nothing wrong with that. It was our American melting pot.

My Mom was great. I was her firstborn son, and her happiness with me was infectious. She used to sing to me when I was little. "You are my sunshine, my only sunshine. You make me happy when skies are gray." She called me Sonny, and it's stuck to this day. Now I'm known as Captain Sonny on my boat.

On the other hand, my Dad wasn't so expressive. He kept to himself. At 17, he started as an apprentice at Warner & Swasey, a huge Cleveland-based machine tool company that had acres and acres of factories right in Cleveland at East 55th and Carnegie. His career was interrupted by World War Two. He came back from the war in the Pacific to complete 45 years at Swasey, rising to Manager of Quality Control.

Swasey also made Gradall construction equipment and textile machinery. They were famous for their telescopes and instruments. Swasey is still regarded as one of the most important companies in U.S. history. Their slogan was "Precision Machinery since 1880." Their ads ran everywhere and were the talk of the industry. My Dad was proud to work for them.

He was precise, meticulous, and very mechanically oriented. He wasn't as much fun as my Mom, but he taught me to dig into things and really try to figure out how something was put together and how it worked.

I became very independent. Being the middle child—my older sister and younger brother were doing what my Dad wanted them to do—my Dad kind of ignored me. So I got to do all kinds of stuff. I ran around as a little kid—going to the library and reading everything I could read, reading adult-level books—religion, history, all kinds of stuff. In the summertime, I'd leave the house at eight in the morning and not come back till seven at night.

I got interested in engineering because of model airplanes. That's one thing my Dad did when he was younger, he built model airplanes and got me hooked on it. I started building them when I was eight years old. I got the first one to fly when I was in the second grade. I actually finished it. A rubber band-powered airplane that flew!

My Dad was a real crazy guy. He would let me work with all these smelly glues and dope and stuff like that—balsa wood kits where you cut out the parts, glue them together, stretch tissue paper over the wings and body, then coat it with dope. I used Gillette blue blades—two sided blades, extremely sharp, no holder. An eight-year-old kid . . . can you imagine that? I would cut out all those parts, and my Dad didn't see anything wrong with that. But I couldn't have a two-wheel bicycle. Too dangerous.

I'm a real fanatic about model airplanes. It's what got me into engineering. I learned more about math. I learned more about engineering by reading airplane plans and building these kit models. As we became more experienced and I got older, we got into the gas motors, then we got into control line planes—the planes attached to a string flying in circles—then we got into radio control. We kept moving up. We read every issue of *Radio Controlled Modeling* magazine. Our hobby became a passion. As we got deeper into it, the capabilities of model airplanes just got better and better. Then came proportional radio controls. That's when flying a model plane became just like flying a real airplane. You had to be really careful you didn't crash.

My Dad, Ed Sr.

My Mom, Cecelia

Mom & Dad on a date.

Mom & Dad married for life.

Dad happy to be heading home. Mom was proud of her Maytag.

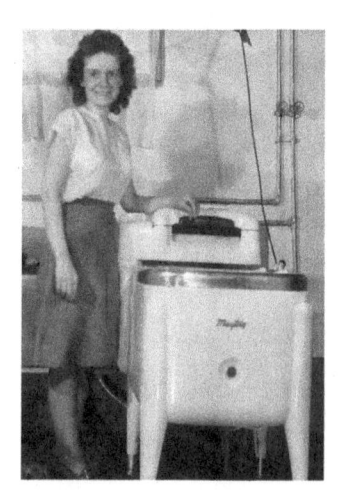

Chapter 3

I Heard a Voice . . .

The instrument panel was glowing, the turn indicator was flashing. The gyroscope was humming. Klaus and Harry were quiet. And I heard a voice inside me: "YOU CAN SURVIVE THIS IF YOU WANT TO."

But I DID NOT SURVIVE premed at Ohio State. I was a straight A student in grade school. I always won tickets to the Cleveland Indians games. The library was my second home. I'm still an avid reader, though my eyes aren't so good anymore. I did OK in high school. But Ohio State? Nah! I graduated high school in '69 and should have graduated Ohio State in '73. Never made it.

I developed all sorts of interests but had no idea of what I wanted to do with them. I only went to college because my Dad wanted me to. He wanted me to be a doctor. When I went to Ohio State, I was in premed. I was going to be a botany major. That was one of the preferred degrees for premed student. It was either that or biology. I thought botany was better because I could get a job as a botany major. I worked at the Botany & Zoology building—the B & Z at Ohio State. That gave me some money.

I worked in the greenhouses watering, fertilizing, and potting the plants a couple of hours a day. In the morning I would open the vents, and at night I would close the vents—control the temperature of the greenhouse—doing stuff like that.

Then I learned how to clone orchids. I amazed myself. A plant grows two ways—it grows up and it grows out. There's a tip called apical meristem where all the cells are dividing and growing up. The lateral meristem allows the plant to grow wider.

To clone an orchid, you chop up the apical meristem into tiny little pieces and put them into a growing medium called agar, a sugary, gelatin-like substance. This is all done under sterile conditions; you can't have bacteria growing in the agar.

If conditions are right, the apical meristem starts growing. Each piece grows an individual plant—an exact clone of the original. All you need is a couple cells of the apical meristem, and you would have the exact same orchid or plant that you started with without going through a seed. When you go through a seed, then you go through genetic variables that plant has and you don't end up with the same plant. With cloning, you have an exact replica—virtually the same plant.

You see, I can be a real nerd. I can become extremely focused and dedicated when something interests me. But becoming a doctor did not interest me. I had a great fear of blood and cutting somebody open. Not for me.

To be honest with you, I blew off college. I never really finished there. I started bouncing around. My grades fell. I was partying all the time. I came from an environment where you couldn't party, so I did it while I had the chance. I had a part-time job and had the money. A beer was about 40 cents. You could have a hell of a good time on a five-dollar bill.

My Dad really got pissed at the whole situation—his money going down the drain, and me not ever having a chance of becoming a doctor. Not on the path I was on, anyway. He didn't see me making any sort of progress toward a career. He said, "That's it! Come on home . . . *Now!*" It was 1971, two years short of graduation. At the tender age of 20, I was a failure.

I came home. Now I had to do something to pay my way. Because I took mechanical drawing in high school and had enough mechanical background with model plane building to get a job—back then there were no computers—I became a draftsman—mechanical drawing, something I picked up in shop class. I was really good at that.

Back in the '70s there were jobs everywhere. You got the Plain Dealer on Sunday, and you got a job on Monday. Quit on Friday and get another one on Monday. It was easy to get a job as a draftsman. My first job was designing power stations. I had enough theory of metals, and I had my math—I could do calculations. Designing power stations and transmission towers was real simple stuff—civil engineering.

If you drive by and see a bunch of transformers, it's a power substation. It's just a bunch of structural steel to support these transformers. All you had to do is figure out the loads on the beams and select the right ones for the job. Easy.

Part of the job was to design power transmission towers too. Why you had to design more than one, I'll never know. But every time somebody ordered one, you had to sit down and draw it. Why they couldn't pull one out of the archives and use it, I don't know. That was the most boring job. I couldn't stand it.

My supervisor really liked me because he said, "You didn't make any mistakes."

Some of these towers had hundreds of pieces. He marveled I could get through one of these things without making any mistakes. That didn't last long. I hated it.

After being a power station designer, I went to United Manufacturing. They made axles and running gear for mobile compressor trailers used in construction. It was during the Vietnam War then, and we made a lot of trailers for the Navy to carry the bombs and wheel them out to load the planes on an aircraft carrier. That was an OK job. At least, it wasn't a pain like the last one. One of my bosses was the treasurer of the Cleveland Yacht Club. He took me sailing all the time. When I was at Ohio State, I used to sail on the Olentangy River.

Then I went to CE Cast—Combustion Engineering which made foundry equipment. CE was a supplier to Kama River truck plant in Russia which began operating in 1976. This was the largest truck plant in the world, covering 22 square miles. CE Cast had the contracts for the foundry. My job was to design the shakers for sand casting.

Then the guys who were running the place got indicted by the FBI for selling production drawings to the Russians. After that, CE Cast just folded up and went away.

When that disappeared, I became a rent-a-pencil at an employment agency. I got sent to Motch & Merryweather, a machine tool company, as a resident rent-a-pencil. That means I was under contract, not an employee, but I made good money. And it was steady work.

In 1973, Motch was a big deal. The whole machine tool industry was. Working at Motch was not only me getting into the same business as my Dad, but the machine tool business was, and still is, one of the most important industries in the country. It's the basic industry that serves as the foundation of all manufacturing. Think about it. Anything that is manufactured, anything that is farmed, and anything that is dug out of the ground depends on machine tools to make the parts and build the equipment that makes all that possible. Let's take Motch whose machines were used to make automotive and farm equipment parts. Motch didn't make cars or farm equipment, but they made the machines that made better parts for cars and farm equipment more efficiently.

My job—my Dad's job—was to help our customers make better parts faster. That created opportunity all up and down the line. I had an opportunity to become a member of the big boys' club. Motch was a big deal—more than 150,000 square feet of engineering and manufacturing on nearly 10 acres. Hundreds of employees. *Boom!*

The first thing Motch gave me to design was a column riser that increased the height of the column so a customer could machine a taller part.

Motch machines were pretty simple. Motch made a line of vertical chuckers—basically a lathe turned up on its end. Let's compare making a metal part on a Motch to making a clay pot. Imagine a pottery wheel, spinning around, and the potter molds the clay with his hands. A Motch machine spins metal instead of clay. A hexagon shaped turret with six tools (instead of five fingers) moves up and down and to the side to cut the metal into a part. The column riser I was assigned was just a three-inch piece of cast iron with holes through it where it was bolted to the base. No big deal. Except I made it one.

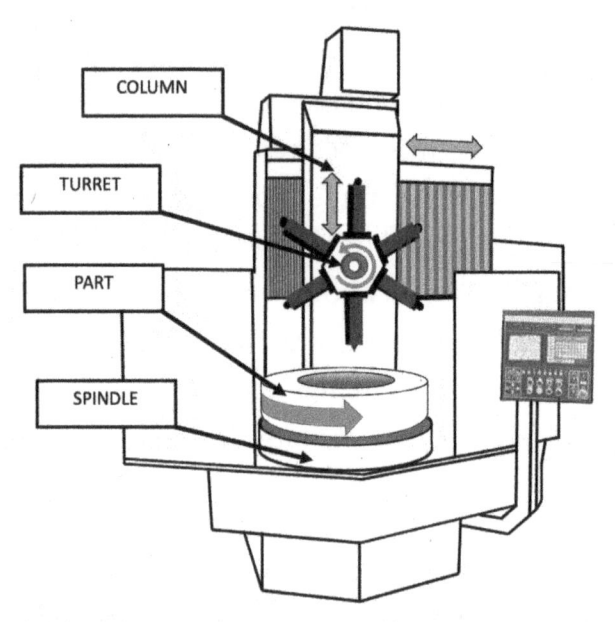

MOTCH Single Spindle VNC: The turret moves up and down on the column for part height and to the right for part width. The tools mounted on the turret can perform a variety of operations—facing, ID or OD chamfering, threading, turning, contouring ... whatever the application requires.

I whipped out the riser drawing in about 20 minutes. The part specification required the microfinish had to be 60 rms, which is very, very smooth (rms is a measure of smoothness; the lower the number the smoother the finish). The problem with cast iron is that it is porous, and it's recommended not to finish it below 125 rms. I took it upon myself to change the spec to 125 rms.

My supervisor, Eddie Smith, came over and said the spec had to be 60 rms. I said he'll waste a lot of money; some guy is going to have to make four or five before he gets one to 60 rms. So he takes it to Pete Forrester, the chief engineer, and Pete says, "Yeah, he's right. It should be 125 rms."

Then I sat down with Eddie Smith and told him, "You're a nice guy and this is a nice place, but if this is all you got for me to do, you're wasting your money. You're spending a lot of money to have me here and doing a column riser from a flat cast iron plate is not really a hot job."

He said, "Yeah, yeah, yeah, OK." I must have made an impression because they started giving me harder jobs—spindles and castings to design. I got pretty good at castings. And I was pretty good with rotating parts. I was hooked. I got more and more and more involved.

Then they came to me one day and said, "We like you and we'd like you to stay, but . . ." There was still some kind of contract where I had to stay there a year or so under the rent-a-pencil agreement before I could become a Motch employee. Otherwise, Motch would have to pay a finder's fee. But I was there. I stayed so one day I could become a real live Motch man.

Pete Forrester liked me for some reason, but he was a really gruff guy. And Eddie Smith was even worse. They used to walk around the department and say, "I want to see asses and elbows. I don't want to see you guys looking up, talking, or anything else." And we'd bend over the tables and keep our heads down.

Because in their mind I had the right stuff, they put me in this program; a kind of unofficial program where they would take the younger kids and move them along at a faster pace. Mind you, these Motch engineers were tough guys—Peter Forrester used to sketch out machine concepts on one-eighth inch grid paper. Who does that?

Then he'd expect me to come up with a real workable drawing. I'd be staring at this grid paper where one-eighth inch was a foot. I'd get my triangle out, trying to convert the measurements, and he says, "What's the matter? Can't you read the scale?" That's how these guys worked. I say, "OK. OK, no problem."

So then when my rent-a-pencil contract was up after a year, I became a Motch employee in '74. I didn't even know about it; they never told me I was official. They kept giving me more and more assignments probably because I was always on time. I stayed late. I liked it. I enjoyed it. They could see that, and took advantage.

That's how I ended up in the machine tool business designing, building, and selling machines that made parts—wheels, brake drums, construction machinery parts; big machines. But even though all the machines were built to the same specs, each one seemed to have its own personality. My experience at Motch just fit in with my life philosophy—everything is its own thing. Unique. With a personality . . . alive.

I loved the machines and going out on the shop floor to see them being built. They let me fiddle around with the machines. They would let me talk to the machinists and assemblers—why doesn't this fit? You learn an awful lot from those guys.

The personnel manager—he must have been reading a book—told the supervisors they have to interview all their guys and see what their goals are. Eddie called me into his office and said, "What are your goals? What do you want to be?" And I said, "Do you really want to know the truth?" And he said, "Yeah." I've never been one to mince my words. I'm always kind of off the wall, so I told him, "I want to be president of the company. Why not? I like the place, you know." He goes, "I can't write that down. I can't." I said, "Write it down. That's OK, I'll do something else if it doesn't work out."

He must have written it down because they started moving me to all these different areas—I went out to the shop for a while, I worked with the assembly guys, and I worked with the machinists. This was the beginning of the end for manual machine operators. The 1970s marked the beginning of wide-spread use of computer-controlled machine tools. The times were changing.

I knew Allen Bradley controls. Through Klaus, I got to know the president of Allen Bradley pretty well, and we used a lot of Allen Bradley controls, so I went there and I learned computer codes. Because I spent time on the shop floor and I knew the machines and designed the machines, they put me in charge of the maintenance school for customers.

I taught the basic elements of computer programming—how to start the machine, how to set the zeroes, codes for spindle speeds, traverse rates, feed rates—mostly related to maintaining the machine. My head computer guy would handle the hard stuff—how to write part making programs. The two of us would teach customers. So I knew how to maintain the machines, I knew how to design the machines, I knew how to build the machines, I knew how to operate the machines, and I knew a little bit about programming the machines. I was hot stuff. Next stop was with John Mylonas to learn tooling and applications for quoting machines.

When I first joined Motch, I told them I wanted to become president of the company. Well, to their credit, they were giving me the

Grand Tour. After about seven or eight years of working in every engineering and production department, Motch decided I should go into marketing and learn that part of the business. I was put on temporary assignment to help marketing get things ready for the big machine tool show coming up in '82. Because I was the newbie, I got all the crappy assignments with none of the benefits.

Chapter 4

Klaus, Is That You?

Klaus wasn't moving. Neither was Harry. I thought I heard Klaus call out. I hope he's OK. He gave me the opportunity to lead the life I love. Now what?

Klaus Eberius was just 53 when he died, about 10 years older than me. But he was in his early 40s when I first met him—his first day on the job at Motch in 1982.

That morning I was in the marketing department. Motch decided before I could go out and sell machines I had to spend time in marketing. So there I was, working for Mike Gendron with our offices just off the lobby. Oerlikon bought us in '79, but the big push on the American market was going to be at the 1982 International Machine Tool Show (IMTS). The show was held every two years and drew about 100,000 attendees. We were going to show up in a big way as Oerlikon Motch, showing a dozen machines with the latest technology—a much greater presence than Motch & Merryweather ever had. A show of strength.

IMTS was so big it overflowed McCormick Place in Chicago. You had to reserve booth space a year or two in advance. For the 1982 show, the Oerlikon Motch booth was 12.000 square feet, second in size only to Warner & Swasey.

This show was so important to Oerlikon they ran four-page ad inserts in the leading trade magazines—their biggest spending ever.

The inserts were printed on heavier paper so the magazines would open right to their ad. The Oerlikon managing director, Dr. Rentz, flew in from Switzerland to hold a press conference in front of 35 editors. Each editor was given a gold-plated business card holder engraved with their initials and containing the business cards of key Motch contacts.

After the press conference, a 110-foot excursion boat pulled up to the McCormick Place dock, and the editors boarded for a three-hour cruise on Lake Michigan with great food, drinks, and a band playing on the bow of the boat. First class all the way. I heard it was a beautiful night and a great time. Too bad I wasn't invited.

I didn't get to go to the show itself, either. I wasn't a real sales guy. My job was to get the product literature—the line cards—up to speed. Doing the line cards required a lot of communication. I called around to the various distributor offices to get details on the stuff they sold. Motch was different from other machine tool companies; we had both manufacturing and distribution. For this project, the distributors were like my clients, so I had to keep them happy, and I had to keep my boss happy.

I worked on the line cards with our advertising agency, Pumphrey Marketing. Gendron hired them for random projects in '80–'81, then hired them full-time for the big push in '82. I brought them along with me to Cone-Blanchard after I left Motch, and they ended up working with Motch for almost 20 years.

I hated doing the line cards. The most memorable part of that project was the after-hours rubber band fights, crawling along floors and ducking behind desks. The Pumphrey people thought

I cheated because I'd put together 20 or 30 rubber bands, making my weapons thicker, longer, and heavier hitting. It was three against one, but they gave up after a couple solid hits.

The distributor line cards included a lot of machines, tools, and equipment that did not compete with Motch. I got to know these field guys pretty well—by phone, anyway—the managers, the secretaries, and some of the sales guys. When we went to IMTS, the first time I went was for the big 1982 show. I was on the setup crew installing the machines, working with the union guys at McCormick Place in Chicago, programming the machines, and doing a runout. I didn't get to stick around for the show itself.

Klaus was born in the Harz Mountain region of Germany in 1940. How he came to Motch is a bit of a trip. He came to the states in 1972 as a well-connected manufacturing engineer working his way up to manager of the metal cutting division of Upton, Bradeen, and James in the Detroit area.

1982 was the year Klaus came on board at Motch. Before that, Klaus was the president of Uni-Sig which was headquartered in the Chicago area. Uni-Sig was a consortium of five Swiss and German machine tool builders. The SIG in Uni-Sig stood for Swiss Industrial Group. Oerlikon had an interest in Uni-Sig. Oerlikon wanted Klaus to work for Motch.

He had been in the U.S. for about 10 years and had proven his abilities. He was well known and well liked in the U.S. machine tool industry. He was the perfect candidate to serve as Oerlikon's man in Motch. e was well known and well liked jjjjjjjjjjjjjThat was already probably in their plans for a while. An inside man; somebody they could count on. But having Klaus on board was potentially good for Motch too. Klaus was friends with a member of Oerlikon's board of directors. His concerns, Motch's concerns, could be heard on high.

When Klaus started at Motch, I was the first guy to meet and greet him. I'd get in around seven in the morning. I was working in the marketing department, whose offices were right off the lobby, with the coffee room down the hall. I was just going to make a pot of coffee when this guy wandered in, looking a little disheveled. He was mostly bald on top, maybe a little fuzz, short close-cropped dark brown hair on the sides, standing about five foot nine, with flashing, squinty brown eyes, and a ready smile that was full of energy. He looked mischievous, sly but in a friendly, disarming way. Quick. Clever. Catlike.

You could tell at a glance he had something up his sleeve, and always would. He played chess while everybody else was playing checkers. Always a step ahead. I introduced myself, and he said he was going to start work that day. I asked him if he wanted a cup of coffee, and he said, "Sure." Was that a German accent?

We sat around and talked for a while, and he told me he needed a tie and a belt; he was going to be in some sort of meeting upstairs. I fixed him up with a show tie—a brown and orange tie, the official Oerlikon colors. We had the ties made up for IMTS so our sales guys would look sharp on the floor and be easily recognized by showgoers. I don't know what he did for a belt. Anyway, that's how Klaus and I got started.

Turns out, he came on board as senior vice president with a very short path to the presidency. Who knew? Oerlikon needed somebody to sell their machines. Motch guys weren't going to do it; they were set in their ways. And you couldn't rely on the distributors who saw Oerlikon machines as competitors to their established lines.

With my background in engineering, tooling, machining, assembly, programming, and distributor support, Klaus tapped me to sell the Oerlikon machines. I was only supposed to sell Oerlikon machines and Boehringer lathes—I sold something out of all the Oerlikon product lines, more Boehringers than anything else. I went to Switzerland and Germany for training, then started selling in '83. The goal was to build Motch into a full-range machine tool company.

Oerlikon was a Swiss-based conglomerate. In addition to European machine tool companies, they owned Bally Shoes and hotels too. Their great plan was to buy Motch for our distributor division. That would give them a ready-made network to sell their machines in the U.S. Ultimately, it didn't work out. Our largest line, Giddings & Lewis, dropped us like a hot potato because now we offered competing machines.

The problem was these European machines were different. They weren't readily accepted by the marketplace; they were all metric. U.S. products were based on the inch system, so metric machines didn't really fit the needs of the marketplace. Trying to force metric machines through our distributor division was the beginning of the end. For both sides.

When sales of Oerlikon machines didn't meet expectations and Oerlikon was getting ready to quit the market, I was asked to sell Motch machines. I said OK. I didn't really have a choice if I wanted to keep my job. They took away all the foreign stuff, and I started selling Motch machines.

Motch was just a small player selling maybe 20 or 30 machines a year or so. And the market niche for Motch machines was very small, according to the NMTBA (National Machine Tool Builders Association, now AMT (the Association for Manufacturing Technology). As a maker of vertical turning machines in the size range that we were in, we had a small piece of the machine tool pie. Giddings & Lewis, the distributor division's largest and most profitable product line, had a big range, and there were other big, big machine makers.

The Motch 152-VNC could machine a part more than 4 feet in diameter.

But in our niche, we were a big frog in a small pond. We always claimed at least a 70% share of that small-range market. And at times we actually got as high as 90%, but our volume was very small. Motch, the manufacturing side, was basically a $20 million–$25 million machine tool builder in its good days.

Motch still believed that they could save the distributor business which was impossible. I mean, even if Oerlikon wouldn't have come in, they would have lost it because they were all associated with American manufacturers, no import lines, and they were all going belly up. And if they weren't going belly up, they couldn't compete. So then they would go belly up.

Oerlikon was not satisfied with our sales of their machines, so they started setting the stage to get themselves out of the machine tool business. All that we were selling from the Oerlikon collection were the Boehringer horizontal lathes. Not enough for Oerlikon. They opened a Boehringer sales office in Atlanta, taking the last European line away from Motch . . . and me.

That's when Klaus came to me and said, "We want you to sell Motch machines, the VNCs." I was given the Detroit territory and told to hit the road. I started selling machines, and my territory was expanded to include Chicago, Ohio, and Kentucky.

Chapter 5

What Is That Voice?

Who is it? Where's it coming from? It kept telling me, "YOU CAN SURVIVE THIS IF YOU WANT TO." Why would I want to?

I didn't think I could survive selling Motch machines. I didn't want to do it. Where was that going to get me? I thought it was a stupid idea. 1986 didn't look like it was going to be a good year.

Motch was always automotive-oriented but this was when the Japanese cars were starting to make big inroads. So the market for American-made cars was starting to shrink. The Japanese had the little cars, and we had the big three. If you went to Detroit, there were huge lots full of big American cars. Nobody was buying them. And we had that gas crisis—gas went from around 50 cents a gallon to two bucks or something like that. There were long lines at the gas station. You could buy gas every other day, odd days only. So I didn't think I could sell Motch machines.

I didn't think there was a market for Motch machines. My job would never amount to anything. I'll never make any money doing this. Why am I doing this? But since I really didn't have any choice, I decided to give it a shot . . . and I went all in. That's how my career started as a regional manager for Motch machine tools. I lucked out. I was given a really good territory—Chicagoland—because everyone else was failing at it.

I was working with LG Evans, our distributor in Chicago who covered Caterpillar and John Deere primarily. Because I had worked in marketing, I had a really good relationship with all of the Motch distributors. I did all the line cards for the IMTS show, so I knew all the presidents and I knew all the salespeople, even though my job didn't involve working with them.

When I was selling Oerlikon machines, the distributor sales guys took me with them to help them sell, and we did sell some machines. So I was in a good position with the distributor sales force. The first thing I did was to go to LG Evans, and I sat down and talked with them. What they had to say was all kinds of bad things about Motch—the machines weren't being built to quality standards; a lot of them were failing.

Dick Legan was the sales manager who became the president of Motch. We used to make all our machine castings and do all the machining at Motch. We had a big machine shop, but Legan sold all our machines—the machines we used to make our parts. At the time, outsourcing was all the rage in business schools. He got an MBA and decided that we didn't need to machine anything anymore. Let full-time machine shops do the work. We got the cash for the machines and cut our labor costs. Short-term gains for long-term grief.

Those machines were irreplaceable. I mean, we had big shaper machines, and we had a huge Blanchard grinder. Big, big expensive machine tools that today I'm not even sure people make those kinds of machines anymore. If they do, they are extremely expensive.

After the machine shop closed, we found a glitch in our system. The engineers would design the part, they would detail the part, and they'd send the blueprint to the machine shop. The machinist would machine the part, send it over to the assembly department, and it wouldn't fit. The assembler would go back to the machinist, and the machinist would fix the part. A hole might be an eighth of an inch off or a wrong thread was used . . . whatever.

They were mostly minor changes. The machinist would then mark up his engineering print with the changes on it, stick it in the drawer, and the next time an order came for that part, he pulled out the marked-up drawing and made the part correctly, sent it over to assembly, and everything was hunky-dory.

Sometimes the marked-up drawing went back to engineering. But for the most part, like in most shops, everybody was too busy. When Legan sold off the machine shop, he fired all the machinists because we didn't need them. He sent out all the parts to subcontractors for machining, but they did not have the right drawings. They had the engineering drawings, not the updated drawings from the machine shop.

When parts came back for assembly, they either didn't fit, or if they did fit, they were wrong in some other way. And so the assemblers, not knowing what to do, cobbled together the machines the best they could and sent them out the door. We delivered a whole batch of machines that created real problems.

We had real quality problems for about a year after we closed our machine shop. Some of the parts didn't fit right, and others weren't heat treated properly so they failed after a couple months in service. The worst example was after about six months of operation, the damn turrets would fall off the machines. I mean, turrets were literally falling off the Caterpillar and John Deere machines! It took a while to figure out what the problems were and get them fixed because we were dealing with outside suppliers where the parts looked good but they weren't made right. The only way you knew the parts were bad was when they failed.

We had all kinds of problems. When I got the Chicago territory, I went to John Deere and I just got my head ripped off over these issues. And rightly so. While we were wading through all these problems, we got down to the fact they had bought some $20,000 worth of chucks that were machined wrong, and John Deere wanted us to take them back.

Dick Legan handled that account personally. Nothing against Dick; he was an OK guy, but he came from the old school of things where the machine tool builder was king and the customer was peasant, so customers had to take whatever the builder would give.

Dick refused to take the chucks back. He fixed the machines the best he could and got the machines working OK. But he wouldn't take the chucks back. He stood hard on these chucks, and he wouldn't take them back. In response, John Deere just gave him the frigging finger and wouldn't buy any machines from Motch. We would get an order for a couple of machines every year from Deere. Even if we didn't have an order, we would go ahead and put a couple machines into our schedule, build them, and wait for the order. Never failed. By the time I came on the scene, Motch hadn't sold any machines to John Deere for over a year and a half.

Oh man, they're beating me up, beating me up. I finally said, "What's the real problem here?" The John Deere guy says, "I've got these damn chucks. Legan made us buy these chucks, and they're no good. And they're sitting here and they cost 20 grand, and he won't take them back!" I said, "Wrap them up, and we'll take them back. I'll send you a check. Forget it."

I said, "I'm here to handle your account, and we'll take care of it. What else you got wrong with the machines?" There were a number of issues, so I sent out a crew of service guys. It cost us some money, but we fixed the machines.

We got over this big hurdle, and it looked like the road ahead would be smoother because all of a sudden John Deere was really happy. And when the next bid came up, we were included. I bid a really low price; almost a break-even price. I talked to Klaus about it, so he knew what I was doing. Sure enough, we got the order. They gave us another chance. I made sure that and the machine we shipped them was one of the best ones that we ever made. It was a 135 VNC (Vertical Numerical Chucker)—our bread-and-butter machine. Then we got some orders for a few 235s, so we were back in at John Deere. Big time.

Our machine model numbers were pretty basic. The first number was the number of spindles (1 or 2) and the second number was the maximum diameter of the part you could make in the machine (15 to 52 inches). If machine model number began with a 2 and ended with a D, then it was a double spindle. A double spindle machine was basically two single spindle machines bolted together so they could be operated by one guy instead of two. You could machine two sides of the same part on one machine. So machine the top on the left, flip it over, and machine the bottom on the right, while the left spindle was machining the top of the next part. Increased productivity, lower labor costs. I could really sell that.

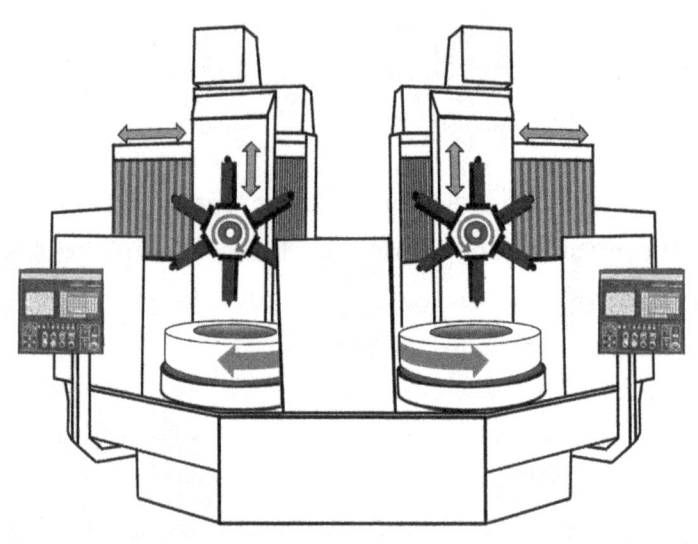

Motch Double Spindle: Essentially two single spindles side by side. Turrets and spindles can rotate clockwise and counterclockwise as required. Machine top of part #1 on spindle #1; turn over and machine bottom of #1 on spindle #2 while part #2 is being machined on spindle #1—increase productivity, lower labor costs.

Problems with Deere were typical of the kind of thing that I ran into when I started selling Motch machines. Motch was its own worst enemy because the people who worked there were so used to dictating to the customer what he could have, and what he couldn't have, and how much he was going to pay.

This was the time the Japanese were turning the whole machine tool marketplace upside down. With the Japanese, the customer was king, not the builder. They would tell the customer, "Whatever you want, I'm going to give you, and whatever the price is, I would do the best I can to make it to your liking." So that started the whole thing. Then the Japanese started building factories in the U.S. to build their machines here. I had to get our company to start listening to the customer to get our sales back on track. It took some work, but the bottom line is we started selling machines again.

We weren't growing, we were just getting back to where we were; where we should have been all along. At least we were back in the game.

While I was selling, no one else could get an order. I don't know why. We had a bunch of guys that they hired but didn't last. They would try this guy, then that guy, but none of them could sell. Maybe they were hiring experienced machine tool salespeople—experienced in the old ways; the failing ways.

I was the only one getting orders. Bob Siewart, who was the general manager for Motch under Klaus, saw this and told Klaus to give me more territory. All of a sudden, my territory got really, really big. I wake up one day and I have the Mississippi River to Los Angeles, to Canada, to Mexico. OK. Then they gave me the South. I wasn't just Chicago anymore.

I had three quarters of the country. The other sales guys split up the rest of the country—basically the Northeast. They were really pissed. They thought I was stealing from them. But they weren't selling machines, and the Northeast—what they had—was the home of a lot of business; potential business, anyway.

But they never sold anything. I kept selling machines and pretty much carried the company. George Simone, who worked out of Cone, did well, too, because he had Blanchards and Springfields too. He had good customers up in the Northeast—Pratt and Whitney, Bell Helicopter, places like that—making jet engines and helicopter engines. Whatever business Blanchard had, George sold. He did OK. The two of us kept things perking along. It just wasn't enough.

The problem was that Motch was an 80-year-old business. The Motch way of doing things was to tell the engineers what the customer wanted, and the engineers then would sit down and basically design a machine, whether it was a standard model or not.

When the customer signed off, Engineering would officially release all the paperwork for the machine. That's when we started to build it. We did that for every machine, even if it was a standard machine, like a 125, for example. In the time it would take to do all this, the Japanese would have delivered a machine at a lower cost. We were lucky. The Japanese were going after high volume machine tools—lathes and machining centers. It was only a matter of time before they came for us. We had to clean up our act.

After all, the only thing that could change on a 125 is the turret, or maybe horsepower, or maybe you put a riser block under the columns and make it a little bit higher or maybe add a chip conveyor—little bolt-on stuff. But engineering redesigned the whole machine—ground up; new drawings every time we got an order. 80 years doing this stuff and we haven't learned to be efficient. Is it any wonder we had problems?

Every time I would sell a machine, the order would be sent to engineering, and they would draw up the machine. If the engineers wanted to change something, they would change it without permission, without a budget, without testing, without letting anybody know, without anything. They would just do it.

When the machine got into production, they'd build it and then they'd wonder why it took 30% longer to build it. There may have been a few options added—bolt-ons—but there were engineering changes to the machine nobody knew about. How crazy is that?

Now we're in a pickle. I'm trying to sell a standard machine. I'm trying to do what the Japanese are doing. And we do nothing standard. Because we did not standardize, it kept our costs up. Our production bottled up, and our integration of new technology became willy-nilly.

Chapter 6

Going Nowhere Fast

Take it from me . . . If you're in a hurry and not looking where you're going, you can slam into a brick wall . . . or a mountain.

The Japanese put a ton of pressure on U.S. machine tool builders. We couldn't keep up. Before they came along, the U.S. machine tool industry was king. We were royalty. We could take as long as we wanted to fill an order, and we could charge practically anything we wanted. That's because we engineered each machine to a specific customer's application. Everything was special. Machine tools were a good business to be in. With no meaningful competition, we could get away with, let's say, inefficiencies. Like making practically every order a big custom expensive deal.

Yet when you get right down to it, a lot of machining applications are standard. You either spin the part up against a cutting tool (a turning machine or lathe), or you spin the cutting tool up against the part (drill press, milling machine, or machining center). Then you scale the machine for a specific range of part sizes. The Japanese saw this, and their solution was to make standard product lines—machine sizes and configurations. Different size machines for different sized parts. Simple and standard right down the line. That meant faster delivery; lower prices.

We argued quality. American machines were better built and would last forever. But for many applications, who needs it? American builders were being put more and more in a bind.

The Japanese were coming in and saying, "Here's my machine." This is it. Part number, blah, blah, blah. OK, now you want tooling and everything else. OK. Tooling packages separate. OK. To customize a machine, you put bolt-on parts. OK. You want a chip conveyor? OK. You want recirculating oil cooling unit? OK. To top it all off, the Japanese were beginning to make their machine tools in the U.S. I think Mazak was first, then Okuma.

As machine tool builders, our job was to help our customers make better parts faster. Our problem was that we took our sweet ol' time to build machines, making every machine a big production. The Japanese changed the game—they made better machines faster.

I had Klaus convinced that we should standardize our machines, like the Japanese. But it never really got done.

We were an old-line American company run by a German. The German way of management is to create conflict. Everyone had to fight against each other. You butt heads until somebody wins. My adversaries were Chuck Hess, a vice president, and Kas Reda, our German head of engineering.

Kas was protective toward his engineers and department, but he could be sold on developing solutions for an application; he could be brought around. He realized if we didn't sell something, he would be out of work. He respected what we did in sales and did come up with some really good solutions.

To understand how there could be a conflict between me and Kas, let's just say that sales guys could have a tendency to overpromise. Not that I did that. Then Kas would have to make it happen.

Kas was tough. I actually broke two telephones arguing with Kas about things. That was one of Klaus's checks on me. I never really figured out what Chuck's job was, other than to cause me problems.

Chuck and I were polar opposites, and, in this case, that was not a good thing. He was short, blond, and had blue eyes. I stood about a half a foot taller, with my black hair and brown eyes. If you could ever get us to stand next to each other, you would immediately think of Mutt and Jeff—the odd couple. If only life were that simple. We were certainly not a couple.

I think Chuck saw me as a rival for Klaus's favor, maybe, and needed a workaround. Whatever he was thinking, my belief was that he thought his job was to put a collar on me; keep me down. Limit my success? That's what it seemed like. Me and Chuck. You can't have everything. I had a good company, good machines, good job, good customers, and Chuck.

I would go out in the field and I would sell something, and we didn't know what it was going to cost. There were custom requirements. It was Chuck's job to cost it out—materials, labor, profit. Chuck had a tough time coming up with a number. And I kept telling him, "Don't send this to engineering."

The engineering department was the kingdom of Kas, and he was their fearless leader. If we had standardized product lines and part numbers, you would not need to devote so much engineering time to each order. Kas fought standardization. You weren't going to take away any work from engineering. Not under Kas. A standard approach to machine building would require less make-work and require fewer engineers. That was a big no-no. A no-win for me and the customer.

This constant internal battling was one reason why we never really made much money. I was able to move the needle a little. I was able to do that after I became sales manager when I was responsible for quoting machines and assigning numbers to them. Back then, when you quoted something, everything was handwritten. I standardized all that stuff, and I assumed that Chuck Hess was following along, standardizing all that stuff too. We actually started making money.

But it was always a roller-coaster ride. The machine tool business is very cyclical. Up. Down. Way, way up. Way, way down. I got to be sales manager because we were heading for a disaster. We were on the edge of a cliff, and I didn't know it. We were coming off a good year. John Mylonas, our tooling and proposal genius, was sales manager. He was way over his head, and he knew it. He was scared.

John was about 15 years older than me; a mature man—dark hair, gray at the temples, glasses. Abrupt. He was under a lot of stress. When I worked in tool engineering, he was my boss. I liked John. John was very good, very intelligent, and thoughtful; almost like an inventor-type guy with tooling and processes. But as a sales manager, he was just terrible. We were in really bad shape. Klaus asked me to become sales manager, and John gave a huge sigh of relief. He was happy to get out of sales and back into applications engineering.

Whatever machines I sold were going through the system, but it wasn't enough. The price was lower than they wanted, but there was a tremendous amount of mismanagement from order input to the factory floor to delivery to the customers. Then I found out what kind of trouble we were really in. "Oh shit, what are we going to do now?"

I was successful. I sold a lot of machines as a regional sales guy. But Motch only had $10 million or $12 million backlog for the coming year, and they needed $20 million to $25 million or $2 million a month. That was the big number—shipping $2 million a month. And if we couldn't get something going, it was going to be bye-bye. We would be done. Kaput.

I put out urgent calls to my buddies at our distributors. I say, "We've got to SELL!" From now on, whatever we do, we just have to sell stuff. First stop was LG Evans in Chicago which was being run by Klaus's buddy, Dell Wrench, who bought the business from Evans. I liked Dell a lot. Dell worked with Klaus at Uni-Sig up in Rockford. They were buddy-buddy. I said, "Whatever you can dig up, let me know." We were in deep, deep trouble. We needed to sell machines. I said, "I'll make it worth your while." So about a week or two later, the phone rings and it's Ron Johnson from LG Evans.

Ron says, "Hey, Caterpillar has this big project coming up for 24 machines." I got Caterpillar to accept double spindle machines instead of single spindle or a horizontal. Ron talked them into 219Ds where you could do first chucking, turn the part over, and do the second chucking in the same machine. Much more efficient.

At Caterpillar we got an opportunity for two 219Ds a month for 12 months. They were installing a new track line—tracks for the bulldozers and excavators. Our machines would make the wheels. Because they would be using double spindle machines (two machines in one), they would cut their labor costs in half. "Great, great, great!" I told Ron. "Do whatever we have to do to get this order." I talked to Klaus, and we worked everything out. I had Mylonas work out the best, fastest tooling package he could. I wasn't sure that we could do it. But we did it.

Because we were trying to standardize, at least pricewise, I got the price down to where we were very competitive. We went back to Cat a couple, three times. I wined and dined those guys pretty well. And Ron Johnson did an excellent job. We got the funding, and that saved the company because when we added the Cat order to our existing backlog, we would be shipping $2 million a month, guaranteed, for the next 12 months—two 219Ds all loaded. Klaus was just happier than a pig in slop because the bank had run out of patience and wasn't going to front us any more money, and Oerlikon was going through that "I don't want to be in the machine tool business anymore" phase.

Up to that point, we were basically doomed. You've heard of the Miracle on Ice where the USA beat the Russian Hockey Team in the 1980 Olympics. Well, 1987 was the Miracle in Peoria. We got the Caterpillar job! Now I'm all happy. Klaus is all happy. Ron Johnson's happy. Dell Wrench is tickled to death. Everybody's happy. I come home with this order, and Chuck Hess looks it over and says, "We can't deliver two machines a month. No way. Don't accept it."

I said, "You're out of your fricking mind!" Klaus, somehow or another, prevailed, and Kas said, "No problem, engineering will do it. No problem." And Mylonas said, "Yeah, yeah, we'll do it. No problem." Tom Daher, our CFO, was all for it. He said we might not make a profit, but we're making money.

Tom Daher said we needed to show that we could make money. Even though we might lose money, we're showing the bank that we can bring money in. We're just not making enough. And that's an easier thing to fix than when you're not making any money at all.

Until that order, we weren't making money. We built the machines and that got us back on track. All I had to do was sell a few more machines at a good fair price to make up for the shortfall.

After all of that was said and done, those 24 machines were delivered as the year went by. On top of that, we sold and delivered dozens of other machines that year, and we made a ton of money. The Cat order was our launching pad. The next year or two, we made quite a bit of money when we got a bunch of John Deere orders.

And that's when Daher remodeled the whole top floor. Oerlikon had just sold us to Pittler, a German company. We looked good because we were profitable. We had all this money, and Daher would not let Pittler take it. So he spent it on decorating the offices. It was beautiful, like the Taj Mahal.

Then we started selling robot brake lines. A big application for our machines was truck brake drums, then disc brake rotors. You could park a robot in front of a double spindle machine, load the left spindle, machine the top, unload, load the right side, machine the bottom, unload, and repeat, day in and day out. Load, unload, turnover load. Repeat again and again. We got to the point where we actually standardized a disc brake line. We also standardized on a drum line. At Wagner in St. Louis, I sold them two or three of those lines, and by the time we were done, we had it so the disk brake or the drum brake was completely finished when it came out.

To finish off, Wagner bought real cheap machining centers—lightweight, inexpensive—and all they did was drill the holes for the bolts. Then the drum went into a wrapping machine—wrapping the drum in an anti-rust compound, putting it in a box, sealing it, and stacking it on pallets at the end of the line. All automated. I sold a bunch of those lines. I sold them all over the place. Then I sold them to Budd Company for the big cast iron truck brake drums. That's another story.

The problem with semitrailer drum brakes is that trucks must stop at those weigh stations on the freeway or turnpike. That's mandatory. They inspect your brakes. Cast iron drums tend to crack. And if you have a cracked drum, you're off the road. You'd either have to have the truck towed or have it repaired on the side of the road.

Budd's solution was to develop a different type of brake drum, which I believe they're still making. They created a stainless-steel cage, put it in a mold, and poured the cast iron around it. It was like reinforced concrete with rebar in it. If the brake drum cracked, it couldn't bust apart. It would not be a road hazard. Budd proved their engineering concept and got a waiver. If a truck had a Budd drum and it showed a little crack, it would be given the OK to drive. The trucks wouldn't be taken off the road.

The problem Budd had was centering the cage in the cast iron. So you'd be machining cast iron, just going like a whiz, then rip into the stainless steel, and then *BLAM!* it would blow apart. The part is spinning at thousands of rpm with a cutting tool. That could be, and was, an explosive machining problem. It was dangerous for the operators and created a real problem in maintaining a production schedule. You had to stop the machine, throw out the part, change the tool, load a new part, start over, and hope for the best.

I was fascinated by this problem, and I thought we could solve it. But, of course, Chuck Hess said we shouldn't even quote on it. So I went to my old buddy, John Mylonas, who, by this time, really didn't have an official position in the company anymore. He was just there. I said, "John, what can you do about this?" He said, "I think I have a way to solve that." I think his solution was some kind of whisker ceramic insert. These cutting tool inserts had ceramic fibers reinforcing the carbide, much like the stainless-steel cage reinforced the cast iron drum.

If you hit the stainless, the tool wouldn't shatter and break. It wouldn't destroy the tool or destroy the part or crash the machine like we worried it would. John's idea worked. It actually worked. We brought a bunch of drums into Motch, and we machined them on a 125 and hit a couple of stainless-steel frames to prove to Budd that we could sustain the process without blowing something up.

Tool breaking technology was just coming on then. If you broke a tool, it would stop the machine. We put that technology on the machine, and it would stop the machine from breaking; stop the machine from destroying the chuck or destroying the part or even killing somebody.

When a tool broke, the operator would just change the insert and off they would go. I sold three or four lines to Budd Company. I think there were three or four machines in each line, plus a robot and all the conveyors and all the material handling and all the tooling that

55

went with it. The package included tool sensing and gauges for part accuracy too.

We had to engineer the first line. We delivered the first production line, so I knew exactly what the first line cost was after we delivered it. We went back and sold them some more at a little bit lower price because we made a fortune on the first one.

Budd needed more lines, so I offered to give them a discount if they ordered them all at once. They were in Tennessee, the Tri-Cities area. I was down there negotiating the deal and something happened. It had something to do with Pittler because it was just when Pittler was starting to nibble at us, and we were done with Oerlikon. It might have been that Oerlikon cut us off financially, and Pittler hadn't quite come on board. Something like that.

Klaus calls me up at Budd, and it was another one of Klaus's "we're in deep shit now" moments. He says, "We need a couple of million bucks. Right now!" I say, "What do you want from me?" He says, "Well, think about it. Figure out where you can get it, either from the distributors or the customers." OK.

Since I was at Budd and I was negotiating the additional production lines, I said, "If you give me two million dollars up front, I'll drop the price another couple of percentage points." And sure enough, they cut a check. They actually wrote me a check. *TWO MILLION DOLLARS!* I had it in my briefcase, and Klaus asked, "Did you get it?" And I said, "Yeah." Klaus says, "Where are you now?" I say, "I'm flying home. I have a six-hour layover. A long layover in Cincinnati."

Klaus flew to the Cincinnati airport! We're sitting at the bar, and he says, "You got it?" "Yeah, right here." We're sitting at the bar drinking a beer, and he goes, "Let me see it. Wow! TWO MILLION BUCKS!" It was a certified Budd check. It was crazy. Absolutely crazy.

Klaus was in charge of money. I'm terrible when it comes to financial stuff. I have no brain for money. My brain just doesn't do that. So it was basically Klaus and Tom Daher who took care of the money. They worked very closely together. Daher was paying all the bills, and Klaus was going to the banks and getting the money. I was selling the machines, and between what I had on the books and what Tom Daher needed, Klaus would put together his plan.

What we did find out—years later—each one of those four identical lines cost us more money to make than the previous one. Each line cost more. Does that make sense? They went up in price for us and down in price for Budd. It wasn't because of the cost of materials because we had the materials. We used to buy spindle housings and keep them in the backyard so that the iron would age. Maybe the controls or something cost a little bit more money, but it wasn't a big inflationary period. That wasn't what happened.

It was Kas. Kas was redesigning the machines and making improvements so that each new line was a little bit better than the previous one, which was a good thing. But it wasn't included in the price. And he was not given permission to do that. All that came out much later.

Chapter 7

Am I Dreaming?

"You can survive this is if you want to . . ." The voice was strong. The message was clear. Where was the voice coming from? Am I dreaming?

One nightmare ends, another begins. Under Oerlikon ownership, we went from a $200 million machine tool company with manufacturing and distribution, to less than a $20 million a year manufacturer. It took only 10 years. That was bad enough. The real nightmare began when Oerlikon sold Motch to Pittler GmbH, out of Leipzig, East Germany. That happened in 1989.

That was the year of the Germans. The Berlin Wall came down, Germany began to reunify, and Pittler, which was an East German company, bought Motch. How did they do that? Where did the money come from? Who was behind the deal? Why Motch? This whole thing was a mystery to me.

There was a lot about Pittler I could never quite understood. When the wall came down, West Germany had all this money set aside to take over and rebuild East Germany. Part of that rebuilding process was taking state-owned companies, privatizing them, and making them West German companies.

Two guys, Dieter Wiedemann and Frank Baumbusch, got the West German government financing to acquire Pittler. Weidemann came from Gildemeister and was a friend of Klaus. Everybody knew Klaus.

Pittler had a line of vertical turning machines and was a licensee to build National Acme screw machines (headquartered in Cleveland, same as Motch) for the European market. Pittler also had a line of automatic horizontal lathes—the Petra machines which they already sold in the U.S. The Pittler verticals competed with Motch, and the Petra machines competed with Cone.

I think they sold the West German government on the idea that they would take the Pittler product and sell it in the United States. Big Market. Motch was low-hanging fruit, ripe for the picking, because Oerlikon wanted to get out so bad.

I think we were a thorn in Oerlikon's side because the whole distributor division, and with it all their machine tool lines, went out of business. Millions in lost sales and revenue. But we, our Motch machine business, kept hanging on through it all; one little miracle after another.

Oerlikon had to sell us. I think Pittler saw this as a good deal and a great opportunity. Their top guy knew Klaus. Everybody knew Klaus. From Pittler's point of view, Motch was a perfect deal because you've got a German running it who can help you do what you want to do.

When Wiedemann and Baumbusch bought Pittler, they had money left over. So they bought Tornos Bechler in Switzerland and Motch in the United States. Cone-Blanchard was not part of the Pittler deal. It was turned over to Klaus. Maybe to incentivize him to carry out their bigger plans.

So Klaus, in an effort to keep everybody happy, turned Cone-Blanchard into an ESOP (employee stock ownership plan). The employees owned 40%, Klaus owned 40%, and a guy named George Caccavero, who Klaus hired to run Cone-Blanchard, had the other 20%. Since Klaus hired George, Klaus had control. But the fact that the employees owned a good chunk and there was profit sharing, too, set the stage for some pretty big management problems down the road.

Why would Pittler buy Motch, a direct competitor who dominated its market segment? Only one reason: put Motch out of business and sell the German machines to customers eager for superior German engineering. That was their vision.

It looked good on paper. So did the Oerlikon deal before reality hit. I think they figured it would be easy to do; thought that they could replace our verticals with their verticals and get in the U.S. market.

So when Pittler came, all they got was Motch—the distributor division was already gone. And Cone was under Klaus. Pittler bought basically the Motch factory.

At this point, I'm the vice president of sales, and Beverly Kozitko is my sales admin manager. Everybody got all upset that I appointed a woman to coordinate sales for a machine tool company—the ultimate man's world—especially because she never sold a machine, was never in the field, or face to face with customers in a selling situation.

I didn't need anybody to sell. I needed somebody to run the department. Beverly knew how to run that office like you wouldn't believe. She could get a quote done; she could get anything done. She knew how to make it work. And that's what I needed.

The boys were upset, but Beverly was really, really surprised and happy. She got a huge raise. She ran our sales meetings, qualified the Requests for Quotes, and tracked the whole quoting process, making sure we were on top of everything.

At that time, I was running the proposal department too. Here Beverly was, and I can't say enough about her. Bev was about 15 years older than me and had been at Motch for, it seemed, forever. She was tall, thin, soft-spoken, had short gray hair, and very professional. She worked for Dick Legan when he was sales manager and when he became president, so she knew everything about Motch. She got things done.

What I did when I promoted her was give her the authority to make things happen. It made her job easier, and the increase in pay was recognition of the value she brought to the table.

To introduce us to the Pittler way, Pittler gave us the Grand Tour. Our European tour group included me, Bev Kozitko, Klaus, Chuck Hess, and our sales guys. First stop was Leipzig, Germany, to tour the Pittler factory and meet our new masters. We figured they had to be really wealthy to buy us, so we were expecting great things. What a shock! Their headquarters was the worst factory I'd ever seen. It wasn't that it was so old; it was just threadbare—everything in the whole place looked like it was worn-out. Even the people. It didn't really dawn on me until later that this was an East German communist factory. I thought there was something wrong with this whole thing.

Pittler management was counting on the allure of German engineering—Mercedes and BMW touted it all the time. German engineering was known to be precise, exact. In those days, that was true for West German products; they were right on spec.

When you're talking about engineered products, like machine tools, you're talking about specs and tolerances. For example, let's say a product was supposed to be one inch in diameter plus or minus 10 thousandths of an inch. The West German product would be right in the middle—one inch—the nominal spec; the exact spec. Let's just say the East German products had a lot of plusses and minuses; still within spec but creating a lot of variables that could affect machine performance.

The Pittler Petra machines were a prime example. As a result, the Motch customers that bought the East German Petra machines were very unhappy. The Petra reputation was an albatross for Pittler and for Motch.

As Pittler was transitioning to Western ways and management and designing new and better machines, they still had to sell their Petra machines. That created problems.

Chuck Hess was a political animal, always looking out for what was best for Chuck. When we did that tour of Pittler, Chuck struck up a relationship with Frank Baumbusch, one of Pittler's owners and their head of engineering. Chuck agreed to take on 50 Petra machines on his own. That made Baumbusch happy. Petra machines were trouble-plagued inaccurate horizontal lathes—not really in my wheelhouse. Not the kind of machines I was used to selling or my customers would buy from me.

The Petra machines carried the Pittler name. Pittler previously sold a number of Petras to Motch customers. Because they didn't work as advertised, that created problems for Motch going forward. Pittler also made vertical machines, but with the Petra reputation out there, that made the verticals a tough sell too.

Frank Baumbusch was a big heavyset guy who enjoyed eating. Chuck made sure that whenever Baumbusch visited us in Cleveland, there would be an ample supply of macadamia nuts in bowls around the offices. To top it off, Chuck would make Baumbusch a special apple pie that he could enjoy when he arrived.

So Chuck was building a relationship directly with one of the owners of Pittler. He was going around the chain of command, going around Klaus. Dieter Wiedemann, the other owner of Pittler, was a friend of Klaus.

Since Pittler also acquired Tornos Bechler in Switzerland, we visited the Tornos plant on the same trip. That facility was fantastic—modern, everybody wearing uniforms; a top-notch operation. The safety lines are painted on the factory floor—the floors are shiny, spotless. You almost felt like taking your shoes off, they were so clean. They had a beautiful showroom with a little bar and cafeteria.

I got in trouble in their showroom because they had these real little machines that make watch parts. An operator was running a demo machine and he handed me this little plastic tub with these little pieces of metal I thought were chips—scrap—so I just dumped them out, and I was firmly told, "Those are the parts!" Real tiny little things. Beautiful machines. High-precision parts.

Tornos even had a bus service for employees. The factory was up in the mountains, a distance from where the workers lived. So Tornos would pick up workers in the morning and bring them to the factory. Since they had a cafeteria, workers stayed there all day. After work, they would jump on the bus and go home.

I remember sitting there with Bev Kozitko, wondering, *Who owns who here?* Pittler can't possibly own this place. We were just mystified because the Tornos Bechler people treated us like we were the best thing since sliced bread.

We went to these fancy Swiss chalet restaurants. It was just a wonderful time. The comparison between the Pittler plant and Motch . . . Motch was a beautiful place compared to Pittler in my mind. Motch was a beautiful place but not as great as Tornos. We just couldn't understand how Pittler was the owner. Our trip to Pittler and our trip to Tornos Bechler had Bev and I wondering what was going on. How was this possible? Very, very confusing.

And then we came back home and, once again, Chuck Hess gets into the action. He made a deal with Pittler's chief engineer, Frank Baumbusch, unbeknownst to me.

Even though I was in charge of sales, Chuck Hess signed a deal with Pittler to bring machines over to Motch. I knew nothing about this. He ordered 50 Petras. 50! We'd be lucky to sell that many machines in a year. Why would we take on machines we knew nothing about? What's going on? Nobody told me, and I'm supposed to sell these things? Turns out, these machines caused us nothing but trouble even with our existing Motch customers.

One of my customers was Reed Tool in Texas who made oil field drill bits. They're a competitor to Cameron Iron, which was another big customer of mine. Reed made rock bits used for drilling oil wells.

Reed had bought a couple of Petra machines to make some of their parts. Except the Petra machines did not do a good job, so Reed dumped them. Reed had them sitting outside, collecting dust and rust. The Reed engineer said, "These are the worst machines I've ever seen in my life. They are unreliable. They're lightweight, they don't hold size, they had European electrics that short out, they blow fuses, so we threw them out. They're sitting in the parking lot. We don't want them." When Pittler bought us, he was the first guy to call me. He asked, "Is it true Pittler bought you?" "Yeah." "Well," he said, "do you want these two Petras back? I'll sell them to you cheap."

I said, "Nope, nope, nope, don't want them." I was going to get a whole warehouse full of new Petra machines. The back bay where the machine shop used to be was going to be filled with 50 Petra machines that our buddy Chuck was bringing over, and I was supposed to sell them. WTF?

If I sold Petras to my existing customers, they would not be happy, so I was caught between a rock and a hard place. Well, get this. After Reed Tool called me and wanted me to buy his machines back, I get a call from Ford. *FORD!*

And the Ford guy says, "We heard you were bought by Pittler, and we're pissed." Now Ford was never a good Motch customer, but they were a terrific Cone customer. At Ford Indianapolis, I sold them tons of machines and all kinds of spare parts and tooling. One of my mandatory stops every couple of months was just to go see Ford, so the buyer for Ford and I were pretty chummy guys business-wise, primarily through the Cones. We had a couple of Blanchards in there too.

But he was just madder than a hornet. I asked him what was wrong. He says, "Does Pittler own you?" Me: "Yeah, I guess so. We're a subsidiary of Pittler." And he says, "You know, we bought a ton of machines from Pittler." I said, "Did you, really?"

He says, "Yeah, Petra machines. We have an entire Ford parking lot filled with Petra machines that are rusting away, and we want you or Pittler to take them back. We talked to Pittler and they won't take them back. So we're putting it on you, Ed. We're not going to do any more business with you unless you get rid of these machines." He was loud and clear. I totally understood. Totally. I'm sitting there, thinking, *How the hell did I get myself into this mess? How am I going to get myself out of it?*

I talked to Klaus. Klaus goes to Ford. He comes back and says, "We're screwed. We're totally screwed." Klaus could usually talk himself out of trouble, but not this time.

I'll tell you a story to give you an idea of Klaus's ability to negotiate. I used to think I was pretty good. But Klaus was a genius. Back before I became the Motch salesman, I used to sell Mandelli machining centers. We were going to import those machines from Italy, and I sold a bunch of them to John Deere. But Mandelli was going to be late—very late on delivery—messing up John Deere's production schedules.

The Italians promised a delivery date, then things went to hell in a handbasket. I had to go back to John Deere and tell him we're going to be late. They weren't very happy about that and wanted to see my boss. At that time, it was Bob Siewart.

Ron Johnson, from LG Evans, and I took Siewart over to Deere, and we were sitting in front of all the John Deere lawyers. There were a half dozen of them. Siewart was just sitting there, and they proceeded to rip him a new orifice.

I never heard anybody get reamed so bad. He probably turned twenty shades of white. He was so scared he was sweating, and the sweat was dripping off his nose. I swear to God, this is the honest to God truth. Sweat is dripping off his nose and hitting the notepad.

We get out of the meeting and get in the car. Ron Johnson is driving us back to the airport, and Siewart is in the back seat. He says, "Well, that wasn't too bad, was it?" *Unbelievable!*

I told Klaus what happened, and Klaus went to see Deere. I wasn't in the meeting, so I don't know exactly what happened.

But Klaus came back out, and everything was hunky-dory. John Deere was loving us. I don't know how he did it or what he did, but Klaus had that magic, you know. But it did not work out that way with Ford on the Pittler problem. After dealing with Ford, Klaus came to the conclusion, "We've got to eat these machines." He went to Germany and it took about six months, but I think eventually Pittler paid Ford some money to destroy the machines.

Back to the Pittler problem. They bought us in '89, just when the economy looked like it was going to head south. Times were tough and getting tougher. A recession was taking hold. Nobody knew how long it would last. What would the recovery look like? Everybody's beating me up because they have Petras that don't work, and Chuck Hess just ordered 50 of them. How was I going to sell them? They were trouble, and everybody knew it—Ford and Reed. I was sure there were more.

I did my best to ignore the whole thing. I didn't order the Petras, so they're not my problem. I kept on selling Motch machines. And then the Pittler machines start showing up. Petras. Oh, God. The first phase. Maybe a half a dozen or so.

With Oerlikon, we were always on the edge, then Pittler came along and showed us what a real disaster was. Why a disaster? They pushed us over the edge. It's my experience that German companies are predatory when they have a U.S. subsidiary. They'd like to go in and raid the bank account. All the time. It happened to us. And look what happened to Chrysler.

Tom Daher was always hiding money from the Germans. That's because Pittler basically wanted to destroy Motch. We dominated the market for small vertical turning machines. They wanted us to sell Pittler vertical machines to our Motch customers.

To me, that was a really bad idea for a lot of reasons.

- Our customers knew Motch and were very happy with our performance. Pittler was an unknown with a sketchy reputation.
- Being European, Pittler machines used metric tooling. Motch used inch tooling; the same as all the other machines in our customers' plants.

- Motch tooling was compatible with Giddings & Lewis machines, which a lot of our customers had. Pittler tooling was not.
- It would be extremely expensive and confusing to run two different tooling systems.
- Because of their design, Pittler machines were not as rigid or accurate in many of our customers' applications.
- If we tried to force Pittler machines on our customers, they would go elsewhere.
- Because we would be importing Pittler machines, complete except for controls and electrics, we wouldn't need as many people in engineering or assembly. We would have to lay off highly skilled people. People I worked with for years. Friends.

For these and a lot of other reasons, I refused to sell Pittler machines to my customers. It was the beginning of the end of my career at Motch.

But I kept selling the Motches. We were making money too. Maybe not a lot, but we were making money. All of this Pittler inventory was a millstone around our neck, dragging us down. We had to pay property tax on our inventory—that was killing Daher. I couldn't sell them. I wasn't going to sell them. Nobody asked my opinion.

Klaus ultimately gave the Petras to Chuck to sell. As far as I know, those machines never got sold.

The 1990 IMTS was coming around, and I wanted to show Motch machines—not Pittler. John Mylonas had just come up with a fantastic aluminum wheel machine—a 219D that could cut aluminum as fast as the machine could go. More and more aluminum wheels were being put on cars. It was a big market with a lot of opportunity. We had the right machine, right size, right price, and unbeatable performance. Easily automated.

John was very good to me, and he was really good for Motch, so I wanted to take a 219D to IMTS to demo wheel machining. This was just at the beginning of the aluminum wheel craze, and Pittler's chief engineer, Frank Baumbusch, was all upset about it. He wanted all these Pittler machines in our IMTS booth. He wanted to spend millions of dollars on the show, and he wanted Motch to pay for it. In Europe, trade shows are a real big deal where machines are bought by the ton. In the U.S., our trade shows are like an auto mall with new car showroom after showroom. Buyers and buying teams come and look, get demos and brochures, but rarely buy off the floor.

I said we should go, but on a limited basis. Let's just show a wheel machine. There's some real opportunity there for that machine. "I would rather take a 219D wheel machine and give it away for free for six months. Let the guys use it. If they like it, they can buy it. If not, they can ship it back. I guarantee you I'll generate more orders that way on this machine that I will spending that money on IMTS. People don't buy machines at the show, generally. They come to look and compare notes, and then they'll make up their minds a month or so later based on the input they had." Then the meeting broke up. We got our way, but the fallout put a target on my back.

We did find a way to make Weidemann happy at the show, though. He came over for IMTS to see how things were shaping up. He was a sailboat racer in Europe. He sailed all over the Mediterranean. He was a highly skilled sailor. He wanted us to rent him a sailboat that had to be more than 50 feet so he could sail Lake Michigan on the weekend of IMTS.

I didn't know anything about getting a boat in Chicago, but Pumphrey did. I called and told him, "We really need a boat." A friend of his belonged to a Chicago yacht club, so we got a 57-footer. It was a beautiful boat. Full crew and only the best food and drink.

The crew could tell right away that Weidemann was a skilled sailor, and I had been sailing for years myself, so they let us put the boat through its paces. We were out on the lake the whole day.

Some people are born sailors, and other people should never set foot on a boat. Two of those people were Baumbusch and Chuck Hess. To say that Chuck tossed his cookies would be putting it mildly. Baumbusch staggered forward where the sails were stored, and the crew told him, "If you get sick on those sails, you'll have to buy a whole new set."

I loved it. Weidemann knew Klaus, and during this outing I warmed up to him. He was not only a good sailor but he also treated the visibly sick land lubbers to an extended nautical experience. And he loved it. I was laughing my ass off.

Around this time, I was negotiating a big Cameron Iron Works deal. Our engineers designed a new big Motch machine perfect for the Cameron application. Cameron was machining big jet engine rings for Pratt & Whitney and GE. These were made from nickel-based superalloys—Hastalloy and Waspaloy—very difficult to machine, very precise in their specifications. They had to go through all kinds of certifications for the parts, so this was a big deal. The machines we were quoting were like our 152, but bigger. They had tool changers and pallet shuttles. Kas and his boys in engineering were going to town. And I got that damned order! *WTF?* Pittler didn't know anything about it. This was a HUGE order!

I'm thinking if we get the Cameron order, we are set. We're going to be making money like crazy. Maybe we'll buy Pittler—*HA!* And they wanted us to spend all this money on the show which was not going to work. Not going to work. No.

We ended up getting the Cameron order, right. *GREAT!* Millions of dollars of Motch machines. The biggest order of my life. We're in business! When Baumbusch, found out about it, he blew his top. Pittler actually had machines in that size range that could probably have done the job, but they weren't Motches. And Cameron wanted Motch. Kas Reda, our chief engineer, was happier than a tornado in a trailer park—he was really going at it—designing all new machines, giving him the opportunity to shine.

Baumbusch just went through the roof because we weren't selling Pittlers. I suspect that Chuck got together with Baumbusch and convinced him that we weren't making any money; that I was giving all the machines away at a discount, which, you know, I was.

I felt great. The biggest order Motch had seen in years, I sold it during a recession—the one that torpedoed George H. W. Bush's reelection. I wanted to make things work. I'm pretty sure that Baumbusch and those guys told Klaus to fire me after I had just gotten this big order. Right. Because there wasn't any money in it for Pittler other than what they could take out of Motch. And knowing Tom Daher, they weren't going to get much.

Summertime 1991, Klaus comes to me. He never really told me I was fired. He just said, "I want you to go up and run my company in Vermont." He fired me without really telling me I was fired. He did a John Mylonas on me. But I was too naive. I didn't realize that.

It was all politics with Pittler and Chuck Hess. Even though I was doing a good job, I was being fired because I wasn't doing what they wanted. Chuck knew his paychecks were being signed by Pittler. I knew I wanted to keep Motch in business, and my customers wouldn't buy Pittler. This was the type of conflict the owners always win.

So Klaus sent me up there, banished me to Vermont, and, reluctantly, I went. I became the executive vice president of Cone-Blanchard Machine Company. Klaus gave me a nice raise to make it worth my while. I was tired of Pittler. I was tired of the politics, the constant internal battles. So I went up to Vermont and I started a whole new facet of my life.

Chapter 8

Am I Dead, and Don't Know It?

My Mom was there, Bobcia was there, even my Uncle Frank was there. But they were all dead. And I was there. What's going on? Am I dead and don't know it?

I never realized that I was actually fired from Motch until about two, two and a half years after it happened. But I eventually realized that Klaus was fired too. I was fired from Motch, and Klaus was fired from Motch at the same time because we didn't do what Pittler wanted us to do. They wanted us to sell Pittler machines. They didn't want us to sell Motch machines. I sold Motch because that's what our customers wanted to buy. They trusted Motch. They didn't want to buy Pittlers. Simple as that.

I was the salesman who was responsible for creating the problem. And Klaus was the guy who OK'd it. I never did anything without clearing it with Klaus. So in Pittler's eyes, Klaus was directly responsible for the orders from Cameron. He was as guilty as I was for selling all Motch machines and no Pittlers. So we both got fired.

When Oerlikon faded away, Klaus got control of Cone-Blanchard. Pittler bought Motch, but not Cone-Blanchard. So when Pittler got rid of both Klaus and me, it's a good thing we had someplace to go. I couldn't believe it. I got fired for bringing in the biggest order Motch had seen in years. Klaus never told me I got fired, he just saved my ass by putting me to work at Cone. He sent me up to Cone-Blanchard which was really in trouble at the time.

I guess the worst thing I ever did was get the order from Cameron. Pittler wanted to bleed Motch out. Without me there, their plan was working. There were times I had to go to Cleveland for a meeting. One time I stopped in at Motch to say hi, and Kas Reda came running up to me and said, "The Cameron thing is done, and we've got nothing. We have no orders. We've got nothing. Come back and work for us." The bosses got wind that I was there. I was told to leave and to never come back. I was escorted out of the building. It was a weird, screwy time.

Klaus had some kind of deal with Pittler where he had a year or two to transition out of Motch. They couldn't get anybody to replace Klaus immediately. So they put Weidemann's son, Svend, in charge. Klaus would serve as a mentor to Svend and hold Motch together until Svend got his footing or until they could find somebody new.

Klaus was eventually going to move to Cone-Blanchard full-time. So when I went up to Vermont, I was just working with Cone, trying to sell screw machines and trying to sell Blanchard grinders.

But Klaus being Klaus wouldn't leave it at that. He was working on a deal where he would buy all the drawings for the Motch machines and move Motch production to the Cone plant. Pittler was willing to make that deal because they thought their machines were better. Pittler couldn't stand Motch. They thought Motch wouldn't be able to compete. Without Motch dragging them down, Pittler would have a clear field. Pittler thought that was a good idea because they would get paid for getting rid of Motch, and Klaus and I would be gone for good. That prospect made them very happy.

Pittler didn't know we had an ace up our sleeve. Cone-Blanchard had a huge machine shop. Cone never sold their machine shop, plus they invested in a Flexible Manufacturing System. With this state-of-the-art technology, we could make money as a machine shop in addition to making and selling machine tools. This machining capability would be great for producing machine tool parts. Perfect for Motch. Perfect for all the lines.

Not only did Cone's machine shop feature advanced CNC-controlled machines but it also included advanced part and tool handling, automatic part and tooling inspection, and automated part washing—all computerized. We could control part flow, tooling flow, and scheduling of all machining operations. Plus they had huge equipment—a gigantic planer mill and a Coordinate Measuring Machine as big as a two-car garage. There was opportunity there.

At one time, Cone-Blanchard was making money hand over fist. They had three product lines—Conomatic multispindle screw machines, Blanchard rotary surface grinders, and Springfield universal grinders.

Conomatics were a big deal. Conomatics were special—an 80-year-old machine that can still make more parts per hour than many brand-new computer-controlled machines; hundreds of parts an hour. Ford and Chrysler had hundreds of Conomatics on their factory floors churning out a wide variety of automotive parts. At its peak, Cone employed more than 1,000 people.

Conomatics were very complicated machines. A six-spindle machine had a six-position bar feeder where the stock tubes were arranged like barrels of a Gatling gun. Each 12-foot-long tube would feed into a spindle, and the six spindles and bars would rotate in unison through six tooling stations in the machine. On the outside, it would look like a huge slow-moving, very noisy 30-foot Gatling gun; on the inside, it was fast-moving and complicated as hell. Each tooling station performed different operations—facing, chamfering, turning, profiling, threading, boring, knurling, etc., depending on what was needed. Every 10 seconds or so, a completed part would drop into a parts bin.

Everything was mechanical—one big motor drove all six spindles through complicated sets of gearing that would make the most sophisticated of watchmakers look on in awe. The machine's functions were controlled by cams, much like a sewing machine. It could take a day or two to set up one of these mechanical wonders, but then the machine could run 24/7 for months or years, making the same parts hour after hour.

I think we had more than 5,000 machines out in the field, with hundreds needing spare parts or service every year. Each machine had thousands of parts. Moving parts could and did wear out, that's why spare parts and rebuilds could be such a good business

But the way Cone did business crippled them. They had a problem with inventory and spare parts because no machine was standard. Each machine was specially designed; specially made for each customer. Screw machines are complicated contraptions with thousands of parts. And Cone made 25 different models of screw machines.

The way Cone built their machines, each part on each machine had a separate part number. They would make the same part over and over again and give each one a different part number. There were thousands of machines out there—millions of part numbers. Bazillions. Nuts. Absolutely nuts.

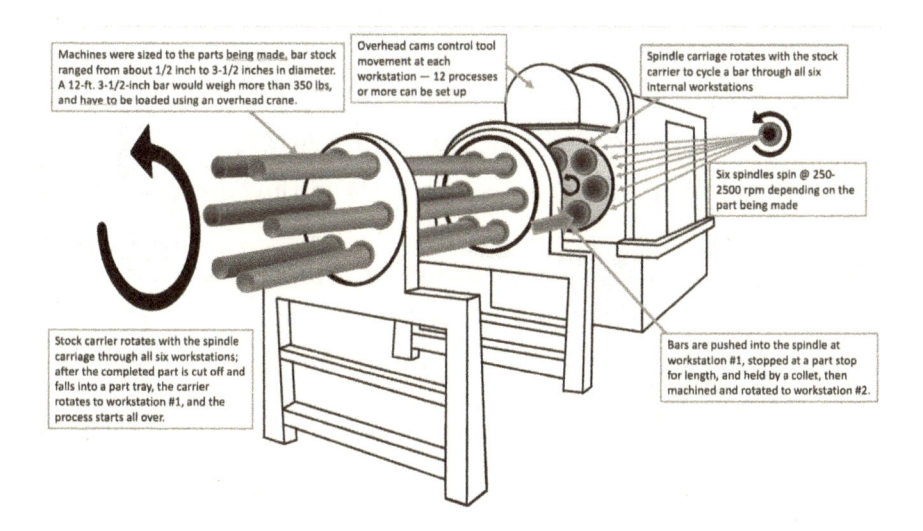

> Machines were sized to the parts being made, bar stock ranged from about 1/2 inch to 3-1/2 inches in diameter. A 12-ft. 3-1/2-inch bar would weigh more than 350 lbs, and have to be loaded using an overhead crane.

> Overhead cams control tool movement at each workstation — 12 processes or more can be set up

> Spindle carriage rotates with the stock carrier to cycle a bar through all six internal workstations

> Six spindles spin @ 250-2500 rpm depending on the part being made

> Stock carrier rotates with the spindle carriage through all six workstations; after the completed part is cut off and falls into a part tray, the carrier rotates to workstation #1, and the process starts all over.

> Bars are pushed into the spindle at workstation #1, stopped at a part stop for length, and held by a collet, then machined and rotated to workstation #2.

Selling spare parts could be a good business. Trouble is, we did not know what part went where. Cone's solution to this problem was as dumb as can be. In their heyday, Cone-Blanchard signed a huge contract with IBM to straighten out their inventory and spare parts problems. And they needed a solution because in their system, each machine was specific to a customer.

Here's the problem: if a customer with 10 machines calls up for a replacement part, you don't know how to respond. You know what customer to look up, but you don't know which machine needs the part, and they all have different numbers. So you can have 10 tries to get it right. Bigger customers, like Ford with hundreds of machines, presented much bigger problems.

Think of an installed base of 5,000 machines, each with a thousand parts. That's five million part numbers. 5,000 different numbers for the same part. That's the problem Cone had. It was probably even bigger than that.

IBM's solution required Cone to buy big, powerful, expensive IBM mainframe computers. In addition to the computers, IBM would provide their programming expertise on a monthly retainer. At the time, Cone was doing really well so they could afford a long-term contract to straighten out their spare parts and inventory problem.

When I got to Cone, the contract was still in effect. They were paying tens of thousands of dollars a month. *A MONTH!* Unbelievable.

This IBM relationship was doing nothing for Cone, except bleed money. IBM was supposed to keep track of Cone's inventory, but it was the blind leading the blind because IBM didn't know the Cone part numbering system, and neither did third-generation Cone employees! Right before I went up there, Cone had shown a small profit, so Klaus was happy. But then, all of a sudden, the inventory fell apart, and Cone showed a huge loss. "What the hell is this all about?"

The problem was the spare parts inventory was counted as an asset, so the company showed a profit based on their inventory, not on operations. They had big assets and small sales. It looked good on paper, so they thought they were in the black. When I got up there, Klaus calls and says, "We're losing money." I ask, "What happened?" He says, "I don't know. Something with the inventory. Find out what's going on."

After a little digging, I found out all about this IBM situation. Because of the part number situation, IBM was counting the same item several times under different numbers. And mistakes were made. A piece of high tensile tool steel two-foot long might be entered as 20-foot long. That extra zero inflated the value.

All these parts they were counting weren't real because they were the same part with different numbers. Because they had different numbers, they were recording them at different values. In reality, they all had one value which was lower than the values IBM showed. Everything just fell apart. The problem was created generations ago, so the people at Cone couldn't help; they didn't know how it got that way. Our inventory profits—our inventory wealth—was a mirage.

Everybody was living in a fantasy land; a circle of blame with each player pointing to the next guy. So when I got there, I called Klaus, "This is a freaking disaster! Nobody knows what the hell is going on here." Getting the contract terminated was difficult, but we got it done.

Cone couldn't sell replacement parts because nobody knew what part was right—you have thousands of numbers for the same part. At the same time, you have all these independent garage shop guys rebuilding Cones and making our parts. For us, we don't know which part is which, and our service and rebuilding are so damn expensive. These garage guys cost a third of what we would charge, and they were faster too.

Our garage shop competitors were killing us. All these guys making our parts, rebuilding our machines. Independent guys. And they're doing it for one-third our price. Me: "What the hell do you want me to do?" Klaus: "Do whatever you can."

Fortunately, our overhead at Cone was less than half the Motch overhead. At Motch, we needed twenty million, twenty-one million dollars a year or so. Two million a month was good. At Cone, I figured out that at nine or ten million a year, we could break even.

So the first thing I did was set up an 800 number for parts and rebuilds. I tried to get 1- 800-CONE. Somebody either had the number or for whatever Vermont reason there was, I could not get it. Everything in Vermont is a problem.

To get orders, I tried to standardize our spare parts. I hired one of the old Coneheads to make up a catalog which turned out to be as a farce because there was no way you could have the same part over and over again with different part numbers. There was just no way.

When I had the 800 number, I started calling on Ford. I begged. I pleaded. I quoted rebuild jobs at the same cost as a guy building it in his garage. But I had an advantage. I could provide a factory guarantee. That was really worth something.

Then I made the big case that you need a Springfield grinder to grind the cartridge and the carriage so the fit was exactly to factory spec. Garage shop guys did not have that capability. We did. Maybe I got a little bit more money than the garage guys got, but I guaranteed the machines. In the process, I proved Cone could make money. Maybe not enough, but we could get orders.

While I was rebuilding our relationship with Ford, I created another problem. I promised to revamp the machines, engineering-wise. A lot of people wanted automatic bar feed added to the back of the Cones. It was simple. You get rid of the manual bar feeder and change it out for a magazine loaded automatic bar feeder. Instead of an operator loading bars one at a time by hand, you just load a bunch of bars on a tow motor and dump them into a magazine. A lot more efficient for the customer, and easy for us to do.

Right. Well, of course, this would require doing engineering, and in Cone's thinking each individual machine had to be engineered separately for each customer. So that was too big a job. But you really didn't need engineers to do it because the bar feed supplier would have done all the work for you. It turns out I had an engineering problem at Cone too. Another old-school internal problem.

Eventually, we got enough Cone rebuilds, plus we got some orders for big Blanchard builds—120-inch machines, our biggest standard machine. So that was really good. We had some trouble building the Blanchards because we couldn't get the tooling to work. I jumped in and helped. I was doing engineering, working on the floor, and trying to sell machines and parts all at the same time. We were beginning to climb out of our hole.

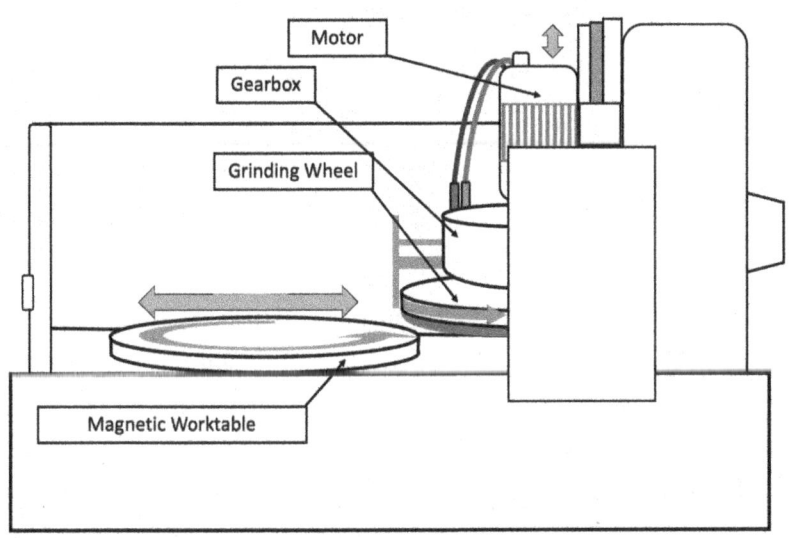

Blanchard grinders are solid, simple machines than can work in a production environment for 100 years. The rotating magnetic worktable holds the workpieces in place and moves under the grinding wheel. The rotating grinding wheel moves up and down to accommodate part thickness.

I was never good with money; Klaus was the money guy. I was the engineer, plant guy, sales guy, whatever you want to call me. We needed money. The machine shop business, it was doing OK, but it wasn't a game changer. With Cone, all we had were some rebuilds and talk about a new mysterious machine. And Blanchards, you couldn't sell new Blanchards if your life depended on it. They lasted for a hundred years. That's why I started rebuilding Blanchards and selling Blanchard parts.

Klaus bought a house in Vermont and was trying to get me to buy one too. He was all in on Cone. He moved to Vermont. His house sat on a mountaintop. It was a new house, had a few acres of land, never lived in, and had a pond down below and a trout stream, so it was a really nice place.

My wife, Nancy, would not move. No way. I had Nancy and the kids up for the summers. We had guests and friends up there. I had her family up there. I spent two years up there. But she wouldn't move.

I had a really good time in Vermont. I was working like crazy, but Nancy was stuck there with the kids, not knowing the lay of the land. She hated it. The nearest McDonald's was an hour away. Can you imagine telling hungry kids, "We'll be there in an hour?" And you didn't shop in Vermont because in Windsor there weren't any real grocery stores. They had convenience stores, and that's about it in Windsor. You had to go across the river to Lebanon, New Hampshire, to buy groceries or really find anything to buy.

We were in the middle of nowhere. That was a problem for us business-wise. Customers had a tough time getting to us. You had to fly to Manchester, New Hampshire, or Boston, Massachusetts.

And then there was another two-hour ride. I complained to Klaus about this too.

Despite all this, we eventually were able to keep Cone going with spare parts and rebuilds because I had finally, finally, finally made friends with Ford again. Ford had forgiven me. Pittler was history. Ford was the one of the biggest Cone customers around. They accepted me as a Cone person, quoting new machines and working on new stuff. We started selling the rebuilt Cones. We started making just enough money to break into the black—this relieved a lot of pressure.

I had already talked to Klaus about running the company and taking over. He would come up and he would take care of the money. I never was any good at taking care of money. While I was at Cone and while Klaus was still at Motch, Klaus hired a guy to take care of the finances at Cone. He turned out to be a real screw up too. He bounced checks at Christmas. Do you believe that?

Guess who had to straighten that mess out? Me. I had to go to the distributors. Cone wasn't exactly rolling in orders, but we had enough orders on the books and enough machines, mostly rebuilds for Ford. I went to the distributors to beg for money. They had the right to keep your money for 60 or 90 days.

I had to get people to pay up by begging them, "Would you do me a favor?" and "We'll make it up to you." That kind of thing. I got enough money together to cover the payroll for Christmas.

But Nancy was . . . Oh my God, my wife Nancy. I never cashed any of my checks, and they didn't have direct deposit back then. My check would come in the mail no matter where I was. And Nancy took care of the family money.

She would always go to the bank and cash my check. Well, our Christmas paycheck bounced. I never heard the end of it. I never know till this day whether I straightened out the mess because of Cone or because of Nancy. But we just straightened it out.

Cone was in kind of a money crunch at the time. And I caused the crunch because we were doing more than we thought we would. You need money to buy the materials to make parts. You don't get paid for months or a year after a machine is ordered. So we needed money. After this whole payroll check bouncing fiasco, Klaus decided to take over the money, and the money guy was gone.

The lesson we learned was that we needed to sell new machines to make real money. But getting customers up to Vermont was a problem. With the Tornos bus experience in mind, I suggested, "Let's buy like one of the super-duper tour buses with a bar in it." I was going to hire some hot Vermont ski babes and fly customers into Boston or Manchester and drive them up to Windsor. That didn't go over too well with the Vermont people. They thought it was too low-class. But Klaus thought it was a great idea.

Let's buy an airplane!

The Cameron order I sold for Motch taught us that we could sell just about anything. New machines. Big deals. So Klaus decides that we should buy an airplane to attract customers because Cone was so far away from everything. The deal was he would buy the plane, he would learn to fly it first, then it would be my turn and I would learn to fly it. We could get customers to Windsor, Vermont.

Klaus thought buying a plane was a great idea. I thought maybe it was not a bad idea, either. Plus, I wanted to learn how to fly, right? The model airplane builder in me agreed, "Yeah, yeah, sure, let's buy an airplane."

So then, of course, we had a big argument about what kind of plane we're going to buy. He ended up buying an SOCATA turbocharged Trinidad TBM. I told him, "No, no, don't buy it. Buy a Beechcraft." In my mind, after I started learning to fly we would get a Beechcraft Bonanza.

The Bonanza is a single engine plane. I think it's a five- or six-passenger. It's like the Porsche of airplanes.

Anyway, Klaus bought this Trinidad, and it was a nice plane, very fast. Maybe a little faster than the Bonanza, but maybe harder to fly too. I was leary of it. Once, the nose wheel collapsed when Klaus landed the plane. I did not like flying in that plane.

SOCATA Trinidad similar to the plane that crashed with me in the back seat.

I kept telling Klaus, "This thing just isn't right. This plane just isn't right." I was taking flying lessons at the time. I was taking flying lessons at Cuyahoga County airport, outside of Cleveland. I had about 40 to 50 hours of flight lessons which Motch paid for. The whole idea at that time was to eventually upgrade the plane. At least that was my idea. I wanted the Baron, which is the twin-engine Beech and a hell of an airplane. And it seats six passengers, so it would have been the perfect plane.

Everything kind of evolved during this year and a half period. That's when I figured Klaus was finished at Motch because he started concentrating on Cone and the airplane. The whole reason for the airplane was so he would get back and forth to Cone. Then Klaus buying a house in Vermont, spending a lot of time up there, sending his daughter, Susanne, up there to work with us—it all added up. Motch was history for us.

Having Klaus and Susanne in Vermont was really a good thing because the Coneheads needed to be kept in line. I don't care what you say; legend has it that the New Englanders are the original Yankees. They're smart, hardworking, with all the traditional American values. Baloney. Those traditional conservative Yankees all moved to the Midwest, and the people left behind in Vermont—in Yankee land, in new England—are all flaming liberals.

They want to be taken care of by the company, by the government... doesn't matter. Whatever work ethic they had in the past is long gone. The only thing those people want to do is join the union. You wouldn't believe the problems we had at Cone with these people. I mean, deer hunting season, really? That holiday that lasted three weeks.

Then, springtime. "Oops, I'm not going to be at work today." "Why not?" "Sap's running." "What?" "It's maple syrup time!" These people . . . I really enjoyed my time up there. I enjoyed the people very much, but they aren't workers. I hate to say that but it's true. Figure it out. Where does Bernie Sanders come from? That's the mentality in Vermont. Their biggest export is their kids. It's the honest to God truth. As soon as you hit age 18 in Vermont, you're on the train out.

Getting the Ford people up to Vermont was a problem, but I did get them to come up. Not on our plane, though. Too much liability—we couldn't afford the risk of killing our customers. So they flew into Boston, rented a van, and made the two-hour drive to Windsor. I did get them to start dealing with us again. First, with rebuilt Cones. We started making just a little, little, little bit of money; enough to get us into the black. We got up to about $9 million to $10 million, and we actually made about five bucks profit. Real profit. Not accounting magic profit. This made Klaus really happy.

Klaus was about 10 years older than me. At that time, I was in my early forties, and Klaus was early fifties, and he says, "Ed, you know, I don't want to do this forever. I'm going to take on Cone, and you're going to run it. And when I retire in 10 years, Cone is going to be your deal."

Then he let me in on his Big Idea. We would move production of the Motch machines up to Vermont. And I said, "Well, we can't sell them from here. This is a real disadvantage from a sales standpoint. We've got to do something else."

Klaus agreed and the idea was roughed out. I was going to move back to Cleveland, and we would rent or buy a small building near the airport, and we would use it as showroom and a service headquarters for Cone Blanchard, Motch, and Springfield. That's what we would have done. I thought it was a good idea to run the service out of there because we could easily get to any where we wanted to go. Plus we wouldn't have to move to Vermont. That would make Nancy happy. I would travel, but I wouldn't be away for a month at a time. it would be like the Motch days.

Everything was falling apart at Pittler. They were going down. At the time when we were talking about this, I first thought all this was pie in the sky. I really didn't take it too seriously, to be honest with you. But then again, Ford wanted us to design a new screw machine, plus they wanted to buy a whole bunch of horizontal single spindle machines. Sunshine broke through the clouds.

I talked to Klaus about designing a new screw machine. He had all these engineering contacts in Europe. He had a guy who designed some big Blanchards for us. He would be the guy to design this new type of screw machine. It was going to be designed and built in Europe. I got a commitment from Ford for $50,000 to do some of the engineering work upfront before even ordering a machine. Plus they gave me a promise to buy 30 or 40 machines. So this was a big deal. I gave it to Klaus. And that's what we were working on before we got on the plane.

Chapter 9

Our Business Was Ready to Take Off . . .

Then Hillary Clinton showed up and my life took a sharp left turn.

We finally got to the point where, on the day of the flight, Klaus had finally sealed the deal with the investment company and we were going to get enough money—$6.5 million—to do what we had to do, which was to cover the finances for Cone and to finance our plan for the Motch machines—buying the drawings and moving production to Vermont. Motch had to be part of the deal, otherwise we didn't have much going for us.

Getting Motch would be like getting a shot of adrenaline. Adding Motch to Cone would be like finding $10 million to $20 million. Even if we just sold half of what we sold before on top of the Cone rebuilds, maybe adding the mysterious new Cone European designed machine, plus the Blanchard parts business, Blanchard and Springfield were always good for a million dollars in parts sales every year. We would be using the Cone plant to its full potential without increasing overhead.

I would move back to Cleveland and open a sales office where we would sell Motch, Cone, Blanchard, and Springfield machines. The facility would feature a showroom, where we could do demos, and it would house our service and parts center. Being in Cleveland, we would have easy access to Detroit and all our customers. And it would be easy for them to come to us. Cleveland made sense—the city had a machine tool heritage, being the home Motch, Warner & Swasey, National Acme, Bardons & Oliver, Lucas Machine, and others.

Our track record with Motch and the orders that we got in the past were a great incentive for a finance company to give us a loan. I'm sure a very compelling proposal was put together with all kinds of pro forma projections. Klaus took care of that. And we could have gotten the Motch drawings cheap because Pittler considered Motch a loser.

A lot of Motch's service business was moving south. President Clinton signed NAFTA into law, and it was going into effect in a month. For the time being, service sales for Motch were excellent. NAFTA created a lot of short-term service business for Motch. Customers were moving their machines to Mexico and paying Motch to install them and get them running down there, especially the brake guys, like Budd and Wagner. They had a lot of those FMS systems I sold. They were all moving to Mexico.

Customers even hired Motch service guys to get their Mexico production going so that at that time, the service business and the spare parts business were very profitable. Budd moved more than $10 million worth of Motch machines down to Mexico, and Wagner did the same thing. Others followed.

Clinton's NAFTA made Ross Perot a prophet. He said the huge sucking sound you heard was our jobs—American jobs—going south. The Tri-Cities Budd plant closed. Budd had an incentive to move their production outside the U.S. Thanks to NAFTA, a lot of my customers were moving out, and my buddies were losing their jobs. Factories were being closed, but, in the short-term, it meant money and opportunity for Motch, which fit into our plans. Motch's customers were jumping on the NAFTA bandwagon. By moving Motch production to Vermont, we wanted to be part of it. I had no clue as to how else Clinton policies would impact me. But I was about to find out.

For us, for now, opportunity was in the air. We had a big meeting at Cone that day, Thursday, December 2, 1993. The basic theme of the meeting was "Thanks for the memories." Everybody was told how different the new Cone would be.

George Caccavaro ran Cone before I got there. Now, Caccavaro would be gone, but he wouldn't really be gone. You know, it was the same with John Mylonas and me. Gone but not really gone. That's the way Klaus operated. George would be still involved with the business somehow, but he would have no authority whatsoever—an ambassador to the past; the way things were. One way to manage change was to make it look like nothing was changing. It keeps people from getting too nervous.

We didn't tell anybody about Motch coming to Cone, but we kind of hinted around at it. Klaus ran the meeting. It was basically about the changes coming up. Klaus would be there full-time, I was going to be there, and Caccavaro and all these other guys would be stepping back a bit. There would be changes in the machine shop. There were some problems with OSHA because some of the machines were old and didn't have the proper guards.

Getting the machine shop up to speed was a central focus of the meeting. We had the money to do it. Making these changes would put us in the perfect position to produce Motch machines. When the meeting broke up, Klaus told me we had to get to Cleveland. I say, "Whoa, why do we have to go to Cleveland?" And he says, "Because we're going to get the drawings and announce that we're taking over the Motch lines." We had to be there the next day, Friday.

"OK. I'll jump in my van, and I'll meet you there. What time?" And he says, "No, no, no, no." He had Harry Frankford, our corporate pilot, fly the plane up. The three of us would fly back to Cleveland. Then we would be bright-eyed, bushy-tailed in the morning for our big Cleveland meeting.

I really didn't want to fly home in that plane. I don't know why. It was a bad day. It was really overcast. It was a sleety, snowy, cold day. I just thought, *I'll just get in the car and drive home.* It was a 12-hour drive. I'd made the drive a million times, so I said, "I'll just drive through the night and meet you there in the morning." Klaus: "Oh, no, no, no, no, no, no." So he talked me into going, which was against my better judgment, but I did it.

So we were waiting at the FBO (Fixed Base Operator—the airport services facility) where the plane was getting gassed up and checked out, and Harry's filling out the flight plan.

Klaus was talking to me and he says, "We're going to really do this thing. We're going to build Motch machines in Vermont." So that's when we finally decided, and we had to decide before we got into the Cleveland meeting that I could stay in Cleveland and we would do the sales office in Cleveland and set up a demonstration room and service and spare parts.

Then we had to decide where we were going to do this. The Germans always had these crazy location ideas. They'd say, "Let's put the sales office in Chagrin Falls. Nice town, harder than hell to get to from the airport." German weird, you know.

I said, "Klaus, Klaus, Klaus . . . The reason we're doing this is because we're in the middle of Vermont and I can't get anybody to come here. I want our sales and service facility right by the airport. I want it so you can get off a plane, get into a cab, and get here in just a few minutes." He finally agreed. "Yeah, yeah, you're right. You're right. You're right. We'll start looking for a building someplace around the airport." Our business was ready to take off.

When we got on the plane, everything seemed fine. But there was a big problem at the airport. Hillary Clinton's plane was there. It was a big commercial heavy jet that looked like a 737. Now we're talking Lebanon, New Hampshire, here—country airport; home of the puddle jumpers. The airport was probably pretty much like any country small-plane airport.

Everything that flew in and out of Lebanon was basically a private or really small commercial plane. This big jetliner changed the whole dynamics of the airport—it was different. Maybe because it just so happened to be Hillary Clinton's airplane. The First Lady.

She was done with her speech on healthcare at Dartmouth, and she was leaving when we wanted to leave. We filed our flight plan to take off at a certain time in a certain direction. All of a sudden, her plane needed to take off, so all traffic stopped, and she got priority over everything.

We were told to get out of the way. We were actually on the taxiway ready to go. We had to pull off to allow her plane to take off ahead of us. Then we were assigned a different runway—the secondary runway; one we never used before. To top it all off, this would be the first time Klaus ever took off at night—it was pitch-black outside. Harry and Klaus had to reprogram the flight path while we were on the end of the taxiway, as Hillary's big jet was taking off in our place.

The Lebanon airport had two runways. If you took off from the main east-west runway, you would be heading east, turn left over the river—north continuing west—and see the lights of Lebanon. On the secondary North-South runway, if you turned left, you would fly east, continuing north toward tree-covered hills. Our new runway, North-South Runway 18, was tricky. It was several hundred feet shorter, with much larger trees closer to the airport.

Tower: *"Trinidad two-eight-one-six-three is cleared to the Charlie golf foxtrot airport as filed, maintain six thousand, expect one-zero-thousand five minutes after departure..."*

Klaus acknowledged the clearance to fly to the Cuyahoga County airport. At 5:26:30 p.m., Klaus said he was ready. Ten seconds later, he was cleared for takeoff.

The plane took off quickly and started to climb at full power—all 250 horses doing their job. The controller watched as we took off. We were just a couple hundred feet off the ground when we started our turn. Turning this soon, this low violated the Lebanon airport's safety protocols. Because of the rough terrain, the requirement was to reach 1,500 feet before executing any turns. That was the minimum.

The controller couldn't believe we were turning so soon, too low—less than 300 feet up—still climbing. We kept turning too early, too sharply, too low; heading for the heavily forested Farnum Hill right next to the airport. Even though we were still climbing, the 800-foot hill was a lot higher than we would ever get.

The air traffic controller was alarmed. *He radioed us.*

Tower: *"One-six-three, you have that hill in sight there?"*

~~Tobago~~ Trinidad **163 (Klaus):** *"One-six-three, say again!"*

Tower: *"Can you see that hill there?"*

No answer. The plane's landing lights were still on as it sped upwards toward the hill. The controller could see the lights shine on the trees. The plane continued to climb, but the trees reached even higher. The controller could see the plane go into the trees, landing lights showing the way, still climbing as it made contact.

For a few seconds the plane held course, still striving to climb through the trees, still climbing, fighting its way through the branches, skimming the treetops until . . .

Crash investigation showed the plane under control and climbing until a catastrophic event. The crash scene was surveyed from the air a few days later. Two trees stood much taller than the rest. They showed significant impact damage. The plane struck those trees with such tremendous, devastating force, it could no longer sustain flight. No hope. It was ripped to pieces.

The plane went down, hitting thicker branches and tree trunks as it fell. Wreckage—bits of plastic, metal, and glass—was scattered over hundreds of yards. Impacts sounded like explosions. The plane struck tree after tree after tree for nearly a quarter of a mile. The plane's top cruising speed was about 215 mph. It took about five seconds for the plane to hit the forest floor. Imagine hitting brick wall after brick wall at 150 mph. Unbelievably violent.

The controller couldn't believe what he saw. The pilot had flown out of the Lebanon airport dozens of times. Why would he fly straight into a hill?

Tower: *"Trinidad one-six-three, how do you hear?"*

Tower: *"Trinidad one-six-three. Tower."*

Silence.

A Cessna Skyhawk N734EE was approaching for landing.

N734EE: *"Find that airplane down there. Is he OK?"*

Tower: *"Calling Tower. Say Again."*

N734EE: *"Did you lose an airplane down there?"*

Tower: *"I think we may have. Sir, if you could make a left turn there just down at the end of runway three-six off to the east of that . . . it looked like he hit the hill."*

A Business Express commuter plane (GAA 524) was on the ground.

GAA 524: *"Yuh. We just . . . Biz Ex five twenty-four . . . we just heard him go in up there."*

Tower: *"Biz Ex five twenty-four, say again."*

GAA 524: *"Yuh. We just heard something crash up there."*

Tower: *"Thank you."*

Tower: *"Cessna four echo echo, it looked like he was up nearer the red light just off to the east of the number of three-six up on the top of the hill there."*

There was a red light on the hill, marking an 800 foot elevation. In addition, the airport had 29 warning lights mounted on poles about 30 feet high, which started prior to midfield of runway 18, and extended 1,200 feet past the departure end of the runway, warning pilots away from the hill.

Biz Ex GAA 524: *"Yuh. That's exactly where it sounded like it came from."*

Cessna N734EE: *"We don't see anything right now."*

Tower: *"Cessna four echo echo . . . you can't see anything?"*

Cessna N734EE: *"Ah, no we don't. We'll probably come in and land if it's alright."*

When a plane crashes in the forest so close to the airport and residential areas, everybody hears it.

The plane was definitely down. The fact that the Cessna pilot couldn't see anything was good news. There was no explosion. There was no fire. And the crash site was just a few hundred yards from the airport east-west runway on property owned by the airport. If there were survivors, maybe they could be saved. The control tower saw the plane's landing lights shine on the trees as it went down, so they had a good idea where it crashed.

Within minutes, more than 100 emergency personnel, volunteers, and local residents gathered at an orchard on Poverty Lane, a two-lane road that cut through the tree-packed hill above where the plane went down. The forest between the road and cleared land at the end of runway 3-6 is where they would find the wreckage.

The rescue parties were made up of state and local police, firefighters from the surrounding communities, local residents, medical personnel, the FAA, Civil Air Patrol, and members of the upper Valley Air Search and Rescue, a nonprofit group put together after a fatal air show accident the year before.

Plane wrecks in Vermont and New Hampshire are sometimes never found; the forests are so dense. Just a couple of months before this crash, they found a plane that went down in the 1960s—30 years earlier! There was a sense of desperate urgency to find this plane. They knew about where it fell. If they found the plane quickly, it could make the difference between life and death.

Searchers were organized into six groups, forming lines of about 12 to 15 people each. They would conduct a grid search until they found the plane. The groups stood about 30 to 40 feet apart and marched into the woods. Slogged might be a better word.

This forest was not like any pristine suburban park. It was wild, packed tightly with a dense underbrush and debris. Slow, dangerous going. The night was pitch-black; visibility was nil. To make it even worse, the ground was uneven, slippery, rocky, and covered with waist-high debris and brambles which tore at their clothes, slowing their progress to a crawl.

It was rough going. Extremely rough. Wet. Boggy. Painful. The dense woods, pitch-black sky, steep terrain, and packed underbrush made the downhill search very difficult and dangerous.

Roger Sharkey, owner of Sharkey's Helicopters based at the Lebanon airport, was in the air almost immediately. The searchlight on his helicopter scoured the tightly packed woods, desperately looking for the wreckage. He crisscrossed the area time and time again, watching for any sign. He ran low on fuel, flew back to his base to refuel, and returned in just minutes, determined to stay with it.

On the second go-round, Sharkey spotted a signal fire and found the remains of the plane. There was at least one survivor! He hovered over the spot, aiming the searchlight on the wreckage so the land-based rescuers could reach the crash site. Even so, Sharkey told the Valley News that the night was so black that, after he found the plane, the rest of the searchers had a difficult time getting to the wreckage. "You couldn't see your hand in front of your face."

Because Sharkey's company was located at the airport, he had seen Klaus land or take off dozens of times. He couldn't believe that Klaus would make such a stupid, catastrophic mistake. Sharkey told the Valley News, "I have no idea what happened. It's not like the hill jumped up in front of him."

That was the big mystery. Why did Klaus turn into the hill?

Short answer: he had to take off from a different, unfamiliar runway to make way for Hillary Clinton's plane. That didn't seem to click with Klaus or Harry, as they tried to reprogram the flight controls—or maybe they overcompensated.

I don't know what they did. I was in the back seat, and they were in the front. I can remember specifically that they are sitting there and their fingers are going like crazy, pushing all these buttons. They rushed the programming. Turns out, they made three mistakes.

First mistake: it didn't sink in that we were on a different runway. Second mistake: they didn't pay attention to the book, probably because they were used to doing things a certain way and didn't think a different runway would make that much of a difference. So they turned way too low, more than 1,000 feet below the minimum for a safe turn. Third mistake: overconfidence. This was the first time they took off at night. Because it was so dark, they couldn't see where they were going. Because they were instrument rated, maybe they didn't think that would make a difference. Hard to say.

The Airport Facilities Book has diagrams of the runways and the taxiways, the FBO operators, the radio contacts, phone numbers, and rules and regulations. When you take off, you're not supposed to make a turn or do anything until you reach a minimum altitude. For Lebanon, it was 1,500 feet before you can make a turn. They were still climbing when they crashed about 250 above the airport. How could that be?

Klaus had 600 hours in the plane. He had his instrument rating, but still, 600 hours is considered a dangerous milestone when you're learning how to fly. You've reached a point where you think you know everything; you have enough experience to be dangerous. Klaus was smarter than that. He did the right thing. He relied on Harry who was the senior pilot, the instrument-rated safety pilot, his instructor, and friend. When Klaus asked, Harry told him to turn on the autopilot.

As the plane went down, it rolled over on its left side in the final seconds, trees tearing the glass canopy off the cockpit before it hit the final tree, and nose to the ground, with only pieces of the right wing still attached; hundreds of feet below the warning light on the hill. Only a about 250 feet up an 800-foot hill. Flight time: less than two minutes.

We were big news in New Hampshire and Vermont.

Fatal Small Plane Crash

1 A single-engine Socata TB 21 Trinidad, piloted by Klaus Eberius with co-pilot Harry Frankford, takes off at 5:28 p.m. Thursday, carrying one passenger, Ed Fiktus.

2 The plane veers left, toward an 800-foot hill.

3 About 100 searchers from police and fire departments, aviation groups and a volunteer search and rescue squad respond to Poverty Lane Orchards, where a command post is set up.

4 Searchers spread out along Poverty Lane and move west-southwest into the woods.

5 At about 7:30 p.m. Thursday, searchers find the wreckage and a battered but coherent Fiktus, who was in the back seat when the plane went down. He is now listed in serious condition at Dartmouth-Hitchcock Medical Center. The bodies of Eberius and Frankford were removed yesterday morning.

Lebanon Municipal Airport
Runway 18
Poverty Lane Orchard
FAA flashing beacon on peak of 800-foot hill.
Trail of debris leading to crash
Crash Site
Poverty Lane
Sources: *Jane's All The World's Aircraft*; FAA; witness accounts
White River Junction
West Lebanon
Map Area

Valley News – D. Marietta

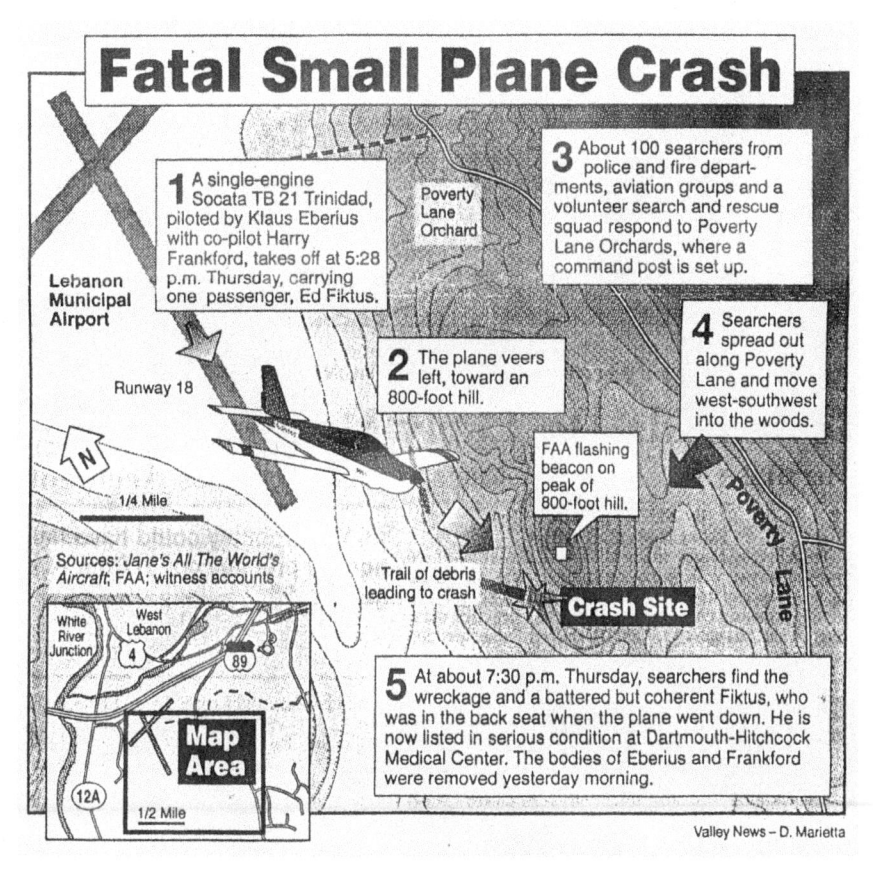

We were in the air for less than two minutes. Nobody could believe what happened. The Valley News drew a picture so people could better understand the accident. With the top two guys at Cone-Blanchard involved, people were afraid this would be the end of the company. Unfortunately, it was the beginning of the end.

Chapter 10

I Think, and Then I Remember I Was Dead.

But I didn't feel dead. I felt wonderful. Yet how else could I see and talk to my Mom? She'd been dead for seven years already. And Bobcia and Uncle Frank . . . all dead. And who the heck was My Friend?

Let's get this dead thing over with. Because when the plane crashed, the adventure began.

George Caccavero was the next guy in line at Cone after Klaus and me. He was the guy on the scene at the crash. I know that for a fact because I saw him. He identified the bodies. He told everybody that Klaus and Harry, who were dead, looked like they were asleep, not a mark on them. But Ed (that's me), Ed looked like death itself. Bloody, bruised, beaten to a pulp. I was the one who looked like hell. Yet here I was.

I did shit and piss my pants. When you die, you evacuate. And I did. Big time. But there was more to it than that. The plane was stopped, I vaguely saw, like through a filter or a cloudy window, that the lights were still on in the dashboard, and Harry and Klaus were there. They looked like they were just sitting there and I was disoriented in the back seat and I didn't feel any pain at all. I felt nothing. I was feeling no pain. I felt wonderful.

There was no sound whatsoever. Total silence. Then I heard this big booming voice inside me, "*YOU CAN SURVIVE THIS IF YOU WANT.*" I heard that voice when we were crashing. That voice. The voice was inside me, but it wasn't me. It was smarter, wiser than me. I call the voice My Friend. My Friend was with me and was guiding me, helping me see.

Then it was like a curtain was thrust open and I wasn't in the plane anymore. The plane was gone. I was someplace else.

I went somewhere, and that somewhere is very difficult to describe. I've been thinking about this ever since. But I don't know what to tell you. Actually, I went to three somewhere else places, like clicking a remote to change places. Click, I was there. Click. Another place. Click. *MOM!*

I first went to a place and I, I . . . there's no way that I can describe it to you. This is the best I could—there was a walkway. There was this path to walk on, but it wasn't natural. It wasn't like a mountain trail or dirt road. Somebody made it. That was what it looked like to me. It was dark, it was black, and it went on very far and all around were lights. All around me were these balls of different colored lights. I can't describe them to you.

They weren't in front of me. They were all around me. I can't describe it. Did you ever take chemistry class? And you know how they had those toy models of a molecule, you know, where they had the interconnected balls, all different colors and they're joined together by these little sticks?

So that would be one way of describing it, but that's not even close. There was all this stuff around me. Like at Christmas time, you know how you had the fairy lights everywhere? And they're all around? In the trees and everything? One thousand points of light? Millions? Something like that.

They weren't points of light; they were balls of light. Well, at least in my mind they were balls of light. All different colors.

It's so frustrating trying to describe what I saw. What I saw is difficult to describe because I really have no reference point from my life. In some ways I can describe my feelings, how I felt, better than I can describe where I was. Where I was, it was like no place I'd ever been.

You see, the whole thing with this and I've thought about this for a long time, I don't believe I'm supposed to remember an experience like this. The reason why I only have flashes of it is because I'm not allowed to remember. I feel very strongly about that. Sometimes I even feel guilty about talking about it because this is the most confusing thing in the world to me.

But I can tell you more about how I felt than where I was. I felt wonderful—no worries, no fear, total peace, serene, curious, confused. Not angry. Not upset. And My Friend reassured me. I was in awe.

So I was on this road, then it was like somebody pushed a button on the remote. Then click. I was gone. I was in the Sound of Music land. Like when Maria was on the hilltop and the grass was a foot tall . . . and I was running through fields and the wind was blowing, and the sun was shining and it was a wonderful place. I was there. I have no explanation.

Then click. I was gone from there. Just like that. It's just, you know, in my mind and my memory, it was like click, click, click. Where was I now? I was with my Mom. My Mom! She died seven years ago. Bobcia was there. My Uncle Frank. How can this be? Yet, in a very matter-of-fact way, we struck up a conversation. We were talking. I was standing there, talking to my Mother, Bobcia (grandma—my Dad's mom), and my Uncle Frank. And behind them, there was a whole bunch of people in a line. I have no idea who they were, but they weren't part of the conversation. Maybe they were relatives from generations past, I don't know, but they hung around.

I remember my Mom, Bobcia, and my Uncle Frank. The thing that mystifies me to this day is why my Uncle Frank was there. I have no idea. Maybe because they were all dead. They were all family. I had a conversation with my Mom, for sure, and Bobcia, but Uncle Frank was a mystery. Maybe he chimed in. I know we connected. It seemed like it in the back of my mind. I know there's a lot more to all of this than I can remember. I believe the reason I can't remember is because I'm not supposed to.

I think the reason that I'm not allowed to remember is because we were talking about a choice I had to make—whether to go back and live, or stay with them, dead. Maybe we talked about my life, my kids, and how my life would be if I went back. And that was the rub. If I knew how my life would turn out, I might make a decision, or a number of decisions that would totally screw things up.

If I remembered, I would not have lived my life the way I should . . . it would have changed. I get the feeling that it would have changed my life in general. Think about it: if you knew everything that was going to happen to you, if you knew what your life was going to be and all the ups and downs, you might try to avoid the downs. And if you knew there was life after life, you might change the way you live your life. And that would be wrong. Having inside knowledge wouldn't be fair to me, to the kids, or anybody else.

Now I don't remember exactly what my Mom and I talked about, but I have an idea. I can guess what we talked about based on the decision I made. You see, My Friend told me from the beginning that I could survive this if I wanted to. Or I could move on and be with my Mom in that wonderful place, feeling wonderful.

But if I chose to go back, then things would be different. Things would never be the same. So I had a choice to make: either to continue feeling wonderful in this beautiful place or go back to the uncertain, the unknown. I think my Mom was there to help me make the right decision.

Chapter 11

My Mom was an Angel...

My Mom was a very beautiful woman, movie star beautiful. Inside and out. She died years ago. How could she be here with me?

My Mom and I had a conversation, and I can't tell you exactly what the conversation was about but it had to do with the kids. My Mom was all about kids; she loved them. I think she wanted me to do right by my kids.

My mother was a very gregarious, outgoing person, and she felt sorry for kids who didn't have a good family life. To help make some kids' lives better, she started becoming a foster parent for Parmadale kids—the local Catholic orphanage. For some reason, she preferred taking care of girls.

The first girl we got was named Norma; she was my older sister's age. My mother believed Norma needed a home, and we were it. Norma would be someone my sister could hang around with, be friends with, be a sister to. My Dad wasn't too crazy about that. Of course, my Mom got her way.

My Dad tried to get Norma to be like him, which didn't work. She stayed with us quite a while, until she was about 17 years old. Then to get out of the whole mess, she joined the Army. She was in the Army for a very long time—about 20 years or so. We still occasionally run into Norma and talk to her. She went to my Mom's funeral.

Norma was orphan Number One. Number Two was this tiny little kid about three or four years old. She was an abandoned baby. Her parents were addicts who abandoned her without food, without anything. She nearly starved. When she came to us, she didn't have any hair, and she had green, moldy teeth. She was so malnourished. She looked like she came out of a prison camp. My Mom nursed her back to health.

But she was, probably because of the malnutrition, a little different. She was a little slow, OK? And she had a wandering eye, where her eyes would cross. Parmadale wouldn't pay for the operation to fix her eyes, so my Mom made my father pay for it. We had her for quite a while. I don't know what happened, but my Mom had to give her up. My Dad would not adopt her because she wasn't right.

My Mom got tired of having the kids around the house for such a long time, and then having to give them up. It was just too hard. Then for the longest time, right through my high school, she would only take care of babies. She took care of newborn babies before they would go to the adoptive homes. The babies would hang around for a week or two or maybe a month at the most. Then they got adopted out.

I remember being in junior high and my Mom would go down the street to her coffee klatch, and she would say to me, "Well, OK. Here's the bottle and here's the diaper." Me: "Oh, Oh OK." That happened a lot. I got good at changing diapers.

When I was in high school, my Mom found my little sister, Lori. My Mom found her at Parmadale. She was Canadian; French Canadian. She was about three years old and very little. She didn't speak

French or much of anything, but she spoke English well enough. She was at Parmadale for a while. And she was a cute kid, with the blondish curly hair; sort of like Shirley Temple.

Lori was just a real trip. We got along from the day we met. She stayed. She was a keeper. When I was a senior in high school, I used to put her on my shoulders and walk to the corner candy store; took her trick or treating. We were became very close. She was our foster child when I was in high school.

By the time I was in college, Parmadale wanted to find Lori a permanent home with people who would adopt her and give her a permanent family home. This set my Mom off. She had a big fight with my Dad and made him adopt her. So she became officially adopted. My Mom wasn't going to give her up. That's the best thing my Mom ever did. I'm closer to my little sister, Lori, than I was to my real sister and my brother.

Lori meets Santa for the first time.

Me and my new little sister, Lori.

Lori and I go Trick or Treating.   Here we are today.

For my Mom, family was everything. For me, this really came to the forefront when my wife, Nancy, was pregnant with our first child, Matthew. I was still working in engineering at Motch. Nancy and I were married, and she was going through some pretty hard times. She was tired all the time; really run-down. She would sleep in till three in the afternoon on Sundays.

At work, my boss got a phone call, and I got called into his office. "You got a phone call from Nancy. It sounds pretty important. You better talk to her." I took the phone; she was crying. Nancy was at the doctor's office and she told me she was pregnant and the doctor inadvertently had just X-rayed her to find out was causing her fatigue. He didn't take any precautions. He didn't know she was pregnant. She was with her mother, and her mother got on the phone and said, "You know, she has to have an abortion because this baby's going to be retarded."

Nancy was crying, nearly hysterical, so I told my bosses, "I have to go home. Nancy's really upset. There's something wrong. I'm not sure what it is." When I got home, I found that her mother tried to take over Nancy's life.

Nancy told me the whole story and the doctor said that just to be safe she should have an abortion because the baby had been exposed to unshielded X-rays. I was stunned. I was really against abortion. I said, "This is too fast. If you're going to have an abortion, you have months before you have to decide."

"You don't have to make that decision right now." I didn't know all the facts, so I said, "We're going to wait, and we're going to talk to other doctors, and we're going to see what's going to happen. And if the baby was hurt, then we'll talk about it, but we're not going to do it now." And my mother-in-law told me right to my face at that moment, she said, "You're taking responsibility for this baby. If this baby comes out retarded or if there's something wrong with this baby, Nancy's out of here. She's out of here!"

We went to Metro Hospital. A team of doctors did all kinds of exams and testing to determine what the problem was—it could be really serious or something relatively minor. We had to wait and see.

In the meantime, it looked like she was going to have a difficult pregnancy. I asked, "What about the baby?" They reviewed the extent of X-ray radiation the baby had been exposed to and felt there's a good possibility everything would be OK.

With the treatment they put her on, she can have the baby, and everything should be OK. It was still a high-risk pregnancy. And she would have to be in contact with the doctors regularly.

By making the decision not to abort Matt, I put Nancy through hell for nine months—most all of '82. It was really hard on her, staying in bed all day and seeing the doctor once a week. So we talked about it. I guess I probably talked her into having Matt. "This might be our only shot. We have to try." I took charge. "Let's do it." She did a really great job. It was a tough pregnancy, but she made it through with flying colors.

When Matthew was born, he was normal; he was fine. He was perfectly healthy. He's OK. He's a great little baby; cute little kid. So now Nancy's mom thinks he's the greatest thing since sliced bread. I'm thinking, *Wait a minute. A few weeks ago, you didn't want anything to do with this kid. You were going to flush him down the toilet. Literally."*

My Mom knew all about what was going on; all the back and forth about ending the pregnancy. My Mom loved kids. She would never allow an abortion, no matter what.

My Mom just went through the roof! That kind of hypocrisy, that two-faced double dealing just set her off. That caused a big break between Nancy's family and my family—a giant sink hole opened up between the families.

My Friend took me to my Mom so she could talk to me about my kids' future. That's what those conversations with my Mom and my Babcia (bob-cha—Polish for grandma, my Dad's Mom, Julia)

were all about. And that's how they convinced me that I needed to be around, needed to live to raise the kids. Otherwise, they weren't going to turn out good. Does that make sense?

Bobcia and my Mom loved kids. Matthew was the oldest. There's six years between Matthew and Taylor because of Nancy's condition. She didn't really want to have more kids after Matt. Since everybody thought Matt was going to be our one and only, they all doted on Matt, even Bobcia, my Dad's mom. Bobcia thought Matthew was a *ładny chłopczyk*; it means "pretty little boy" in Polish.

About six months after Matthew was born, Nancy went back to work. Matthew was just a little baby. For Nancy's mother, taking care of Matt was beyond her. She was not going to raise a kid.

So my Mom raised Matthew when he was a little kid. When my Mom passed away, Matt was maybe two or three; my dad still watched him. Matt could do whatever he wanted to do during the day. It was kind of a weird situation because Nancy's mother always made a big deal out of Matthew, but all she ever did was buy him stuff. She spoiled him rotten.

I guess in retrospect I don't know if Nancy was the right choice for me. We were diametrically opposed, personality-wise. It worked for my Mom and Dad, but not for me.

If you looked at my mother and my father, my mother would be me, and my father would be Nancy. My Mom always managed to keep my Dad pretty much under control. He wasn't that bad of a guy. He had his moments, and a lot of it had to do with my Mom.

My Mom made him a much better person and I tried to do that with Nancy, but that didn't work out. Maybe I wasn't good enough. Or maybe it's a one-way street where a woman could make a guy a better person, but a guy can't make a woman a better person. I was always traveling—that might have had something to do with my efforts falling flat. It loosened our connection. Then Nancy had her mother too, and her mother was . . . *oh God!*

I think when I was with my Mom and Bobcia, wherever it was, the message was that if I left the kids, there would be trouble. At that time, Adam was two, Taylor was five, and Matthew, 11 years old or so. I got the feeling that if I didn't do something, if I didn't make it back, they would end up in terrible shape.

If I didn't make it back, Nancy's mother would be more involved in my kids' lives. Nancy relied on her mother, and her mother and I didn't get along.

When we got engaged, her mother threw a fit, I think, because I was more or less Polish. Her mother was married to a Polish guy, Nancy's father, so Nancy is half Polish. She won't admit it, but that's what she is. And Nancy's mother was pure Italian. She got a divorce early on and remarried, so Nancy never knew her father; never been in contact with him.

Her mother kept her away from the whole Polish side of the family. Nancy refused to believe she was half Polish. This was a problem during the pregnancy with Matt because the doctors wanted to know about her parents' medical history so they could better understand what was going on, but her mother would not allow anybody to contact her father's side. We were flying blind on half of the baby's family—Nancy's side of the family—in the middle of making life-and-death decisions.

As long as Nancy wasn't around her family, she was a great person. But as time went on, she got more and more connected to and more dependent on her mother, probably because I was on the road a lot. She called her mother twice a day.

I think my Mom and Bobcia were right, convincing me to come back for the kids. There was no question about it. They convinced me to go back for the sole purpose of the kids.

The whole reason for my life is the kids. That was really interesting because I was never really that crazy about kids. When I was younger, my attitude was "Yeah, they're OK as long as they're cooked properly." After Nancy got pregnant, that all changed.

My Mom and Bobcia convinced me to come back for the kids to make that decision. But how did my Uncle Frank fit in?

Uncle Frank was a drunk. But he was a great drunk. He was a great guy, but he was not a good father. I can remember being a little boy and my dad driving out to a bar and picking him up drunk and dragging him home. But he did like Matthew at the end of his days. He got throat cancer, and he talked with one of those things you hold to your throat.

Matthew used to get a big kick out of the way Uncle Frank talked. He used to call him "Uncle Robot" because back then Matt had these Transformers. Uncle Frank's voice sounded like a robot. So maybe that has something to do with it. I don't know, maybe Uncle Frank was concerned about Matthew. I don't know.

Uncle Frank was my father's brother. My father was the youngest of 10 kids, and Frank was the second youngest. They were very close. My Dad would help Uncle Frank and his family as best he could. Maybe Uncle Frank was thanking me or telling me my kids needed my help. I don't know. No clue as to why Uncle Frank was there. Don't remember.

I always was pretty close to Uncle Frank's kids. He had five kids and one adopted daughter. They were always living on the edge because Uncle Frank used to drink his paychecks. Uncle Frank's son, Clarence, is 10 years older than me. Clarence went to work when he was 16, got into steel mills, and worked there all his life and pretty much supported his whole family. My dad helped them out as best he could.

My Friend told me I had a choice to make. I could survive this if I wanted to. But if I chose to go back, things would never be the same. My old life was over. Gone. No Cone-Blanchard deals. No big shot machine tool sales. That life was over. I would begin a new life. It would not be easy.

I decided to come back for the kids. Now, what my Mom said, what Bobcia said, what my Uncle Frank said, I have no idea. I have a feeling. It was about family.

I have no real memory. If I knew what was ahead of me, I might not want to go through with it. I had to live my life. I can only guess based on the choice I made. I could stay or I could come back—come back for the kids.

But being there, wherever it was, with my Mom, Bobcia, and Uncle Frank was a really great experience. To be honest with you, that was just my feeling. I needed that clarity of purpose. That was how I see it. And that was how I feel.

My decision to live for the kids was more of a commitment than a deal. I wasn't promised anything in return. The easiest thing for me to do was not to come back. I mean, it was very clear to me that I didn't have to decide to live. I didn't have to do this. I had the feeling that if I didn't want to do this, it would be perfectly OK. I would not be judged. Yet I didn't choose the easy way out.

Because I made my decision, it was time to go. My Friend was with me. The whole time. In the plane. No pain. Click. I'm on a road. Click. In a field. Click. With my family. Click. Behind a curtain. ZOOM! The curtain opened, and I was back in the plane. Thank God My Friend was still with me. *"YOU CAN SURVIVE THIS IF YOU WANT TO."*

I wanted to live. My new life was about to begin.

Chapter 12

I'm Back . . .

EEEEYYYYAAAAHHH! What the hell? This is not right . . . this is not fair . . . why do I hurt so much?

I woke up in the plane without any pain at all. My Friend told me I could survive, if I wanted to. Great. The first thing that I remember was that I could smell gasoline everywhere. The plane was full of gas—the tank held a little more than 80 gallons. We just took off. It was a real terrible smell. I yelled to Klaus and Harry, "There's gas everywhere! Get out of the plane!" How do I get out? "Get out of the plane! Get out of the plane!"

When we took off, Klaus was in the pilot's seat—the left-hand seat, the driver's seat. And Harry was in the right seat as the copilot instructor. I sat behind Harry. Behind Klaus, wedged in between his seat and the back seat, was this big case, like a traveling salesman's catalog case. In it was this really big book with hundreds of pages—the Airport Facility Book.

It was printed on vellum; real thin pages like onion skin. It tells you all your approaches and all the rules and regulations for each airport. This pilot bag was behind Klaus, so I sat behind Harry. When we came to a stop in the trees, I was behind Klaus because I had ripped the seatbelt out of the floor.

I decided the first thing I should do was get out of the plane. I was worried that the plane might catch on fire because the dashboard, the instrument panel, was still lit up. The turn indicator was still on.

You could hear the gyroscope spinning. We had electricity and we had gas leaking all over. I remember going through the safety drills. When you're in the back seat, the back window was a punch out.

You have to kick the window out to get out of the plane. When I kicked, there was nothing there to kick out. *There was no friggin' glass!* It was blown out! I kicked air. I was surprised. "Holy crap, there's no window." I was worried that I wouldn't have the strength to kick it out. I was worried that the plane might catch on fire because the dashboard was still lit up.

I had to get out of there, but my feet just kicked air. I went into the air and landed on the ground outside the airplane. It was only a couple feet off the ground, but when I landed, I really felt it.

EEEEYYYYAAAAHHH! Jesus, Mary, and Joseph, why the hell did I come back? The pain was un-f**king-bearable. You wouldn't believe how bad it was. *PAIN!* Everywhere. I couldn't stand it. Constant. Unrelenting. Piling on. Ramping up by the second.

My back was broken. My ribs were so broken they crossed over. My chest caved in. You wouldn't believe how screwed up my chest was. Smashed in. I'll let you feel it. My guts were ripped. I had burns on my stomach and ruptures from the seat belt. You don't even know. You can't. Just can't.

It was like the worst pain you could ever imagine. I don't, I can't even describe it. Every frigging part of my body hurt. I was crying in pain, like a baby. The pain was so bad, I didn't know how bad I was hurt. I just was overwhelmed in pain.

When I was in the plane there was no pain. When I came back, I crashed all over again into unrelenting pain. When that pain came, it was . . . big. Geez, I never thought I was ever going to survive. It was just totally unbearable.

That was the craziest thing. It was like no pain, and then, OK, we're going to live now. *EEEEYYYYAAAAHHH!* All of a sudden, I'm back on earth. Unbelievable pain.

That was when it hit. Right? That was where it was like crash, *boom*. I was actually on the ground outside the plane, smelling the gas, and I was telling Klaus and Harry to get out of the plane and . . . Jesus Christ! "I can't help you! I hurt like hell!" You know, I was crying like a baby here. I was really, really, really in pain.

"I smell gas. Get out!" There was no response from Klaus or Harry. They were just sitting in their seats. They weren't slumped over or anything. They were just sitting there.

I tried crawling away but didn't get that far. I couldn't. Maybe 20 feet away or so, that was as far as I could go. And then the pain kept hitting me. I could smell gas everywhere. I mean, it was just smelling like crazy and the lights of the dashboard were still lit up and you could hear the turn indicator beeping. So I thought right away, *FIRE!* I told Klaus and Harry, "Get out of the plane. It smells like gas."

I was trying to crawl back to the plane, but I stumbled and slid down a gully. I tried to get up. I couldn't. I didn't realize I was so hurt. I fell and I, you know, we were on the side of a steep hill, and I slipped down this hill and I landed on this ledge in this big pile of leaves.

I don't know how far it was. Maybe 10 or 15 feet. It seemed like it was far, but who knows? I stopped in a pile of leaves; ended up on the edge of a cliff. I didn't know it. It was dark; too dark to see anything. The ground was wet. The leaves were wet. Another foot or two sliding down that gully, I would have fallen off a cliff. Dead. Again.

I was under the leaves. I was cold. I was going to give up. I crawled out of the leaves and ended up sitting on a ledge. My Friend and me. I was sitting on the ledge, ready to give up, thinking how I would miss Nancy and the kids; how we might work this out. I was thinking I was going to get better. I was going to go back to Nancy, and we're going to live happily. You know, hunky-dory. Everything was going to be great.

As we sat on the ledge, I wondered about the future. I hear, *"THE DEAL WITH KLAUS AND GETTING MOTCH IS NOT GOING TO HAPPEN."* I'm thinking, *OK, but I'm really worried about the kids and what will happen.* *"YOU SHOULD BE."* Some Friend.

I was thinking about Nancy and how we might work this out. My Friend interrupted me and said, *"IT'S NOT GOING TO BE THE WAY YOU THINK IT'S GOING TO BE. IT'S GOING TO BE OK, BUT IT IS NOT GOING TO BE THE WAY YOU THINK IT'S GOING TO BE."*

He says, *"THE CONE THING IS OVER WITH. YOU MIGHT AS WELL JUST KISS YOUR JOB GOODBYE."* He knew what was going on politically and everything at Motch and Cone. And then he told me that my life with the kids and with Nancy was not going to be hunky-dory. It was not going to be the way I thought it was going to be.

We were sitting on the ledge—it was a rock outcropping—and we were talking about Cone, and I was going to smoke a cigarette. I had cigarettes in my pocket. I always tell everybody that smoking saved my life because I had a cigarette lighter in my pocket and we were here and we were talking, and I was going to light a cigarette, and he said, *"YOU PROBABLY SHOULDN'T DO THAT."* And so I didn't.

I had a tough time breathing. My chest rattled. The seatbelt caved my chest in. But I didn't realize it then. Did you ever, like, when you were a kid, did you ever play marbles, and did you ever keep your marbles? My dad used to smoke pipe tobacco—Prince Albert in a can. He used to get these tobacco tins, and I used to keep my marbles in there. And if you walked around with the marbles in your pocket, they would rattle. Remember or imagine that noise. That's how my breathing was. I rattled like marbles in a tin can—a death rattle. I couldn't breathe. I was gasping for breath. It was scary.

When we got on the plane, I had this really nice warm coat, scarf, and hat—the executive look, you know. I took that all off when I got on board. So I just had my suit pants and a white shirt on, and it was really freezing cold. I couldn't walk. I couldn't move.

Then I got to the point where I just said, "I can't make it. This is bullshit." My Friend said, *"YOU CAN MAKE IT. YOU'RE GOING TO BE OK. JUST RELAX."*

I almost gave up. Like I said, I slid down a cliff and landed on a ledge in this big pile of leaves. I started getting really cold, so I curled myself up, trying to breathe, trying to walk, trying to move. Everything hurt me. I had a hard time moving my arms; a really hard time with my hands, and my leg was . . . my right ankle hit one of the feet on the seat in front of me. The little feet bolted to the floor. I didn't know if it was broken or not, but it didn't work. Nothing worked.

I was ready to give up, and I was covering myself with the leaves . . . and My Friend stayed with me. We were sitting on a rock. These ledges were common in Vermont and New Hampshire. The mountains had these rock outcroppings and you can sit on them. It was like a ledge. From that ledge, it just went straight down. George Caccavaro later told me it was 30 or 40 feet straight down.

So we were on this ledge—me and My Friend—he said, *"DON'T GIVE UP!"* We actually had a conversation there. I could look down on the city of Lebanon. I knew the river was there, and I knew Windsor was just across the river and the Cone plant was over there.

And here we were. Klaus and I finally got this deal with Cone going, and I could really see where it would work. I didn't think we would have ever been huge machine tool company, but we could have had a real viable long-term company. Yup.

I already made the decision to go back, to live for the kids. I was thinking, *There's Cone.* And My Friend told me, *"YOU'RE GOING TO BE OK, BUT THINGS ARE NOT GOING TO BE THE WAY YOU THINK THEY'RE GOING TO BE"* Almost those exact words.

Here's the thing. I was really miserable. I got the leaves off me, and I was talking to My Friend. We're on the ledge looking over the city and thinking about Cone-Blanchard, but he really had to make me understand that the thing with Cone was done.

One of the reasons why I never really went back to work was that My Friend finally got me to understand that no matter what I was thinking I could do, it was not going to be that way. I just couldn't pick up where I left off. My kids and my family . . . it was going to be OK, but it was not going to be the way I thought it was going to be.

"IT'S NOT GOING TO BE THE WAY YOU THINK IT'S GOING TO BE." In other words, I was thinking everything was going to be hunky-dory, back with Nancy. But My Friend was telling me that was not how it was going to be. It was not going to be picture-perfect, but it would be OK. How many times would he have to tell me before I finally got it? Because I wasn't getting it.

While we were sitting on the rock and he was trying to make me realize things would be different, I wanted to have a cigarette. Do you believe that? I could barely breathe and I was thinking about having a smoke, and he talked me out of it and he said, *"YOU'RE GOING TO NEED THAT LIGHTER."* I think maybe he didn't want me to fumble around and lose my lighter, so he talked me out of smoking. If I fumbled and dropped the lighter off the cliff, I would have never made it. I would have been screwed.

I almost gave up. I was getting cold. So I covered myself up with these leaves. I figured, OK, I'd bury myself in these leaves and maybe I'd take a little nap, you know. My Friend said, *"NO, NO, NO, NO, NO, THIS ISN'T A GOOD THING. GET BACK TO THE PLANE! YOU'RE GOING TO BE OK. YOU'RE GOING TO BE OK!"*

And then I thought I heard Klaus's voice. My Friend encouraged me to go back to the plane. I gotta get back to the plane to get the guys out of it. And then the pain. It was not only the pain; my body didn't work. I couldn't walk.

I want to make it clear. My Friend wasn't just a random thought in my head. His voice was amplified—loud—BOOM, BOOM, BOOM. In my head, the voice was extraordinarily strong.

But the strange thing was that when I was talking to My Friend, the pain went away. At least it seemed like it did. It probably didn't go away, but it was pushed far back in my mind. Sitting on the ledge, talking—no pain. When I started climbing up off the ledge, the pain kicked in again. Big time.

I had to make it back to the plane. I started crawling. I couldn't walk. I started crawling up the ravine—it was pretty steep—back up to the plane. I started calling out, "Klaus! Klaus! I can't get to you. I'm down here. I fell. I'm down here. I'm coming up there. Get out of the plane! Get out of the plane!"

I could swear I heard Klaus call my name. Later on, the people from the FAA said that no, Klaus and Harry were already dead. But I swear to God, I could hear him call me. That gave me incentive to get back up to the plane, and maybe save them.

I started crawling and crawling. I didn't know how long it took me, but it took me quite a while. I could hear a helicopter flying around. They were looking for us. They sounded like they were really close. You could see he had had spotlights on, but it never came close to us. The helicopter was always far away. Then it went away. As I was crawling up this ravine, the helicopter disappeared. "Oh shit. That's the end of that." They've given up looking for us.

Again, I was almost positive I heard Klaus call my name, and so I just kept crawling up this mountain. The helicopter was gone. And My Friend wasn't saying much, but he was not discouraging me, either.

I'm probably not doing a really good job of describing what happened. None of the doctors, or the FAA guys believed I slid down the mountain and crawled back up. They couldn't believe that I would have had the strength or the stamina to do that. And they didn't believe that I heard Klaus call.

Years later, thinking about it, I believe Klaus was dead, but I believe I was maybe in between at the time—dead and not dead—so I could hear him. That was what made me climb up the hill back to the plane. Between My Friend and Klaus calling, I felt I had to get back to the plane, no matter what.

I finally got to the plane. During this whole time my breathing sounded like marbles. Rattling in. Rattling out. Nothing was working, and I was freezing cold. Then all of a sudden, I was not cold anymore. I couldn't figure that one out. By the time I got to the plane, I wasn't cold. And it was sleeting and snowing. It was a December day. It was cold, and I wasn't cold. Not anymore.

I got up to the plane to Klaus's side of the airplane and I was saying, "Klaus, Klaus, come on, get out of the plane!" The smell of gas was everywhere. I put my right hand against the side of his head and neck. He felt warm. Warmer than me, for sure.

I figured, *OK, he's alive. He's knocked out.* So I kept yelling at him, "Come on, Klaus! Come on! Get out of the plane!" No response.

I never worried about Harry. I probably called his name, too, but I don't remember doing that. I sat down; nothing was happening. Klaus wasn't moving. I was pretty sure he was alive because he was warm. "What do I do now?"

The helicopter came back! It was flying back and forth. I figured they must have gone for gas. That was probably how long it took me to get up the hill. The timing was perfect. The helicopter was a Godsend. I had to do something. I went into the window I thought I kicked out but I didn't have to kick out, and I knew that the case with the book was back there. I reached in. I opened the case. Inside was the flight book with all the airports. I ripped out a handful of those vellum sheets. They would burn. Then I found some insulation from the plane and got back outside the plane. The helicopter was flying overhead.

I had got to get their attention somehow, so I would start a fire. I had everything I needed—paper, insulation, and a lighter. I always say that smoking saved my life because I had a pack of Salems in my pocket . . . and a lighter. A lighter!

I pulled back out of the plane with all this stuff. It smelled like gas. I figured I couldn't light a fire here or the damn thing was going to explode. I would start a fire and burn us all up. So I crawled away. I didn't know how far away, but it seemed like an eternity.

I crawled to a point where I didn't smell the gas anymore. I set the stuff down and got my lighter out. Then I realized I didn't have a thumb.

My thumb was bent back parallel to my arm. I couldn't work my thumb. I couldn't light the lighter! My right hand . . . the right side of my body took the brunt of all of this—my right ankle, my right leg, my right chest, my right rib cage, my right arm, my right shoulder, my right hand, and my right thumb.

I was sitting in the right side of the plane so I was up against the plane and that was where the shoulder belt came across from right to left—high on the right, down low on the left, buckling across my left hip. My whole right side still bothers me today. I still drag my right leg. If you look at my shoes, I wear out the right shoe heel before I wear out the left one because I'm always dragging my foot.

So I got away from the plane. I was ready to start this fire. I made a little pile of paper and insulation, and I realized I didn't have a thumb!

It took me a God-awful long time to figure out how to use the lighter. My little Bic was not working too well, either. I know I could strike the flint on the lighter—get a spark—but I couldn't hold down the little lever to keep the gas going; to keep it lit. It was one of those 19-cent Bics. But it saved my life.

I could use my index fingers. I could hold the lighter in my left hand; use my index finger to flip the wheel, but I couldn't hold down that little red lever. It took me a while to get that going. Try and try again. I—the engineer in me—finally figured out a way to do it, and I set the pile of paper and insulation on fire.

Before you know it—five minutes later, ten minutes later—the helicopter came. He shone a light down on me! He saw me! I waved to him with my left hand. At that point in time, I was at the end of my rope.

I couldn't move; couldn't get up. Breathing was really hard for me. So I just sat and waited. I was having a tough time. I was sitting up somehow, trying to keep vertical so I could breathe.

After a time, I might have even passed out. Sometime later, these guys showed up; surprised me. "What the hell?" They were rescue people from the fire department and the airport firemen. They were looking for me.

I didn't know this at the time, but they sent out a rescue party right away, and they had people searching the mountain for us. Then what I learned later, the air traffic controller was looking out for us as we headed for the mountain. He saw our landing lights shine on the trees as we went down, so they had a pretty good idea of where to look for us.

These guys showed up, and the helicopter left, and the firemen were there. They wanted to put me on a stretcher. I said, "No, I can't. If I lay down, I'm going to die. I can't breathe." They heard me rattle as I struggled to breathe. I asked them to hold me up so I could breathe.

Two guys—one in front of me, one behind me—held me up vertically. I offered to buy them dinner if they got me out of there, but I was in no condition to do that. Another guy went to get an oxygen bottle. The two guys held me up there for quite a while; maybe a half hour. They were strong. And kind. I was no better than a 220-pound sack of potatoes with wobbly knees. The guy came back, and they put an oxygen mask on me, and I felt better.

They put me on the stretcher. I didn't know how far it was, but someone said a quarter mile, half a mile up the mountain. They had to walk downhill, you know. A helicopter couldn't take me out because there were too many trees—no place to land.

The only way to get me off that mountain was to walk me down on the stretcher with my oxygen bottle. One guy was looking over me all the time. It was such a long trip; such a hard trip because I'm a big guy.

They became a relay team. These guys were great. The four guys carrying me would get tired, another four guys would come up and get in front, they would pass the stretcher to them, then the first four would go ahead and have the stretcher passed to them. It was a relay team, like passing me along in a bucket brigade. I was the bucket. They might have substituted too. It was a rough way down. Through the woods, dense underbrush, over stone walls; steep, muddy, and slippery—no place to be with a stretcher. We eventually made it down to the grassy part of the airport where it was flat.

There was an ambulance waiting. It was from Dartmouth-Hitchcock Medical Center. The doors were open. There were nurses and EMTs. They got me in the ambulance.

The first thing I said to the nurse was "How bad is it? Am I going to make it?" And her answer was "What religion are you? Are you a religious man? What faith do you belong to?"

I said, "I'm Catholic." She turned around and called the hospital to make sure there was a priest there. I was scared. "Oh shit, this doesn't look too good." But then again, I didn't worry about it because I felt that My Friend was almost laughing, or maybe it was me. I didn't know what, but I didn't worry about it at all.

The next thing they did—I don't know if it was her or somebody else in the ambulance—they took a bag of . . . it wasn't blood, it was plasma—the clear stuff. And they put the bag of plasma in the microwave. I thought, *What's this about?* Then they stuck the needle in, hooked me up with lines, and they pumped me full of this warm plasma.

"Oh, MY GOD!" I'll tell you the feeling of that warmth coming into my body was the best feeling ever in my life . . . better even than sex. I can't describe it any other way. It was absolute pleasure. Pure joy. It wasn't a drug at all. It was warm plasma. It was bringing me back to life. I never felt anything so good in my entire life! Not ever!

I found out later on that I was within like a half a degree of being dead. That's how cold I was. When I touched Klaus's neck, I was so cold, so near freezing, so near death that he was warm compared to me. The plasma they put into me in that ambulance was life-giving. I'm sure it saved my life. I'll tell you that being brought back to life was a very, very unbelievably joyful moment. Orgasmic. *WOW!!*

When we get to the hospital, who was there to greet us? Who was the first guy I saw? The head of trauma? You'd think I would see a doctor, right? No. It was a priest. Father . . . I don't know who. He gave me the last rights right there on the stretcher before I got into the ER.

The medical staff thought I was going to die. They must have gotten word from the ambulance. They made sure I would go to heaven, but I just came back from a wonderful place on my own free will. I knew I wasn't going to die. Not now. I had My Friend's word. The doctors weren't so sure.

Then they took me into the emergency ward, and somehow or another they got my clothes off me. The first thing I remember is I was on my stomach, and they were pushing on my ass. I think they pushed my intestines back into me. Could that have happened? They pushed so hard, I thought, *Oh my God, what the hell are you doing?* I was half out of it.

I was in pain the whole time. I remember the bleeding. It was terrible. But the first thing they did was they did my ass. Whatever they did to it, I don't know. But they did something. They pushed really, really hard. It was like somebody taking their fist and sticking it up your ass. I have a hunch that I must have blown something out there.

Then the next thing they did, the doctor came in, turned me over, and it was my right lung. They cut a hole in my chest in between my ribs, and they stuck a tube in.

They reinflated my lung. *JESUS!* I thought I was going to die right there. I mean, the pain was like, Holy crap. Oh my God, did it hurt! Screaming pain. God! My lung popped like a balloon. More drugs. I passed out, so that was that.

Remember when you were a kid and had all those pimples that that had to be popped? Well, I had plexiglass pimples. The windows of the plane just exploded, and I got all these little shards of plexi embedded in my face. I must have looked like that pinhead guy from Hellraiser. They cleaned that up, too, not that it made me any prettier. Thank you, Dr. Plexi Popper. Overall, I guess I looked like a midlevel member of the walking dead.

On Saturday, I got a visitor. I was groggy; drugged up. This guy was from the FAA wanting to know what happened. He was Johnny on the spot. An eyewitness account was important. But the doctors didn't know whether I would live or die. He made sure he got me on record right away, just in case I didn't make it. I never knew the government to be so efficient. Maybe because Hillary's plane took off just before ours made it more important. I don't know.

The crash happened the night of the second, a Thursday, and here the FAA guy was in my hospital room on Saturday, the fourth. He asked me what I thought caused the crash. I'm always kind of flip and so I told him, "Hillary Clinton." I said we were scheduled to take off one way; everything was computerized to go a certain way. And we got switched, switched around because Hillary Clinton's plane was taking off, and Klaus and Harry got our flight plan wrong, so we ended up crashing. If she wasn't there, I don't think we would have crashed. That was it.

Being a smartass under the influence of drugs was not the best way to be when talking to the government. I thought I was being funny. But the FAA guy wrote it down in his report. Little did I know, it would come back to bite me in the butt.

Chapter 13

The Burgundy Bed

When I woke up, I was rocking back and forth. Back and forth. Rockabye baby in the treetops . . . Treetops! What the F**k?

Where am I? The next thing I remember was waking up in this narrow burgundy bed. I don't know how to describe it. It was like you're in traction. It wasn't an ordinary bed. On a boat when you're sailing, the boat leans one way or another. Back and forth. Right? You're never straight up and down on a sailboat . . . it rolls with the waves.

Well, that was what this bed was like. It had rails on all sides, padded all around, and it was so narrow the sides almost touched me. That was how narrow it was. And I thought I was sailing. It was rolling left and right. Left and right. Left, right, left, and right. I don't know why it did that, but that's how it was when I woke up.

None of the doctors believed that I would survive. But I never felt I was going to die. Not again, anyway. I had confidence in what My Friend told me. So I never felt I was hurt that bad. But I really, really was hurt so bad most people would have died. Not me. Not again.

I guess I wasn't afraid because of what I went through—meeting My Friend, talking to my Mom . . . and the promise My Friend gave me. *"YOU CAN SURVIVE THIS IF YOU WANT TO."* I took that as an actual promise. I really wanted to live. I was ready to do what it took to make a life for myself. I felt that My Friend was looking out for me and would help me.

I was stretched out in this burgundy red bed. I felt like I was trapped, and the bed was rocking back and forth, back and forth. I had all these tubes going into my arms. It was kind of weird. I wasn't uncomfortable because, after they inflated my lung and did all that stuff that hurt, they put me on some heavy narcotics, and I think I probably went to sleep or passed out from whatever they did to me.

The burgundy bed moved back and forth like a hammock, but it wasn't a hammock. It was stiff. It was firm and held me tight. I was stiff in there, and I could feel the padding up against my head and up against my sides. It was up against my legs. All around. I think I might've been Velcroed into it somehow because I was stuck to it. I could move my hands, but I was stuck in this bed. I was trapped in this thing. What the hell was this? If it rolled over, would I come loose or still be stuck?

It was rocking me back and forth, back and forth, back and forth. There were these machines behind my head. I didn't know what they were. I didn't know what they did. I couldn't look around to see them, but the one thing I do know was that the machines controlled the painkillers; maybe some kind of morphine drip.

When I woke up and I realized I was in this bed and it was moving, and I said, "What's going on here?" I guess I startled the nurse. She said, "You're OK! You're OK!" She reached up and pressed the button on this machine behind my head. And, oh jeez, I was off to La-La land again.

I was just lying there. I didn't feel any pain. I felt nothing. I was just swaying back and forth, back and forth in this burgundy bed. I felt like I was out on the boat sailing, you know, because I was moving around back and forth, back and forth. I guess I passed out again because of whatever they were giving me. The drugs worked. I guess I sailed through a lot of pain.

The next thing I remember it was daylight when I woke up. I was in this bed. I don't know how to describe it to you. I was hurting all over, but I was not really feeling any pain. You know, the one thing about narcotics is they don't really take away the pain. At least they didn't for me, but they make you feel better about it. You don't care about the pain. And so I was just swinging away and swinging away. And I had to go to the bathroom.

I had to take a dump. Right. I guess I had a catheter in me for number one. I don't remember all of it. I was so out of it. But I remember there was a trapdoor on the bottom of this bed. Yeah. The nurse came in and stuck a bedpan or something down there. She said, "Whenever you gotta go, just go." And that was what I did. OK. Then she took away the pan and closed the trapdoor. And I went back to just swinging away, swinging away, swinging away.

I don't know how much time went by, but I was slowly coming to my senses. Every time I asked "What's going on? What's going on? What's going on?" The nurse would come in and said, "Don't worry about it. Don't worry about it." Then she'd press this frigging button. And there I was off into La-La land again.

Every time a nurse walked by, she would press that frigging button. I had no control over it. I wanted to say, "Don't press that button. Let me do it." Then she pressed the button. And I was down again. Not a care in the world. Right. I don't know how long this went on, but it went on for a while, I guess. A few days, anyway. It got to the point where I started to hallucinate. One day I woke up and there was my wife, Nancy. "Holy crap." Is this real?

I didn't think it was a good idea for her to come, for a lot of reasons. I wanted to have her wait. I wanted to be in better shape. But when I woke up, there she was. And she brought my Dad with her.

I didn't want her there, especially with my Dad. I told Caccavero, "Tell Nancy what happened, but don't have her come up." Lickety-split. She was there.

She had the kids to take care of. She had things to do. And to be honest with you, I didn't know if I was going to make it or not. The doctors and nurses did their best to scare the crap out of me. What would they do to her?

When I was getting in the ambulance and the nurse asked me what religion I was, a priest met me at the entrance to the hospital to give me last rights. I was banged up, bloodied, and bruised all over. The doctors gave me the impression I wasn't going to make it. The looks of concern on the nurses' faces . . . Even though I couldn't see what I looked like, I knew I was a mess. I thought it might not be good for Nancy to see me like this. If I did die when she was there, I didn't think she could handle it.

When the kids would get hurt, Nancy would lose it. Part of Nancy's Italian culture is to get little girls' ears pierced very young, so Taylor got her ears pierced as a baby. One day she was laying in the neighbor's hammock playing with the dogs and she hooked her earring in the rope of the hammock and pulled it out of her ear, right through her earlobe. Blood was everywhere. She was bleeding like a fountain. Nancy freaked out. I said, as calmly as I could, "Don't worry. Don't worry. Get a washcloth." Meanwhile, Nancy was a basket case.

I didn't want her to come out here and see me all beat-up, with tubes everywhere. I was afraid she would freak. So I wanted her to wait. Anyway, she showed up with my father, who was over 70 and was starting to show signs of dementia.

My Dad would lock his keys in the trunk of his car at the grocery store ... do things like that. We all knew where he was headed, so he was the last person in the world I wanted to come up there. Not that I didn't want to see my Dad. And not that I didn't think he was worried about me, but I just think, physically, he shouldn't have come. It was too tough on him. Then, again, Nancy needed a crutch.

Of all the people to pick, you don't pick somebody who's losing it.

I said, "Hi, Nance, I'm glad to see you. I'm OK." But then I said, "You brought my Dad? Geez, why didn't you bring your mother? Why didn't you bring your dad? Why did you have to bring my Dad? Why not my brother or somebody else?"

Even though I didn't care for Nancy's mother, for Nancy's sake, it would've been better to bring a relatively sound person with her. It really didn't matter to me who she brought to support her, but, in my mind, my Dad was the wrong choice. So now it turned out I was not only half dead, but I also had to worry about my Dad because he couldn't even remember to turn off the gas on a stove.

I didn't know what Nancy was told about my condition. Maybe she thought I was about to take my last breath and she wanted to give my Dad the opportunity to say goodbye. I don't know. But the bottom line for me was that instead of bringing in somebody to help, Nancy brought somebody she needed to care for. Nancy had to worry about him and me too. More trouble. This wasn't good. It was bad.

Anyway, I was swinging away in the bed and Nancy was there. She didn't know what to do. I didn't know what to do. Nothing I could do. And my Dad was just taking it all in, not saying anything. I don't remember how long it took me, but somehow or another, I convinced Nancy to stay and send my Dad home. I was worried about my Dad. But he got home OK, and Nancy stayed.

I think Caccavero or one of the guys from Cone got him on an airplane. Nancy made arrangements for my brother to pick him up at the Cleveland airport. We got him home. I figured that was the best thing to do. I told him, "OK, Dad, I'm going to be all right. I'm just all beat-up. You know, don't worry about me. Everything's OK. You go home, and we'll all be OK." The folks at Cone put Nancy up at the Sheraton, and she hung around for a couple of weeks. It was getting close to Christmas.

Chapter 14

Bye, Bye, Burgundy Bed . . .

She drove my van to the land with me in a cast,
had no drugs, didn't think I could last . . .

Nancy: "I want you home for Christmas." Me: "Holy crap. How the hell am I going to get home for Christmas? Look at me! I can't get out of bed. I can't stand. I can't walk. How can I go home? I'm all drugged up. I don't care. Honestly, I don't."

I hope to God you never have to get in a situation where these people just keep pressing a button on a machine, loading you up with painkillers. Whenever I became a little clearheaded, somebody came along and asked, "How are you doing." "I'm doing great." Hello! They pressed the button, and then I was off to La-La land again.

I don't know what they were giving me, but it worked. You know those miracle drug commercials where the side effects are longer than your arm? Well, with my PTSD- rocked brain, I started hallucinating. I started having the weirdest dreams you ever heard of! Terrible dreams. The girls from Cone brought a bunch of those balloons that float around; those silver helium balloons.

One night, I think the nurse pressed the button. I was sleeping and having this dream. These balloons were flying around my room. The heater was on, and the air was pushing them around faster and faster. And they became Harry's and Klaus's faces being smashed against the wall. I was freaking out!

Then I was having this strange dream where Nancy was all alone and she was in trouble. And I freaked, I totally freaked!

I told the nurse, "Call Nancy! I've got to see her!" I had no sense of reality at all. I didn't know where I was. I didn't know what I was doing. I saw crazy, horrible stuff. I panicked. I wanted to talk to somebody I knew. I knew that Nancy was somewhere around. I begged, "Could you please find Nancy?" It was in the middle of the night, and I was really scared; sweating scared.

The nurses called Nancy. She showed up and was she ever pissed. "Why are you waking me up in the middle of the night?" I said, "I just had to talk to you. I just had to see you. I had this bad dream." She was in a rage; no calming her down. My reality was worse than my nightmares.

I thought, *Oh, Christ! Now I'm really screwed!* I felt I couldn't count on her anymore. She didn't understand. She couldn't understand. I was all alone. The nurses didn't know how I felt. Nobody could. So their solution—well-meaning, for sure—was to calm me down with painkillers. I had lots of terrible dreams from there on in, but I kept them to myself. Nancy shut me down. I didn't call her anymore. I just gritted my teeth and got through it. I had dreams like you wouldn't believe.

It was a frustrating, grim struggle trying to get through this because I was hurt so bad, and the drugs with their side effects. It didn't matter to Nancy. She told the doctors, nurses, everybody, "I want to get him home for Christmas." That caused an uproar.

I could care less about Christmas. But she was worried. Her mother was having problems with the kids. The kids were hyper. They didn't know what was going on. It had been a week or so—forever in kid and babysitter time, not much in healing time. But Nancy wanted to go home.

I said, "I'll be OK. Go home." She said, "No, I'm not going home without you. You have to go home. The kids want to know if you're OK . . . yada, yada, yada, yada."

Later I found out that the night of my accident she had an accident too. Nancy always wanted a BMW 325i convertible. One year I sold enough machines to make lots of money, and I had enough money to buy her a BMW 325i for Christmas.

She wanted a red one. So I bought her a red one with a tan leather interior. I gave it to her for Christmas. And she said, "That's a wonderful car, except I can't stand the interior." Me: "What's wrong with the interior?" She: "It's tan. I want black." OK.

I felt like a jerk, but I called the dealer and said, "Hey, I got a problem. This car has a tan interior. I need black." Thankfully, they took it back. I had to pay some more money. They had to ship one in from New York, but it had a black interior. Great!

The night we crashed the plane, when she heard about it, she put the kids in the car, going to her mother's. She was so nervous, so upset. She had the doors open. She backed up and ripped off the passenger door of the car. She was frantic. Adam was in in the baby seat. Thank God he didn't get hurt.

She was insisting that I go home for Christmas. When she gets an idea in her head, you can't shake it loose. She grabs hold and won't let go. Meanwhile, her mother took the car to the BMW dealer to get it repaired without telling me anything about it. I didn't find this out until later. My car, my company minivan, was at Cone. So in her mind, we were going to drive home to Cleveland for Christmas in the minivan. That was it.

I had no clue whether I was even going to be able to be released by then. Christmas was just a couple of weeks away. Right? The doctors told Nancy, "It's not a good idea. You shouldn't do this. He should be here a lot longer. He's got so many things wrong with him."

But Nancy being Nancy, she won. She was taking me out of there no matter what. Their solution was to put a big heavy full torso cast on me to stabilize my back. That way, I could move without doing any more damage. They said if I could get up and walk, they would let me go home. One condition: I had to go to University Hospitals in Cleveland and check in with the head of Orthopedics as soon as I got home.

This was Nancy's plan for getting me home. I was all drugged up. I was out of it. I was not thinking straight, but I thought it was a bad idea. I was in no shape to argue or put up a fight. I thought I should have stayed there, but like the idiot that I was, I just did what they told me to do. Nancy hounded everybody to get her way. We were all scared—doctors, nurses, me. Resistance was futile.

To get the cast on, I had to get out of the burgundy bed. This was not good. You know, when it comes to bones, a lot of medical treatments are pure agony. Question: how do you put a full body cast on somebody who can't stand up? A heavy plaster cast from the neck down to the groin? Their answer: they hung me like a hammock and wrapped the cast around me.

I'm a big guy—six feet four—with a broken back, crushed chest, and broken ribs, and they were going to hang me horizontally to put a cast on? They were going to stretch me out, almost to the point of dislocating everything to wrap the cast. They pulled and pulled, stretching me out from both ends. For pure torture, the rack had nothing on this thing. To get this cast on, I was held up by my neck and arms and by my feet, and there was nothing in between. I was a human hammock. *I was a friggin' HUMAN HAMMOCK!* They were like a spider wrapping up its dinner.

My back hurt so bad. They kept pulling me to get me as straight as they could. I screamed and I was yelling and swearing and I was screaming at the #@!&%^#* nurse and the doctors. You wouldn't believe the pain. They started wrapping this plaster around me. But I had no support. Absolutely no support because they had to wrap it all around me. Human hammock. They were plastering all around, layer after layer. It was getting heavier, but they couldn't put the cast on right if I sagged, so they pulled harder.

The pain was so bad. I swear to God. I swear to God, I would kill every #@!&%^#* doctor, every nurse in that whole damn place. I used every swear word I knew. I had to apologize to them afterward.

Remember my medication? All this pain, and I was in La-La land when they did it. Oh, geez. You don't know. This was like somebody taking a hot poker right above your ass, like three inches from your ass, and sticking it in your back. And they were rolling you around and wrapping you with all this wet crap. There was no support. It was just unbelievable pain. At the same time, I was pissing blood, spitting up blood. I was in just terrible, miserable shape. And they did this to me. *Oh my God! Un#@!&%^#*believable.*

When the cast hardened, they put me in a regular bed. No more burgundy bed. The cast went from my neck over my shoulders and chest, down past my hips. It was hard and heavy, but it got me out of that burgundy bed. That was when I started seeing what I was peeing. They took the catheter out of me, and I was peeing blood. My pee was like wine. It was really, really scary. I couldn't walk. I couldn't move. I couldn't do anything.

Nancy kept insisting that we were going home for Christmas. The hospital assigned a very nice young woman—a physical therapist, I guess. She told me, "You're not getting out of here unless you can get up and walk on your own." I had her on one side, and Nancy on the other. And we walked. And walked. And walked.

Nancy to the therapist, "Yeah, well, he's going to get up and walk on his own." In a couple of days, I did walk on my own. It wasn't normal walking—the cast prevented a lot of hip movement. It was a rocking Frankenstein walk. Think of Lurch. It was the best I could do. They released me, reluctantly, with the idea that I would go to University Hospitals in Cleveland. The minute I got to Cleveland we should make an appointment. I said, "OK."

Nancy was dead set on getting me home. She wanted to show the kids that I was still alive. I could understand that. Nancy was large and in charge. "OK, you got me out. Now what?" The doctor gave me all these prescriptions for painkillers, and I had been on these painkillers for weeks already.

I was addicted. When you're an addict, you can have cold turkey withdrawal. I wasn't an addict because I wanted to be one. I was addicted because, in the shape I was, pain killing was a medical necessity. Maybe the doctors and nurses thought I was going to die, and I should die happy or maybe I needed that much. I don't know. But I was dependent on them, physically and mentally. I couldn't do without the painkillers.

Nancy decided we were going to drive home in the van. Me: "I don't know if we can do this. I don't know if I can do this. If we're going to do this, we got to stop at a drug store to get the painkillers." I had these prescriptions; there was a drugstore in town, not too far from where she was staying. Easy.

I needed the painkillers for a 12-hour trip like that. Twelve hours. In the snow. In a stiff, heavy body cast. With the seat reclined all the way back. No way I can bend in the middle. I needed the drugs. No way I can make it without the drugs. But Nancy was focused on getting home, not thinking about a drugstore.

I got in the van—half in the bag, three sheets to the wind . . . whatever. She had to drive to Windsor to pick up her luggage. So we were driving down the main street of Windsor heading to the freeway and, honest to God, she stopped at the florist and bought Christmas wreaths. Huh?

I said, "Did you stop at the drugstore? Did you get my pills?" "No, no, no. Not now, I'll get them on the way." All right. I was miserable.

I was so damned miserable, you wouldn't believe. It was a 12-hour drive. I had driven that drive a million times. It was 12 hours, right. We got on the freeway, and we started driving, and you know what she did next? She stopped for a Christmas tree.

She bought a Christmas tree and had the guy tie the tree to the roof of the van. I still didn't have my drugs. I didn't have my pills. When was she going to stop? I needed my pills!

We drove all the way home with a Vermont Christmas tree on the roof of the van. Twelve hours. No painkillers. Couldn't even sit straight. We got home. It was snowing, and everything was crazy. The Christmas tree was one giant block of ice. I really hurt. I needed my pills. I had it with this. Humbug!

I just wanted to go to bed. I couldn't even walk up the steps to get to bed. Nancy's dad, Mike, helped me get upstairs. Nancy would not let me sleep in my bed, our bed. I had to sleep in Taylor's bed which was a kid's bed—too small. I could not bend to fit. No rest. Not for me.

I always had an extra-long mattress to hold my six-foot four frame. Putting me in Taylor's bed—me with a cast—was heartless. It was mean. She could get a good night's sleep in her bed. Not me! The crazy, crazy stupid crap I had to put up with. Unbelievable. Once we were home and I was settled in, she finally went to the drugstore and got my pills. Finally! I spent the whole 12-hours drive and then some in an unholy combination of pain and withdrawal. My own special little hell. Maybe I would have been better off dead.

I guess it was my fault. I should have told her going home was nuts. But I let her have her way. I was so screwed up. What would you have done?

Chapter 15

The Stuff of Dreams

I had nightmares all the time. Really, really vivid. I thought I'd be living in the sun, but I'm trapped in the darkness.

I told you about the dreams I had in the hospital; about Klaus and Harry's faces being on those balloons, with their faces being smashed against the wall. My nightmares didn't stop when I came home. In many ways, they just began. I was living the dream.

They were so real. Before, when I had dreams, I could tell they were dreams. Now I couldn't. I was so much in the dream, I couldn't tell it was a dream. That scared the hell out of me. I didn't know where I was or what was real. It had nothing to do with drugs. I didn't take any painkillers now, except beer. It had everything to do with what I went through, where I've been—a different reality.

I couldn't psychoanalyze myself, but If I tell you about these dreams, they wouldn't sound that bad. There were no monsters, devils, or demons. I didn't feel like something was going to tear me apart. When I describe the dreams, they would sound normal to you, maybe. But to me, the way I felt, they were very disturbing. It might be because I couldn't tell dream from reality, or maybe because I was so emotionally involved. I don't know.

Let me tell you about a dream I had about Svend Wiedemann, the son of Dieter Wiedemann, one of the owners of Pittler and Motch, my old company. When Klaus negotiated his departure from Motch, Svend was made president, and Klaus was going to help him for a couple of years—to gain a foothold for the Pittler machines in the States. In return, we would get the Motch drawings and be able to build the Motch machines at Cone-Blanchard in Vermont. The plane crash blew that whole thing up.

I knew Svend. The company bought him a house in Bainbridge, near where Klaus lived. I went over there for cookouts. He had a nice wife and a baby. I liked him.

I saw him . . . this is going to sound really weird, OK? I saw him in a tree. A big tree, out on a limb. And I kept yelling at him, "You're going to fall! Watch out! You can't do this! You're going to get hurt!"

His wife and his baby were at the base of the tree, yelling at him. I was there, but I don't know where—not on the ground. I was someplace in the middle, somewhere floating, suspended. I shouted, "No! you can't do this! You're not ready! Get down from there! This is bad for you! Get down!" I was scared for him. Really scared. Weird.

I don't know why. Maybe because I really liked the company and was afraid for the people there too. Does that mean, as president of the company, he would fall? Was he going to get hurt? I don't know what being up in a tree meant, but that was what I saw. This dream happened when I was in the hospital, in the burgundy bed, under a lot of drugs. I guess what rattled me was that I had lost my sense of reality. I didn't know where I was. Does that make any sense to you?

But seeing him up a tree seemed like it was really happening. It wasn't a dream. It was like life. Real life. I didn't know where I was or how I got here or how this was happening. I was afraid. Where the hell am I? What the hell is going on here? Is this real? I was probably more afraid for myself than I was for him. Does that make sense?

For the record, under Svend, Motch was sold. After some initial success, the new owners eventually closed Motch, and it no longer exists as a company. For all I know, Svend is back in Germany. There was truth to the dream. That's the really creepy part.

That other dream with the balloons flying around . . . Klaus and Harry. I could see Klaus and Harry's faces smashing, constantly slamming into the wall. It was just like the crash. It scared the crap out of me!

I had other dreams; good dreams too. But what was so unsettling—the thing that scared me so much—was that I always thought they were all real. I believed them. See, feel, and touch real. In the dreams, I didn't know where I was. There was no inner voice challenging what I saw or felt. I didn't know what was going on. I didn't feel any pain or anything. I was just somewhere else. What was happening?

These things were not like dream nightmares. These were like real-life happenings. Everything felt real. The tree was solid; the ground was solid. It was real. I didn't feel it was a dream. Everything was so real, but a different reality. I couldn't understand that.

Later when I was home, I would have dreams about Klaus. I felt bad because I was so hurt and beat-up. I missed the company memorial for him in Vermont and the funeral in Ohio.

I had a dream shortly after the funeral, when I was back home, and I was on the drugs. I dreamt I was in his house. I had been to his house many times. He had a unique house. It was a modern-style house.

He had a fireplace in the living room, but it was open on both sides. And on the backside was his den. Sometime back, we both got the idea that we were going to buy these leather-bound classic books from the Franklin Mint.

We both signed up for this book club, and we were both getting these leather-bound books every month or so. We put them in our libraries, so our bookshelves would have a touch of class—a nice collection of classic leather books.

In one dream, I was at a funeral reception at Klaus's house, and everybody was walking around, talking about how great Klaus was and how they would miss him, and the fire was burning. I walked around the other side of the fireplace, and there was Klaus. He was looking at the books. He asked, "Did you get the latest one?" Me: "I don't know. I haven't checked." He said, "It's *The Three Musketeers*. It's pretty good. I read it." I said, "Isn't this your funeral?" He said, "Yeah. Don't worry about it."

I actually had that dream. It was real. He was real. What did that mean? That he lived on in another reality?

It was one of those dreams where I didn't know where the hell I was. Everything was so real; almost like an alternate universe. I've had many dreams about Klaus since then.

He was alive in my dreams. Some are memory dreams when I dreamed about Motch and I needed to talk to Klaus and he was not there. He was out of town. And then there were dreams when I would see him in totally different surroundings. Nothing to do with work or Motch or anything else.

I had dreamed of him in some kind of a big business. He was running this big, colossal company where I didn't know anybody. I didn't know the building. I didn't know anything. He was there in his big office, laughing, clowning around, and enjoying being Klaus. I was happy for him. I didn't know what any of it meant. Sometimes I just had little dreams about him where he just popped up and asked, "What are you up to?" "Well, nothing much." That kind of a thing. He's always with me.

I know Klaus is OK. That much I can tell you. In whatever he's doing. But as time went on, the dreams got further and further apart. But it was as real now as it was in the beginning, and I was not taking any drugs or anything else for that matter.

I still have these really vivid dreams. I don't know how to describe them. They're not like regular dreams that when you wake up, you can't remember. These dreams are . . . real. I remember.

Sometimes when I wake up from one of these dreams, I don't know whether I'm still in the dream or I'm at home. I ask myself which one was real. What's real—this one or that one? The sense of reality in my dreams is so strong, I'm confused.

Yet the reality I had to deal with in the real world was to get better. To heal. I was miserable. Constant pain. Drugs. Very slow improvement. Snail slow. I was missing dinners. I was missing everything in the kids' lives, events, gatherings. I got my wish. I was with my family, but I wasn't.

Nancy would get more and more angry when I didn't participate in family activities. Even coming downstairs to eat dinner, I just couldn't do it. Physically, I couldn't do it. I got to the point where I thought, OK, I'm going to take care of me. I'm not killing myself to please her anymore. I have to get well. So I did what I thought I had to do. That drove a wedge between us.

I probably missed a lot too because of what I went through—the crash, getting to the hospital, and that burgundy bed. It was almost like a blur. I was so drugged up and I was so hurt, so broken up. Really, the most important part of the whole thing was physically recovering from this. It was really, really a difficult time for me. Add all the extra worries about my Dad's decline, the kids, everything. It was tough.

I think back on the mountain when My Friend told me, *"IT'S NOT GOING TO BE THE WAY YOU THINK IT'S GOING TO BE."* Right. So this is the way it is. It was not how I thought it would be; it was much worse. I could see what he meant. *"I TOLD YOU SO."* I've realized now what he told me, and it got worse. I had to go through lots of operations. It took me two years, maybe three, to recover to the point where I was close to a functioning human being.

When I did start feeling better, I started doing kid stuff—building model airplanes, coaching my kids' baseball, soccer, and basketball teams, taking them sailing; having fun. I spent a lot of time with my Dad. He was still functioning to a degree, but he had to be watched closely. We both spent a lot of time with the kids.

All this just made my situation worse with Nancy. I was home all the time, not on the road. All the time meant ALL the time. Plus, as I was healing, I had special needs. This put more of a burden on her. I was her ball and chain.

When I got more mobile, I didn't focus on her, I focused on the kids and my Dad. That made it worse because now I was home and I was mobile, but I was invading her space and butting in on her life, dragging her down. She did all the work; I had all the fun.

There were storm clouds on the horizon, and I still had a way to go.

Chapter 16

Home Sweet Home.

Back to reality. My new reality. The reality I have to live. It isn't what it used to be. Not what I hoped it would be.

Nancy was dead set on getting me home. She wanted me there. I guess she wanted to show the kids that I was still alive, and everything was going to be OK. I can understand that. She wanted to get back to normal as soon as possible. Even though that wasn't going to happen, she wanted to make believe it would. I just couldn't make her wish come true.

Home at last and I got my pills. I was feeling better, but I was just out of it; really out of it for the first few days I was home. Right? Lori, my bubbly little sister, maybe in her late twenties at the time and recently married, decided to pay me a visit. She and Nancy belonged to a yoga group, and the instructor thought it would be a good idea if they all came over to cheer me up. They brought a lot of food over to help Nancy out and take a load off her. So Lori and a bunch of her and Nancy's yoga friends came over, along with Lori's high school friend, Froggy.

We were all in the library, and I was on the couch in my cast, just totally out of it; not so much from the drugs but from the pain and just feeling terrible, rotten, lousy.

Lori has this gift of making me laugh. And I was saying, "Lori, don't make me laugh. Please don't make me laugh." I was laughing. Can you believe it? I was laughing so hard I was afraid my gut would split open. "Stop. Stop. It hurts." They didn't pay any attention to me. It was great.

Those girls brought over tons of food. She and her girlfriends cooked all kinds of stuff—my favorites, like pigs in a blanket and casseroles. All this great food. She made an apple pie. I love apple pie. It's my favorite; the best.

Nancy threw them out of the house! She said, "I can take care of him. I don't need your help!" I went from having so much fun and laughing with Lori and her friends to "What the hell? Why did everybody leave?" Nancy said, "We don't need this. We have food here." This was her group too—her yoga buddies!

Oh, my God. This was when I started wondering whether this was the real Nancy.

On edge. Frustrated. She told Lori and her friends to leave. She made Lori take the pigs in a blanket back with her. I didn't get to eat them. It sucked.

Then Christmas rolled around and all I wanted to do was rest. I finally moved back into my big bed—a four-poster Queen Anne's bed; a wonderful, big bed. And I was just relaxing. I was starting to feel a little better, and I was starting to pee not exactly blood anymore but it was not exactly right, either. I was just starting to feel better.

Nancy insisted that we visit Marsha, her sister, for Christmas. Let's stop and take an inventory here. In the last few weeks . . .

- I was in a plane crash that killed a good friend and partner and hurt me terribly;

- I almost froze to death;
- I lost my job;
- I lost my big deal;
- I broke my back;
- My hands were ripped up, my right thumb was flopping around;
- My lung collapsed;
- My guts were hanging out my ass and had to be shoved back in;
- My guts popped out the front too. I had two inguinal hernias where part of my intestine poked through my abs;
- The seat belt really messed me up—I had broken ribs that crossed over each other; overriding ribs that were never fixed. They fused that way. My chest was a tangled mess;
- I was in constant pain;
- I looked like hell—bruises, cuts, and scabs all over my face;
- My back needed to be operated on;
- My front needed to be operated on;
- My hands needed to be fixed;
- I was in constant pain; and
- I was in a cast that must have weighed one hundred pounds.

Yeah, it was all good. Let's go see Marsha.

I told Nancy, "I don't think I can do this." I could barely walk. I wasn't walking. I was stumbling. Baby step stumbling. The cast made normal walking impossible. To please Nancy, I got dressed and, like an idiot, went to her family's Christmas celebration. What fun. I couldn't sit at a table and eat. I just couldn't. I ended up laying on Marsha's couch all day, alone. Nancy got mad at me because I couldn't get up and do stuff. What did she expect? Seriously. She had no idea how bad a shape I was in.

That event made me realize this was the beginning of the end. Christmas 1993. Nancy never understood how bad I was hurt. No clue. She was oblivious to me. To make matters worse, I got hooked on painkillers and there was nothing I could do about it because if I didn't take those drugs, I was just totally miserable. I would not have made it.

I think one of the reasons why I let Nancy treat me this way was that My Friend did not object. He kind of agreed with me being passive. He didn't say it was a good thing for me to do, but I kind of got the feeling that it might have been what I had to do, the way I had to be, to recover, to get through it.

It came back to the kids. If Nancy was really interested in showing the kids that I was still there, that was a good thing to do. If it made the kids feel better, I was all for it. My Friend's influence probably helped me make that decision—right, wrong, or indifferent. And I guess it was the right decision because everything now is as it should be. It was just hard getting here. My Friend didn't object to it. On the cliff, he objected to my smoking, so I didn't try to light up then.

He didn't object to Nancy dragging me home. Not at all. I never felt like my free choice was taken away from me. No. He always let me decide what I wanted to do. And it's still that way. I think I'm kind of weird because of this whole thing. I don't think like you do, and I can be very naive about certain things. I guess that's one of my flaws. All my life I just accept things at face value, until proven otherwise.

Long story short about my recovery, I had lots of major operations. I had drainage tubes in me all over the place. I would come back from the hospital and I couldn't walk. I couldn't. I was just miserable.

Our marriage fell apart then because I couldn't do anything. And I couldn't do anything about not being able to do anything. I was a lump. I was dead weight, of no use. For me, being alive was being a burden. Nancy would make supper. "Come on down for supper!" There was no way I was going to get out of bed and make my way down all those stairs, eat supper, and drag myself all the way back up. No #@!%&^#* way!

She used to get mad and stay mad; always frustrated. Those were bad times, dark days . . . not what I wanted them to be. But when it came down to the point where it was time to make a decision about our future, I didn't. I couldn't.

Chapter 17

Two Years in Hell

Misery. One word that can describe more than two years of my life. Pain. Frustration. Operations. Drugs. Isolation. Anger. All rolled up into one word.

When I first got home, I was an invalid. It was so bad that I had all these little gizmos to help me function; do little things. One of these was a stick where you put the toilet paper on the end so you can wipe yourself. I couldn't bend down to do that, so Nancy had to help me. That was how bad it was. It was a terrible thing to go through for both of us.

After the holidays, I started seeing the doctors. I had my family physician, and I had the back guy, the hand guy, and the foot guy. I was going to all these doctors, and they were all saying that at this point in time I had to take these pills. I might have to take them for a while.

They put me on OxyContin. They gave me videotapes of how OxyContin was, for a person in my condition, the best choice. I wouldn't have to take one every four hours or so, just one or two a day. That was it because the painkiller was timed-release. That was what OxyContin is all about. It was a timed-release pill. And I said, "OK. Let's do it."

I started taking those and, eventually, I went to see the doctors at University Hospitals. Dartmouth let me go home for Christmas because I agreed to go see the back doctor at University Hospitals.

Dr. Sanford Emery, an orthopedic surgeon at University Hospitals, took care of me. A young guy, he was a great doctor. I trusted him. The first thing he suggested we do was get rid of that big, hard, heavy cast and put me in a removable cast.

When they got that miserable cast off, I took a look at myself. I was a walking bruise. You know, those multicolored Easter eggs where you take a couple of dye pills and swirl the egg in and get an abstract look to the egg? That's how my body was. Somebody took black, blue, purple, brown, and little bit of yellow, and made me into a work of art. I was one big multicolored bruise. Head to foot—front, back, face, arms, legs, hands, feet—colorful splotches—nothing was left untouched. You might say I was a real bruiser. And this was nearly a month after the crash.

Anyway, getting this new cast on me was no big deal. They cut off the old one and molded the new one on me. It was two pieces, front and back, where the back was a little longer—down to my tailbone—and the front was just below my belly button. No pain. No problem. The great thing about this cast was that it weighed less than half of the old one. It was a lightweight clamshell cast that closed over me. It was held together with Velcro.

The idea was that during the day the cast would keep me in shape, but at night I could take it off and sleep without the cast on. I think it was fiberglass. Because it was so lightweight and shorter, I had a lot more freedom of movement. It was easier to walk, and I could take care of my bathroom business by myself.

I could sleep on my bed without a cast which was really great. But outside of the bed, I was like one of those used-car lot, floppy noodle guys. That was how I looked trying to get up and walk without my cast. I was a regular Gumby. It may sound funny; I'm sure it looked funny, but believe me, it wasn't funny. I couldn't support myself without that cast.

The cast was green. The front and the back were green. The Ninja Turtles were a big thing on TV back then and in the movies. The kids called me the big giant Ninja turtle. They had fun with it.

I was definitely going to need back surgeries—more than one. The cast stabilized my back, giving the back doctors time to come up with a surgery plan. The next thing on the list was to do something with my hands. Remember my thumb that couldn't work a lighter? It was still with me.

We went to this clinic where they were going to put a pin in my right thumb—the one I had trouble lighting the fire with. They took off the cast and I freaked, really freaked. I said, "Forget it! Cancel the whole thing! I'm not doing it."

I don't know why I freaked. I just felt enough is enough. I've had enough. No more. So the doctor did something to my thumb where he didn't have to put a pin in, and I went home; done with that. I probably should have had the pin put in; my right thumb still bothers me.

There were problems with my left hand too. I ripped apart tendons in my left hand, so they did something to fix that too. I still have a tendon that's not connected in my left hand. If you ever want to see it, I'll show you the lump where it's curled up on my wrist.

The tendon damage affected my finger movement—the middle finger on my left hand. It screwed up my left hand for piano playing. Now I can't play the left hand on the piano anymore.

My hands were bad because of my thumb and because of the tendons. That was why we had to take care them first. The fixes weren't major. I didn't have to spend time in the hospital and weeks recovering, so we got that out of the way first. Getting my hands working better was important for me to be able to function. I had no idea how many tendons they reattached on my left hand, but my hands hurt. I have a hard time moving my fingers and my hands, but I get by.

I had problems with my ankles too. You know, the ankles hit the support on the front seats; my right ankle, especially. But I don't remember them doing anything about that. It might have healed as best it could. I still have problems with my whole right leg, and my right foot was totally screwed up.

Meanwhile, I was walking around in the Ninja Turtle cast, and I was somewhat mobile. I couldn't walk without it. I refused to use a walker. In the beginning I got crutches, but I got rid of the crutches. Then I had canes—the old-fashioned ones that look like umbrella handles. I still have one that I use from time to time.

Anyway, a couple of months after Christmas, I was told I would need three surgeries on my back. When I went in for the first back surgery I had no clue what they did, but it was a horrible operation. Horrible!

The first operation was just to clean out the chips. I had a burst fracture where my L-1 vertebrae burst into little pieces of bone that flew into my dorsal cavity, which runs up your back and protects your spinal cord. Getting that cleaned out was the first step, and an important one to prevent further injury.

The first back surgery didn't really improve my function or help me walk any better. At least it didn't seem to because it was just to clean things out, not rebuild my back. Even so, I still had to go through rehab and physical therapy after that surgery.

I couldn't walk at all for probably a month after that first operation. It just didn't seem to really help. I finally was able to get up and walk around with the cast and I was semimobile. I couldn't walk without the cast. Then it was time for the next surgery.

OK. The first surgery was cleanup. The second surgery was to stabilize my back. To do this, they used a bunch of stainless steel and titanium pieces and parts, screwing dozens of them into my spine. They fused vertebrae. I'm two inches shorter than I was. I lost two inches from the accident right out of my back. My back was shorter, but my front wasn't, so I bulge out in the front.

The third surgery was to strengthen my back by putting some more bone in my backbone. They took a piece of my hip and stuck it in my back. These surgeries were going on every couple of months. Every four or five months, a new surgery, a new procedure, and more rehab. Those were the things they did. This lasted over a period of a couple of years. For a couple of years, I was out of it.

While I was trying to put myself together, my marriage fell apart.

That was my memory. The whole period we're talking about is from that Christmas I got home in '93 till about two years later. Doctors,

X-rays, consultations, blood transfusions, operations, rehab, physical therapy, exercises . . . all kinds of work to make it back. I was in and out of the hospital all the time. And when I was home, I was lying in bed. I still had to deal with that cast. I was having a hard time walking around. I remember one springtime going outside for a walk with the canes. It was great.

My neighbor Jack was like a surrogate grandfather to the kids. Jack was a great guy; great friend of mine. Jack gave me a cigarette when I hadn't had a cigarette in a while. Remember, smoking saved my life. So I started smoking again. Loved it. That got Nancy mad . . . what didn't? There was a period of about two years when I was always drugged up. I had to be to survive all these surgeries and rehab.

I had to learn to walk again. I got to the point where I was supposed to start walking around the house which was very painful. It was a nice big house with large rooms and high ceilings. I stumbled and dragged my foot. I was in constant therapy through this whole thing. It started out with little things like riding one of those air cycles where they had the fan blade in place of the front tire. And I was going to swimming pools where they had the current you walk against. I had to basically learn how to walk again; to strengthen my legs and back.

It was a really strange, difficult time. I never realized how frail I had become or how beat-up I was. Neither did Nancy. I just did what the doctors and nurses said I had to do. I did it. I took the drugs. I followed doctors' orders. I didn't have a choice. They told me I had to do it. And I did it. Simple as that. It was a miserable, depressing time for the family because I was an invalid, basically useless.

I would take off my cast and I would lay in bed. It was the only place I was really comfortable—getting out of that damned cast, laying down in bed, and going to sleep. That was all I wanted to do. When Nancy called me for supper, I didn't go down. It was too much of an effort for me to get up, put on my cast, walk down the two flights of stairs to the dining room, and eat. Too much work. It really upset Nancy. She wanted things to be normal, and I wasn't normal. I wasn't then, and I would never be normal again. I was changing and adapting to my new reality. Nancy wasn't.

The kids were a lot more flexible. Adam was just a little baby. I think Adam was two years old when the accident happened. We played around while I was in bed. We had a cat back then and we played around with the cat. I read stories to the kids and played games. We had a good time. Nancy wasn't really a part of that. The bed, the kids, the cat, the games—those were my world.

These were the two or three years of my life that I really don't remember much. People don't believe me. But if you go through this kind of trauma, you sometimes just run out of gas. In the movies you see a guy swimming away from a shark and he's just one foot away from the boat. He runs out of gas, and the shark gets him. I was that guy.

Your body only has so much energy. And when you run out of that energy, no matter what your mind says, you can't do it. I was running out of gas every day. And that was where I was for two years or maybe more. Always low on gas. Breaking down.

As time went by, I started to walk more and more, getting active, doing better all the time. Then the hernias. I had two grade A extra-large eggs popping out of my abdomen. These were inguinal hernias—my intestines popping through my muscles. That was where the seatbelts were.

If I remember correctly, I had one surgery for the hernias that was supposed to fix them. And then later, one popped out again, and they had to go back and fix the second one. To hold everything in, they installed hernia mesh—some kind of flexible plastic, I think. Now, the only six-pack I'll ever see is beer. Preferably PBR.

This whole time—two years, maybe three—I was living in La-La land, drugged up so I could survive surgery after surgery. It was like a blur to me. It was survival, not living. But I had to survive so I could live.

When they looked at my chest, they said there was no hope for that. They couldn't do anything about my ribs or my chest. My chest was totally, totally crushed. My sternum was hammered and caved in. My ribs were so broken the doctors couldn't do anything about them.

They told me my ribs have overridden—overriding ribs; sort of like crossed fingers—fused together and never to be separated. They rode on top of each other when they broke. My ribs didn't just crack, they rode up on top of each other and that was how they punctured my lung. They healed that way. Now there was calcium build up too. It was like cement holding the ribs firmly overlapping, not to be undone.

There was no way to get my ribs back in place. You know, if you ever want to feel where the seatbelt goes, I'll show you exactly where

I broke my ribs—just put your fingers there. Really weird. After more than 25 years, you can still see the burn marks on my stomach where the seat belt was.

Every part of my body was affected by the accident, but they never did much about a lot of things—my shoulder, my teeth.

At first, nobody ever noticed the small cracks in my teeth until they started rotting away. My teeth had microcracks. I don't know if that was from the accident or from me clenching my jaw when I was sleeping. Or both. I went to the dentist, and he kept trying to fill all the cracks with epoxy, and it lasted for a while. And then it would get worse, and eventually I lost all my teeth.

I have dentures for my uppers, but I don't wear them. I never got my lowers done, and my kids tease me about having only one lower tooth. Matthew and the kids say I only have one tooth, but that's not true. It's a front one, and it is really noticeable. Call me Fang. But I have more than one tooth. I have a couple. I have one, two, three, four . . . four of those teeth where they drill into your bone and put in implants. I have more than one. I can chew.

Now through all this I haven't mentioned My Friend at all. He never actually said anything during my recovery. He didn't say goodbye, either. To be honest with you, and this might sound a little weird, but I think he's still with me to this very day.

Chapter 18

End of the Beginning

There was a big storm brewing ahead . . .

I was lucky. While I was struggling to get better, Cone-Blanchard kept me on the payroll, paying my full salary. We never had a problem with money. They paid me for a long time after the accident; at least two years or more, before the insurance and the lawsuit kicked in. Cone and Motch paid for all my medical expenses.

After a couple years, they finally said we're putting you on disability, which was 80% of my salary . . . still substantial. Not only were all my medical bills paid, but Klaus made us get AFLAC, so we had that money too. We had plenty of money. No worries. Nancy never had a problem with money.

Cone and Motch took really good care of us. Then we got settlements from the lawsuits which was great. I don't know who all the lawyers sued. This was all going on when I was half in the bag. I think we initially sued Motch and maybe Cone-Blanchard, then Klaus's estate, which I really regret. I never wanted to hurt his family. I was out of it. Maybe we should have sued Harry's insurance company. I don't know. What difference at this point does it make? None, really.

I think after the second year I was feeling pretty good, then I tried to go back to Cone. They had hired somebody to fill my spot, but I thought he was an empty suit and couldn't do the job.

I had a deal with Ford where they were going to pay us $50,000 upfront to develop a new computerized automatic screw machine to replace our outdated line of cam-driven machines. I worked with Klaus who knew some German company that could help us. He had gone over there with our engineers to develop this new machine. That just started, then the accident happened.

This new guy canceled all that. Hey, I wasn't going to design that machine, the Germans were. Klaus wasn't going to build it, Cone was. It could have and should have gone forward. Now all the time and effort we put into that project was out the window. A total waste of time. I was shocked. It made me feel completely worthless.

I stayed there for maybe a week. I just came back home and said, "Well, that's the end of that!" And I didn't even consider going to Motch with Svend Weidemann or whoever was running it. I didn't go back. I wasn't mentally fit to do any of that anymore.

That was the end of my business career. Soon it would be the end of Cone. They missed their opportunity. They could have survived. But financially, Nancy and I were fine . . . until we weren't.

So here I was. Getting better. Feeling better. With nothing to do. I was home all day. Nancy was used to me going off to work; sometimes being away for weeks or months at a time. Now here I was, home all day. Every day. And needy. I needed to be taken care of . . . for the first couple years, anyway.

I was home 24 hours a day, seven days a week, 365 days a year. Nancy was trapped. Nothing can push you further apart than full-time togetherness, especially when I devoted all my energies to the kids.

Nancy had a lot tougher time than I realized. Looking back, we should have hired a nurse for me. We had the money, but she wouldn't do that. Even if she thought of it, I don't think she would have done it. She wouldn't even let my sister bring us food. And I was in no shape to come up with ideas.

It was a sad situation. Yeah. But I needed help. I couldn't move. Just getting to sit down on a chair was a big adventure for me. I don't think she really understood that.

Remember how Nancy reacted when Taylor's ear was ripped open? All the blood freaked her out. With me, she seemed like she was dazed; shell-shocked all the time. Disoriented. Confused. Frustrated. I don't blame her. I was too. She needed help. No way did she think of hiring a nurse. Maybe she needed somebody to tell her to do that. But nobody did. Not me. Not her mother. Nobody. So that was how it all started. I was becoming an outcast in the family.

I was doing my best to get better. I honestly was. This meant I had to stay upstairs in bed, doing what I had to do. Nancy was doing her best to get back to normal. That meant cooking family dinners; dinners I wouldn't come down for. Every time I refused might have seemed like a slap in the face to her. But there was no way I could do it.

Her insistence on being normal was very frustrating for me, just like my insistence on getting better my own way was very frustrating for her. We were together, but apart.

If she needed affection, there was no way I could do it. I was in such bad shape I was in no position to do any of that at the time. There was no way. Probably it was my fault too. To be honest, all I wanted to do was get out of that cast, lay down, and relax. Whatever affection I had I gave to the kids. They were the reason I wanted to live.

All my waking hours, I was in the cast if I wasn't in bed. I wouldn't be out of bed that long because I didn't have enough stamina to really walk around and do stuff. And then years later, when I felt better, I couldn't stand all those screws and metal in my back. I told the doctor that when the weather changed or when I took a hot shower, I would get terrible back pain from those things heating up or cooling down.

I had another surgery to take all that hardware out. The insurance paid for that too. Dr. Emery gave me those metal pieces as souvenirs; more than 40 pieces of metal, mostly stainless steel, including a half dozen two-and-a-half inch screws, two six-inch rods, some god-awful titanium contraption with four big screws with nuts attached—some kind of fixture.

Putting these things in and taking them out cost thousands of dollars. I can't imagine all that stuff being in my back, how it was put in, how it was arranged, how it worked. I just know how bad it felt.

Now I suffer because I had all that metal taken out. I suffer with back pains now, but I was suffering with those pieces in my back too. I couldn't stand it. I just couldn't. Not after what I went through. It was just too much. And changes in the weather really drove me nuts. It wouldn't take much to push me over the edge.

My back is still fused. It's still weak, but it's healed to a degree. And I'm probably better off. I did a lot of research on back surgery and reconstruction after I got well. Everything I read said that eventually all those screws and fixtures should come out because your body moves even when you're sitting down in a chair. You don't realize it, but your back is constantly moving around. This can eventually cause metal fatigue—the heads pop off the screws, the nuts come loose. They would have had to come out eventually. I might have just been ahead of schedule. Getting those pieces out was my fourth back operation.

Today, I don't go to the doctor unless I really think I'm dying, like when I fell off my old boat a couple of years ago. It was 38-foot sailboat out of the water, on the hard (dry land). I fell off the deck and landed on asphalt. It was about 15 feet down to the hard. I broke three ribs. The doctors couldn't really do anything about it, but they did discover I had pneumonia and had been walking around with it for quite some time; years maybe.

I could hardly move for a couple of months. It takes me a while to recuperate these days. That was the last time I saw a doctor which was about 25 years after the accident. I'm basically doctor-free. I least, I'm trying to be.

I had another encounter with doctors about eight years after the accident. I like working with my hands—fooling around with cars, building model airplanes; all of that. I was working on a car, I think an Austin Healy, and bumped my hand on something. I didn't think anything of it. In a day or two, it got really inflamed.

Then my arm blew up like a balloon. It looked more like a leg than an arm; hurt like hell too.

When I showed up at the doctors', I was put in the hospital right away. I was put in a tent. The doctors and nurses had to wear HAZMAT suits to come into the tent. I had a very potent, virulent strain of MRSA—an almost impossible infection to treat. I don't know how long I was in the hospital, but I do know I got the Church's last rites. Again.

Over time, I've developed this allergy to doctors. I'm allergic. Not really. But I really seem to have a lot of problems when I'm around doctors. I try to stay away as much as possible.

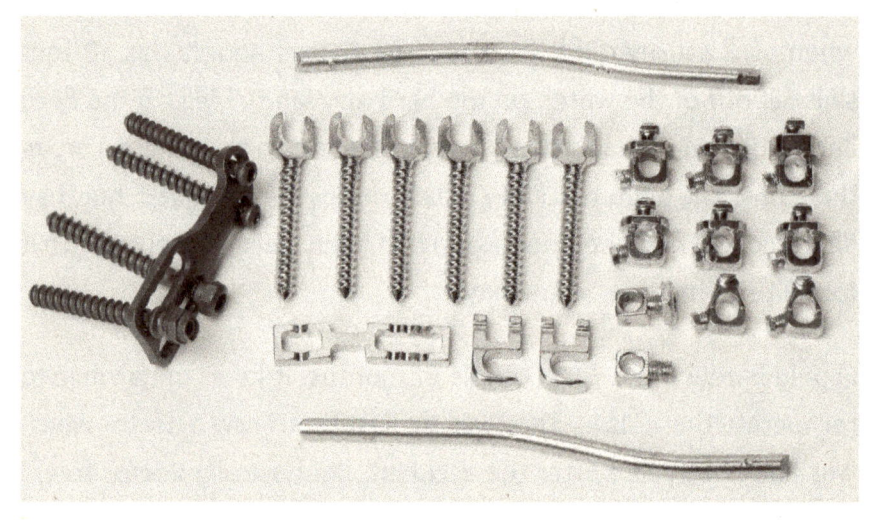

Metal fixtures removed from my back.

Chapter 19

Dad Again.

Being a bedbound Dad was no way to live. But I couldn't help it. It was the best I could do.

It took two to three years of recovery before I could actually get up and stay up for a full day without the pain taking me down. Even so, I still got really tight with the kids. They would visit me in my bed. We would play games, read stories, play with the cat. But when I finally got up and could move around, then I was really dad again.

Being a good dad was why I wanted to live; that was what I told My Friend. I wanted to be there for my kids. He told me I could do that, but things would be different . . . not what I expected. And he was right.

- I didn't expect to lose my job.
- I didn't expect to lose my company.
- I didn't expect a long, hard recovery.
- I didn't expect constant pain.
- I didn't expect endless surgeries.
- I didn't expect so many physical limitations.
- I didn't expect to lose my marriage.
- I didn't expect to lose my daughter.
- I didn't expect to lose my money.

But you know what? I got my wish. I could be dad, and I couldn't be happier. I'm having a wonderful life.

I've always worked with my hands. My hands hurt like hell—floppy thumb on the right; torn tendons on the left. I couldn't move them the way I wanted. I used to play keyboards all my life, since I was in about second grade. I started with the accordion, then the organ. I played the piano. I lost all that with my left hand not being up to snuff.

Not being able to work my hands was a big deal to me. And to be honest with you, I think part of my success in life, as an engineer or problem solver, revolved around a simple little thing—building model airplanes.

My Dad was kind of a model airplane freak when he was a kid, and he got me going on them when I was young. I could show you pictures of me when I was in second grade building rubber band-powered airplanes. I was terrible at it. I was absolutely terrible at it, but, you know, I kept doing it and doing it and doing it.

I decided that, to get my hands going again, I was going to build some model airplanes. It was therapy. I had something meaningful to do; something to show for my efforts.

It just so happened that Matthew, he must've been about 12 years old back then, was eager to help. We built this real little model airplane. It was really basic. It was an Ace Grasshopper with a Coxwell 049 gas engine. As easy as it gets.

And I bought a little Cox three-channel radio control and, like a couple of dumb clucks, we built the plane. It got us off the ground. We went to St. Peter & Paul's parking lot behind the house to fly it and almost wiped out a neighbor.

I got into building this stuff with Matt. He really took to it and learned how to fly remote control planes. Now he's a licensed pilot in real life. Then I built a model plane for Taylor, and I built one for Adam. He was little, so Adam's planes were held on control lines. And we were building model rockets, just having fun.

The kids and I really got into this stuff. My Dad was showing signs of Alzheimer's, but he was still pretty coherent. Back in the sixties, when I was a kid, I belonged to the Cleveland Radio Control Club. I rejoined that club, and we flew our planes at Harvard and Richmond roads, where there was an airfield for radio-controlled planes.

We would pick up my Dad at eight o'clock every morning during the good weather, and we'd go to the Big Boy on Granger Road. I had all the model airplanes in the back of the van. We'd have breakfast—the kids, my Dad, and me. We'd go out to the flying field, and we would stay out there until two or three o'clock every day.

For lunch, we'd go up to one of those lunch trucks that would serve businesses in the area. We'd have lunch out there and do all kinds of kid stuff. We did that almost every day. We had a great time. It was glorious.

Taylor never really got into flying model planes, and Adam was a little too young to really get involved, but Matthew really enjoyed it. Matthew got to the point where I started building contest aircraft for him—racing planes. We'd travel all around to air shows and flying contests. He did pretty good in a couple of them. This all started out because of my hands; I wanted to get them working again.

To my great surprise and satisfaction, my idea worked. I got to the point where I was pretty good at building those planes. That was back before you could buy them already built. I enjoyed it so much, I even built planes for neighborhood kids.

I think the most expensive one I ever built, if you count the radio, was probably $300—the engine was probably $100 and the model itself is probably another $100, maybe $150. So we're talking about $500, $600 for the contest planes that Matthew flew. But once you buy a radio, you can use it for a lot of different planes.

Each plane had to have its own receiver. You can just switch it from plane to plane. But receivers were cheap, like 50 bucks, so I just bought one for each plane. We probably had four or five airplanes at any given time. At most, we probably had a couple of thousand dollars invested in them.

I was a full-time dad, a big playmate for my kids, and I became a coach too.

Matthew was in peewee baseball. I had the time and involvement with my kids, so I started coaching that. He was in Cub Scouts and Boy Scouts, so I got involved in that too. And then he got into soccer. I never played soccer, but I became a coach. We were doing all this fun stuff. Depending on the season, we were busy year-round. I was having a blast.

All the kids played sports, even Taylor who played city soccer which I also coached. And Adam was probably the best of them all. He played for a private traveling baseball club. It cost me about five hundred bucks a month to keep it going—the Lake Erie Waves or something like that.

The airplanes were for my hands; coaching was for my soul. I loved working with kids. We were doing baseball—Little League, Cub Scouts, Boy Scouts, soccer, basketball. I think even one year Matthew played football in eighth grade. He was a good soccer player. He made the all-city team in high school playing for Benedictine. He almost got a soccer scholarship to college, but he blew out his knee in the last game of the high school season.

Taylor was really good at soccer. She played in the Garfield Heights city league. She played soccer and she played softball. This is where more problems piled on in my marriage. Nancy didn't want me to be getting too involved with Taylor. I wasn't allowed to be Taylor's dad, let's put it that way; not like I was for the boys. Maybe she was jealous. I don't know.

But I was able to get all the kids involved in music. The first was Matthew with the saxophone. He played in St. Peter & Paul's band. Then he graduated to the guitar.

Taylor wanted to play music, too, so I got her into piano. I bought a piano for the house. I took her to the Broadway School of Music every Saturday for lessons. She is an excellent pianist. She could make her living playing the piano if she wanted to. Really. She could be a lounge player or more. She was given a tremendous gift.

Adam played the sax for a little while and he still plays the guitar. That was one of my rules. Whether they liked it or not, the kids had to try music. Had to. I didn't care if they would do it for six months and quit. They had to give it their best. And, thankfully, it all stuck. To this day, Taylor has her own piano, and she's a lot better than I ever was. Matthew is an excellent guitarist these days. And Adam still plays the guitar.

The kids were doing all kinds of things, getting more and more active, having more and more fun. But I still had pain. The trauma of the crash will be with me always, just fading more into the background. Thank God for OxyContin. I hate to say this, but I was an OxyContin coach. Back then, Oxy didn't have the bad reputation that it has today. I was tired of taking drugs. I did cut down on the other drugs because they were driving me crazy. Oxy was different.

During my coaching days, I would usually wake up in the morning and take an OxyContin. And that would be all I'd have to do for a whole day. It helped. It really did. I never overdid it. I did what the doctor said. To this day, I can barely swing a bat, but somehow or another, I did it, and I had so much fun coaching baseball.

There was constant pain even with taking the OxyContin. It doesn't make the pain go away. It just makes you feel better about it. You feel like you can get through it.

I got to be a pretty good baseball coach. My teams won two championships. Oh yeah. Please understand that when I came out of my funk, I cut down on the pills. I was taking OxyContin, but I would take just one a day. I wasn't out of my mind. I wasn't crazy hooked. I was not an addict. And I'm not in denial. No way. It didn't do that to me. I was fine. I could drive. I never had a DUI or a speeding ticket . . . anything.

I became a certified CYO coach. I coached for St. Peter & Paul for basketball and soccer. You had to go through training at Borromeo Seminary to get certified, qualified for coaching.

They gave me a badge. I was certified, so I didn't see anything wrong with taking Oxy at the time. It wasn't like before when they were loading me up with so many drugs that I was having nightmares. With Oxy, it was not that bad. It was nothing.

In Garfield Heights, they had a baseball league, though it was independent from the city. We were allowed to use city baseball fields, bats, and balls. The guys that ran the league always rigged the draft where they would end up with the kids they wanted—the best players. The only kids I could get for my team were my own kids and the rest nobody wanted.

It turned out Adam was the only natural player I had. I had a team that would lose every freaking game. It was depressing as hell. I finally told them, "Look, guys, do you want to get your butts kicked every day or you want to learn how to play baseball?" They said, "Let's play baseball!" It was like the Bad News Bears all over again.

I bought our own bases. I bought the catching gear. I bought all this equipment. I went to Garfield Park where they had these old baseball fields. The city was dismantling them because it became a Metro Park; back to nature. But we found this one field that they left up. Every day the kids would ride their bikes there, and we would practice.

I would buy a 12-pack of Coke, hot dogs, and chips. And we would spend every day—all day—learning how to play baseball. I'm talking about kids who could never hit the ball. Then, suddenly, something clicked. They started to hit the ball. They started to make plays. They were starting to realize what the game was all about. It was Adam's team.

I had a lot of fun doing that. That team came within one game of getting into the world series. Wow. I earned a trophy that says *Coach of the Year: 2004*. I have the trophy in my apartment here. It has all the kids' names on it. It took years to get there.

We were one game away from the city championship. We lost, but we had a hell of a ride. Adam was our catcher; that's what he liked. If you're a baseball coach, the greatest thing in the world is to find a kid that can catch; one who really wanted to be a catcher. Adam was a natural. He had the skill. The kids called Adam "The Rocket" because he could throw a kid out at second base from a crouch. He was a great catcher.

I remember the semifinal game we played to get into the championship game. The other team had this hotshot kid at third. He kept leading off, leading off . . . There were two outs, and we were down a run. And this kid was leading off . . . leading off. Taunting us. So Adam came to me and said, "We're going to play the game."

Me: "What are you doing? What are you talking about?" He said, "You know, the game." We practiced this play where you fake a throw to second or to the pitcher, and you get the guy to lead off third far enough so you can throw him out.

Adam did it. He pulled it off! He threw this rocket to third base. He faked everybody out. They thought he was throwing to second, trying to get the guy from first to second on a fake play, then he threw a rocket to third base.

The kid was halfway down to home; couldn't go back to third. Our third baseman threw the ball back to Adam, and Adam tagged the kid out. Adam was a great catcher.

That's what I did as dad—play with model airplanes, coach sports, enjoy music—and we went on vacations a lot too. We used to go to Hilton Head once or twice a year; the whole family—all of us going out to restaurants and having a good time. That was a great time. It was a good time.

I helped some kids who turned out pretty good. Many of them came from screwed-up families. Playing baseball, soccer, or flying model airplanes were things they probably would have never done if it weren't for me. I did my best. A whole bunch of them never caught on. You wonder. A lot of Matthew's friends—kids I coached—are dead now—drug overdoses from heroin. You just have to wonder, and be thankful your kids turned out OK. I tried to help them. I couldn't save them. Not within my power.

There was this one kid, a friend of Matt's, named Joe. He came from a pretty strange family, and he got into building and flying model airplanes with us. I don't know how many I gave away in my lifetime; at least seven or eight radios and airplanes to kids that wanted to fly. Free of charge. I gave one to Joe, and he stuck with it. He turned out to be a pretty good kid.

I'm proud of my kids. Nobody's in jail; nobody's doing drugs or ruining their lives. They want to be happy, so that's a good thing in my mind, you know. Live your life the way you want. I never pushed them into anything.

But Nancy could never relate to any of it. She never went to the ball games. She never went to fly model airplanes with us. She would never do any of that stuff.

She always called me "The Good Time Dad." I don't mean to knock Nancy so much; that's just the way Nancy is.

Chapter 20

Bye, Bye, Love. Hello, Happiness!

I begged Nancy not to get a divorce. I didn't want a divorce. I still care for her to this day . . . some.

Nancy is Nancy. I don't mean to make her out as a bad guy. We both struggled through this. But our struggles didn't bring us closer together. They drove us apart.

That was the thing I could never understand. We had the world by the tail. We could have done anything we wanted to do. We won the lawsuit and had even more money. Money was never a problem for us. But Nancy just couldn't adapt to our new life. Maybe it was just me being home all the time. She wanted me to go back to work or at least get out of the house every day. She wanted her space. And I was a space invader.

I said, "Why don't you go back to school?" She only had one year at Kent. "Why don't you go back to school? I'll watch the kids, no problem." "Why don't you do this? Why don't you do that? Come on!" I don't think she was comfortable being challenged like that.

At the time, we were chummy with Artie and his wife, Carol. Artie was a boyhood friend of mine who handled my finances. Carol decided to take flying lessons, and she became a pilot. She also went back to school in her thirties and became a doctor. Artie paid for her to go back to school. She became a radiologist.

Why couldn't Nancy be like Carol? Right. "Why don't you do the same thing? Do anything you want to do. Go become a teacher. Go become whatever you want to be."

Nancy is a type of person who wanted to be taken care of. She was taken care of all her life. When I first met her, I knew she had to be taken care of. It was probably one of the reasons why I fell in love with her.

She wanted to be taken care of in the traditional way—me going to work, and her staying at home. But it didn't turn out that way. We were provided for financially, but I was home all the time. Not only that, I had a better relationship with the kids. That's not what she signed up for.

I was oblivious. I didn't realize how unhappy Nancy was. She would get away from the house, go out shopping, get something to eat, and come back hours later. I didn't care. I saw as much of her, maybe even more, than I did when I was working. We were together. I didn't get that she was seeing too much of me. And I wasn't the me she married.

I wasn't attentive. I needed attention. I wasn't taking care of her; she was taking care of me. I used to have ambition—to grow in my job, to make more money, to strive to improve our life. Now I didn't need to work. We had all the money we needed. I was having the time of my life, having all the fun I wanted with no money worries or responsibility. That can change a person.

She held the family together while I was recovering. She took me to the doctors, helped me recover from the operations, got my prescriptions, took me to physical therapy, took care of the house, fed the kids, did the laundry, and took care of the finances. She stayed with it, while I adopted the role of The Good Time Dad.

If this happened today, I might be compared to an online video gamer—all wrapped in my little world. In my defense, I could say I built model airplanes, I worked with the kids, coached them in sports, encouraged them in music. I helped them grow. I taught them things. I loved them. I poured my life into them. Right? Yes, that's true.

But our marriage wasn't a partnership. I didn't realize that all the stuff I was doing with the kids was on an exclusionary basis. The kids and I did things that didn't interest Nancy. She didn't want to build model planes. She didn't want to coach. That's OK, but it was excluding Nancy. Maybe she sensed that when we asked her along, we really didn't mean it, or she might have felt that way.

It was my fault, too, because I was just floating along. I was happy with Nancy, even though we weren't very romantic, to say the least. But I was happy with the kids. And I was happy with the family. I was happy with where we were. I thought everything was OK.

After nearly 10 years of doing this, nursing me from the wreck to The Good Time Dad, Nancy had enough. She was alone in our house. When she was out with her friends, I think she saw there was greener grass; more to life than what she had. She wanted a divorce. I didn't.

She divorced me. I didn't want a divorce. I begged her not to get a divorce. But that's what she wanted.

We ended up standing in front of the judge, and he asked if I was OK with this. "Do you want a divorce?" I was almost ready to say, "No, I don't!" But we went through so much aggravation to get to this point. The lawyers already took about a hundred grand of my money, so I just said, "Yeah, yeah, sure. Yeah, let's do it." I often wonder if I should have said no, I didn't want it. What would have happened then? The divorce was finalized October 31st. I celebrate every Halloween.

That was the worst. But a burden had been lifted. For both of us. After the worst, the good times came. I really had a good life after the divorce. I really did. I had a lot of fun. I had about $250,000 in the bank, and I was making monthly payments to Nancy.

I had to pay her $1,400 a month until things changed. She had enough money from the settlement to buy a house, which she did. I was living off the insurance and using my money to pay her. I didn't change my lifestyle and I didn't realize that all my resources were just being drained away.

I could have gone back to court after a few years and stopped those payments. I had no income, no chance to work. My circumstances were terrible. I believe the divorce settlement could have been modified if I went to court again. I could have gotten out of it. Artie warned me about paying too much, but I thought I was doing the right thing. So I didn't go back to court. She collected that money for 11 years! More than $180,000!

That was what paying her $1,400 a month added up to by the time I was 62. That was when we went to court for the last time. The payments stopped. I was broke. The disability was good for only another couple of years, then nothing. No savings. No retirement account.

I paid her that money all those years. Taylor was living with her, and I thought the money was going to her, so I paid. I paid it, and I felt sorry for her. I paid it because I didn't think I was going to live this long, to be honest with you.

I kind of frittered all my money away. It's my own fault. Artie warned me, but I didn't listen. I did what I thought was right. I wouldn't be hurting at all right now if it weren't for that. I would not have been rich, but I would have been OK. I am OK, though. Yeah, it's true. Sort of on the low end of OK.

I still can't believe the whole thing with Nancy. I feel sorry for her. I really do. You know, I still care for her, and I still worry about her. I gave her way too much money. I shouldn't have done it, but I did it. I don't really know if I regret it. Sometimes yes, sometimes no. Since I'm satisfied with my life, it's mostly no. I tried my best. Wasn't good enough.

Ed & Nancy: RIP (1975–2002).

Chapter 21

Hillary Makes a Comeback

I told the FAA our plane crashed because we had to use a different runway to make way for Hillary's big jet. Then I tried applying for Social Security disability.

Five years after the divorce and nearly 14 years after the accident, I was contacted by the insurance company who was paying my disability benefits. They were paying me 80% of my salary which was substantial. Every month I would get a check. Up to that point, they had already been paying for about 10 or 12 years. It kicked in after Motch and Cone stopped paying for me as an employee—when it was clear I wasn't coming back. According to the policy, they still had about nine years to go—until I turned 65 and "retired."

They thought I had a good case to go on Social Security disability, and they wanted to pursue it. It didn't make any difference to me. I would still get my monthly benefits, but it would make a difference as to who signed the checks. It would have been good for them. Since it would not be bad for me, I said, "OK. Why not?" Something to do.

The insurance company hired a firm to represent me, and we went through the steps to get in front of a judge. I had to be examined and evaluated by a team of doctors. I went through all that. I guess we had a pretty good case.

I met the attorney working my case, and she went with me to the judge. She told me, "You have a really good case!" We got a date to appear before an Administrative Law Judge in the Social Security court. I was walking with a cane back then.

The FAA report on the plane accident was part of my case file. So the judge decided to take a look at it. When he saw that I involved Hillary Clinton in the crash report, he blew up. Really blew up. He was mad. Veins popped out. His face turned purple.

It was 2007, and Hillary Clinton was no longer First Lady. She was a Senator from New York and running to become the Democratic Party's candidate for President of the United States. Her main opponent was a little-known Senator from Illinois named Barack Obama. Hillary could be the next president.

The judge was not going to tolerate giving credibility to anything he considered so outlandish, so ridiculous. Who knows? He might have even been a Hillary supporter. But he lost it. "Hillary Clinton had nothing to do with it! Are you nuts?" He was livid.

He looked at me and basically said, "You're not disabled. You can walk. You can talk. You can move around. You can get a job. Be a greeter. Take tickets at a racetrack or a movie theater. Whatever. You can work. Get a job. Request denied!"

The doctors' reports didn't matter. The medical evaluations didn't matter. My broken back didn't matter. My caved-in chest didn't matter. My screwed-up hands didn't matter. The fact that my innards were held together by plastic mesh didn't matter. The fact that everything hurt all the time didn't matter. What mattered was a wisecrack I made a couple days after the accident when I was all drugged up and expected to die.

My attorney was shocked. She was really upset. She couldn't believe it. Normally, it can take anywhere from two weeks to three months to arrive at a decision. The average is eight weeks. We had a ruling on the spot. Talk about a speedy trial.

My attorney was visibly shaken. I asked, "What do we now?" She said, "There's nothing we can do now. There's nothing to do." She doubted an appeal would do any good.

She said, "Don't worry about it. You're OK. Go home. Live your life."

My life was so screwed up. I felt really dumb. Why couldn't I keep my mouth shut? I felt stupid that I let this happen to me. If I didn't have that insurance, I would have really been screwed. I guess things worked out in the long run, though. I still have a good relationship with the boys, and I'm not hurting. I eat too many bologna sandwiches, but that's OK. You know, been there, done that.

My favorite sandwiches are turkey, bologna, ham, Swiss, tomato, mayo, all on one sandwich. It's kind of like a Dagwood. Sometimes I switch it up and put salami on there. It's OK. You know, you can appreciate simple things again when you're broke. I appreciate having a beer or two every now and then.

I sense the end is near. I think I really should have died permanently some years ago. Maybe I'm trying. After all, I've fallen off a sailboat a couple of times. A few years ago, it was a 15-foot fall; broke three ribs. I told myself, "Be smarter."

I sold that boat and worked on Matt's 27-footer, which is now in great shape. But I think it's too small, and the boys agree. There's a 36-footer that's been on the hard for about five years—the owner has been paying storage all that time. He might take Matt's 27-footer plus spare parts in trade. It would be a real upgrade for us, but the boat needs a lot of work.

So we were inspecting it one night in the dark, and I decided to get off the boat. I tried using the ladder, but my old friend—gravity—took over and I fell. Again. But it was only about 10 feet this time. I landed on my left side. I landed on wet ground, not pavement, and cracked some ribs; couldn't really walk. The boys heard the ladder fall and helped me up and got me home. That was me being smarter.

Hurt like hell, but I was not going to the doctor. It would just be more bad news and I've had enough of that. I was out of commission for about a month or more. The boys and my sister Lori were bringing me food. I was told I stunk like hell because I hadn't taken a shower in weeks. If I fell in the shower, I would never be able to get up, even with Adam's help. So after a couple weeks of the boys complaining about my smell, I started doing spit baths at the kitchen sink. Once a week, maybe.

I was bored. Frustrated. Bad winter. I couldn't close the boat deal, couldn't go out and drink beer, and couldn't go shooting. A buddy of mine from the Motch days was a member of a sporting clays club and had me and the boys out as guests. We were doing it about once a week. The boys loved it. We all did. I wish we did it years ago; can't do it now.

I don't have a TV or a car that's reliable. My disability has stopped. I gave all my money away. I didn't have enough money to pay for my daughter's wedding, but I chipped in my last $5,000. She didn't invite me and might still be mad. I don't know. I have seen her kid. She brought him down to the boat one day to show the boys. We said "Hi." That was about it.

I have no savings; no house anymore (a generous contribution from the Lebron James Family Foundation to Boys Hope Girls Hope of Cleveland helped them buy my Garfield Heights house). My house money is long gone. I have a one-bedroom apartment and four garages. Two are for the cars that don't work, one for a dinghy that doesn't sail, and one for Adam's truck. We just got it running again.

I've grown a pretty good-sized pot belly, unless it's an oversized hernia that popped out. I'm not going to get that checked out. Since I got the screws out, I've found that beer and an occasional Delta 8 really helps with back pain.

When I look in the mirror, I don't think I look that bad. I've got all my hair—thick, wavy, and gray. My one visible lower tooth does make me look a little like a toothless old man, but I get by. I can tell you this, if my young basketball star self could see me now, he'd probably want to drive over a cliff. But looks aren't everything.

With all that, to be honest with you, I'm having the time of my life. I don't have any worries. I have enough money to stay in my apartment. I have my boys, my buddies, my smokes, and my beer.

My kids don't understand why I believe I've had a wonderful life. I'll tell you. On that mountain, with My Friend, I decided what was important in my life. My kids. My Friend told me I could have that life. It wouldn't be easy. It wouldn't be what I expected. But it would be OK. That's the life I fought for. That's the life I won. That's why I have had a great life.

Someone once said we lead lives of quiet desperation. Not me. I always speak up. I know that nobody's responsible for my life but me. I can't blame anyone else. I also know that I have to live my own life. Nobody else is going to live it for me.

I may have died, but I decided to live. Dying is the easy part. Living is hard. It's worth fighting for. I have had so much joy, so much happiness seeing my kids grow up, I would do it all over again.

Sometime in the not-too-distant future, I'm going to die again. I won't come back. I will die my own death. I'm not afraid. Do I believe in God? Yes. Do I believe in an afterlife? Absolutely.

A lot of people are afraid of dying. It's not so bad. Their real problem is that it makes them afraid to live. To give it their all.

You have to live. You have to fight for it. You have to want every minute. It's worth it. You might not think you're important. That what you do isn't important. But you're contributing to humanity. The human experience. That is important.

I'm at peace with my life, even the most difficult times. That peace has brought me happiness. To live in the moment. To enjoy every bit of life I have left.

Who could ask for anything more? I've experienced more life and lived more life than most people. I'm happy with my life and proud of my kids—all of them.

And who do I have to thank for it? Well, without a doubt, I wouldn't be here in the state I'm in if it weren't for Hillary Clinton. Am I going to thank her? Hell no! Not on your life. I didn't vote for her, and I'm not going to thank her. Ever.

And if my attitude causes a bolt of lightning to strike me dead, I don't care. I know from experience there's nothing to be afraid of. Now don't get me wrong, I would never wish her ill.

But here's to you, Hillary! I'm glad you didn't win! Hear that? I'm glad! Ha!

Introduction

Welcome to the *Easy Slow Cooker Recipes Cookbook for Two: Effortless & Delicious Meals Perfect for Couples with Pictures*! Whether you're a busy couple juggling work and life or simply looking to enjoy more quality time together, this cookbook is designed to make mealtimes more manageable, healthier, and enjoyable.

Cooking for two doesn't have to mean leftovers for days or complicated recipes that leave you exhausted. With your trusty slow cooker and this thoughtfully crafted recipe collection, you can create mouthwatering meals with minimal effort. From hearty breakfasts and comforting soups to savory dinners and decadent desserts, each recipe is tailored to serve two, ensuring you can savor every bite without waste.

What sets this cookbook apart is its focus on simplicity and flavor. Every recipe is easy to follow, with clear instructions and readily available ingredients. Plus, each dish is accompanied by a beautiful photograph to inspire your cooking and help you visualize the final result. Whether you're a seasoned home cook or just starting, these recipes will help you create delicious meals that bring you closer together.

This cookbook is more than just a collection of recipes, it's a celebration of shared moments and the joy of cooking for someone you love. So, grab your slow cooker, gather your ingredients, and get ready to enjoy effortless, delicious meals that are perfect for two.

Thank you for choosing this cookbook. I hope it becomes a cherished part of your kitchen and helps you create countless memorable meals together.

Table of Contents

Chapter 1: Hearty Meats for Two 6
- 01: STRACOTTO DI Manzo 6
- 02: Lamb, Carrot and Chickpea Tajine 8
- 03: Lamb Knuckle 10
- 04: Ribs with Pasta and Grilled Vegetables 12
- 05: Beef Brisket 14
- 06: Slow Cooked Pulled Beef 16
- 07: Beef Stew 18
- 08: Irish Stew Made with Beef 20
- 09: Cannellini Beans Beef Stew 22
- 10: Slow Cooked Pot Roast 24

Chapter 2: Chicken Delights Duo 26
- 11: Chicken Cacciatore 26
- 12: Chicken Stroganoff 28
- 13: Fricassee 30
- 14: White Chili Chicken with Beans 32
- 15: Shredded Chicken Breast Stew with Broccoli 34
- 16: Chicken Stew with Vegetables 36
- 17: Korean Traditional Food Chicken Tang 38
- 18: Moroccan Chicken Tagine with Potatoes 40
- 19: Thai Green Curry with Chicken 42
- 20: British Chicken Thigh Fricassee Stew 44

Chapter 3: Veggie Comforts 46
- 21: ESCALIVADA Roasted Eggplant 46
- 22: Stuffed Sweet Peppers 48
- 23: Collard Greens 50
- 24: Karnataka curry dish 52
- 25: Braised Red Cabbage 54
- 26: Cottage Cheese Posto Masala 56

27: Dhaba Style Sev Curry 58

28: Baked Potatoes with Mushrooms and Dill 60

29: Ratatouille 62

30: Lebanese Vegetarian Eggplant Stew 64

Chapter 4: Ocean Bites for Pairs 66

31: Octopus With Vegetables and Sauce 66

32: Slow-Roasted Citrus Salmon 68

33: Kerala Fish Curry in Coconut Milk 70

34: Slow Cooked Salmon Fillet Steak 72

35: Delicious Risotto ALLA PESCATORA 74

36: MOQUECA BAIANA 76

37: Spicy Curry with Shrimp 78

38: Salmon Masala 80

39: Seer Fish Curry 82

40: Thai Curry Orange with Prawn 84

Chapter 5: Cozy Soups Together 86

41: Turkey Soup with Vegetables 86

42: Slow Cooker Corned Beef and Cabbage Soup 88

43: Chicken Soup 90

44: Norwegian Soup with Cream and Salmon 92

45: Chickpea Soup with Pumpkin 94

46: Indonesian Chicken Soup 96

47: Slow Cooker Vegetable and Beans Soup 98

48: Creamy Garlic Carrot Mushroom 100

49: CALDO de Gallina Chicken Noodle Soup 102

50: Minestrone Soup 104

Conclusion 106

Chapter 1: Hearty Meats for Two

01: STRACOTTO DI Manzo

STRACOTTO di Manzo, an Italian pot roast, is typically slow cooked in red wine and herbs, producing tender, flavourful beef.

Serves: 2

Prep Time: 20 mins

Cook Time: 8 hrs

Ingredients:

- 1 lb beef chuck roast
- 2 tbsp olive oil
- 1 medium onion, sliced
- 2 garlic cloves, minced
- 1 carrot, chopped
- 1 celery stalk, chopped
- 1 cup beef broth (no alcohol)
- 1 cup crushed tomatoes
- 1 tsp dried rosemary
- 1 tsp dried thyme
- Salt and pepper to taste

Instructions:

1. Heat olive oil in a skillet over medium heat. Season the beef with salt and pepper and sear until browned on all sides.
2. Place the seared beef into the slow cooker.
3. In the same skillet, sauté onion, garlic, carrot, and celery until slightly softened, about 5 minutes.
4. Add the sautéed vegetables to the slow cooker over the beef.
5. Pour beef broth and crushed tomatoes into the slow cooker. Sprinkle with rosemary and thyme.
6. Cover and cook on low for 8 hours until the beef is tender.
7. Once cooked, shred the meat lightly with forks and stir to mix with the sauce.
8. Adjust seasoning with salt and pepper if needed.

Nutritional Facts (Per serving):

- Calories: 510
- Protein: 58g
- Carbohydrates: 14g
- Fat: 25g
- Saturated Fat: 9g
- Cholesterol: 170mg
- Sodium: 510mg
- Fiber: 3g

This simple, savoury dish is perfect for a comforting meal. It can be easily prepared in the slow cooker for effortless cooking.

02: Lamb, Carrot and Chickpea Tajine

A tajine is a North African stew named after the earthen pot it's traditionally cooked in.

Serves: 2

Prep Time: 15 mins

Cook Time: 4 hrs on low

Ingredients:

- 300g lamb shoulder, cut into chunks
- 2 medium carrots, sliced
- 1 can chickpeas, drained and rinsed
- 1 large onion, chopped
- 2 garlic cloves, minced
- 2 tsp ground cumin
- 1 tsp ground cinnamon
- 1 tsp ground coriander

- 400g can diced tomatoes
- 1 cup beef or vegetable broth
- Salt and pepper to taste
- Fresh cilantro, chopped for garnish

Instructions:

1. Place the lamb, carrots, chickpeas, onion, and garlic into the slow cooker.
2. Sprinkle with cumin, cinnamon, and coriander. Add the canned tomatoes and broth.
3. Mix all ingredients, ensuring the lamb is well-coated with the spices and liquid.
4. Cover and cook on low for about four hours or until the lamb is tender.
5. Season with salt and pepper to taste. Garnish with chopped cilantro before serving.

Nutritional Facts (Per serving):

- Calories: 600
- Protein: 35g
- Carbohydrates: 45g
- Fat: 30g
- Fiber: 10g
- Sugar: 12g

Enjoy this comforting and flavourful dish that brings a piece of North African cuisine to your table.

03: Lamb Knuckle

A slow-cooked lamb knuckle, braised in a rich red wine sauce with herbs, is a culinary delight rooted in traditional European cooking.

Serves: 2

Prep Time: 15 mins

Cook Time: 8 hrs

Ingredients:

- 2 lamb knuckles (approximately 1 lb each)
- 2 cups red wine
- 1 cup beef stock (ensure no alcohol content)
- 1 onion, chopped
- 4 garlic cloves, minced
- 2 carrots, sliced
- 2 stalks celery, chopped
- 3 bay leaves

- 1 tsp dried thyme
- 1 tsp dried rosemary
- Salt and pepper to taste
- 2 tbsp olive oil

Instructions:

1. Heat the olive oil in a skillet over medium heat and brown the lamb knuckles on all sides.
2. Place the browned lamb knuckles into the slow cooker.
3. In the same skillet, sauté the onion, garlic, carrots, and celery until slightly softened.
4. Add the sautéed vegetables to the slow cooker over the lamb.
5. Pour the red wine and beef stock into the cooker. Ensure the liquid covers at least half of the lamb.
6. Add bay leaves, thyme, rosemary, salt, and pepper.
7. Cover and cook on low for 8 hours or until the lamb is tender and falls off the bone.
8. Remove the bay leaves and adjust the seasoning if necessary.

Nutritional Facts (Per serving):

- Calories: 600
- Protein: 48g
- Fat: 30g
- Carbohydrates: 18g
- Sodium: 340mg
- Sugar: 5g

This comforting dish pairs perfectly with mashed potatoes or fresh bread to soak up the savoury sauce.

04: Ribs with Pasta and Grilled Vegetables

A dish with roots in rustic cooking, slow-cooked ribs with homemade pasta, and grilled vegetables meld tender meat with fresh, hearty sides.

Serves: 2

Prep Time: 20 mins

Cook Time: 6 hrs

Ingredients:

- 1 lb beef ribs
- 1 cup homemade pasta dough
- 1 cup cauliflower, sliced
- 1 red bell pepper, sliced
- 1 tablespoon olive oil
- Salt and pepper, to taste
- 1 tablespoon barbecue sauce
- 2 cloves garlic, minced

- 1 teaspoon dried oregano
- 1/2 teaspoon smoked paprika

Instructions:

1. Season the ribs with salt, pepper, garlic, oregano, and smoked paprika. Place them in a slow cooker and coat them with barbecue sauce.
2. Cook on low for 6 hours until the meat is tender and easily separates from the bone.
3. About 30 minutes before the ribs are done, prepare the pasta dough and cut it into your preferred shape.
4. Boil the pasta in salted water until al dente, approximately 3-4 minutes, then drain.
5. Toss zucchini and red bell pepper with olive oil, salt, and pepper. Grill over medium heat until charred and tender, about 5-6 minutes.
6. Serve the ribs alongside the homemade pasta and grilled vegetables.

Nutritional Facts (Per serving):

- Calories: 620
- Protein: 35g
- Fat: 30g
- Carbohydrates: 45g
- Fiber: 4g
- Sugar: 6g

This satisfying dish combines the heartiness of slow-cooked meat with the freshness of pasta and grilled veggies for a balanced meal.

05: Beef Brisket

A slow cooker beef brisket recipe offers a tender and flavourful meal. It originates from the traditional practice of long, slow cooking to soften tough cuts of meat.

Serves: 2

Prep Time: 15 min

Cook Time: 8 hrs

Ingredients:

- 1 lb beef brisket, trimmed
- 1 tbsp olive oil
- 1/2 tsp salt
- 1/4 tsp black pepper
- 1/2 cup beef broth
- 2 cloves garlic, minced
- 1 tbsp fresh thyme leaves
- 1/2 tbsp apple cider vinegar
- 1 tbsp brown sugar
- 1 medium onion, sliced
- 1 bay leaf

For the coleslaw:

- 2 cups shredded cabbage
- 1 carrot, shredded
- 1/2 small red onion, thinly sliced
- 2 tbsp mayonnaise
- 1 tbsp white vinegar
- 1 tsp sugar
- Salt and pepper, to taste

Instructions:

1. Rub the beef brisket with olive oil, salt, and pepper.
2. Place the sliced onions at the bottom of the slow cooker and set the brisket on top.
3. Mix the beef broth, garlic, thyme, vinegar, brown sugar, and bay leaf, then pour over the brisket.
4. Cover and cook on low for 8 hours or until the brisket is tender.
5. Combine cabbage, carrot, and red onion for the coleslaw in a bowl.
6. Mix mayonnaise, vinegar, sugar, salt, and pepper in a separate bowl.
7. Pour the dressing over the coleslaw and toss to coat evenly. Refrigerate until ready to serve.
8. Once cooked, remove the brisket from the slow cooker and rest for 10 minutes before slicing.
9. Serve the brisket slices topped with the chilled coleslaw.

Nutritional Facts (Per serving):

- Calories: 540
- Protein: 38g
- Fat: 35g
- Carbohydrates: 18g
- Fiber: 3g
- Sugar: 12g

This delicious slow cooker beef brisket paired with fresh, tangy coleslaw is perfect for a comforting meal any day of the week.

06: Slow Cooked Pulled Beef

Slow-cooked pulled beef is a comforting dish rooted in Southern barbecue tradition. Spices season the meat, which is smoked for hours to tender perfection.

Serves: 2

Prep Time: 20 mins

Cook Time: 8 hrs

Ingredients:

- 1 lb beef chuck roast
- 1 tbsp smoked paprika
- 1 tsp garlic powder
- 1 tsp onion powder
- 1 tsp black pepper
- 1/2 tsp salt
- 1/2 tsp cayenne pepper (optional for heat)
- 1 cup beef broth
- 2 tbsp apple cider vinegar
- 1 tbsp Worcestershire sauce
- 1 tbsp brown sugar

Instructions:

1. In a small bowl, mix the smoked paprika, garlic powder, onion powder, black pepper, salt, and cayenne pepper. Rub this spice mixture all over the beef chuck roast.
2. Place the seasoned beef in the slow cooker.
3. Combine the beef broth, apple cider vinegar, Worcestershire sauce, and brown sugar in a separate bowl. Stir until the sugar dissolves.
4. Pour the mixture over the beef in the slow cooker.
5. Cover and cook on low for 8 hours or until the beef is tender and shreds quickly with a fork.
6. Once cooked, remove the beef from the slow cooker and shred it using two forks.
7. If desired, skim the fat from the liquids left in the slow cooker and use the remaining liquid to moisten the pulled beef.

Nutritional Facts (Per serving):

- Calories: 480
- Protein: 58 g
- Fat: 24 g
- Saturated Fat: 10 g
- Cholesterol: 160 mg
- Sodium: 620 mg
- Carbohydrates: 8 g
- Fiber: 1 g
- Sugar: 6 g

This dish pairs well with coleslaw and cornbread for a complete meal that brings a taste of Southern cuisine to your table with the ease of slow cooking.

07: Beef Stew

Beef stew is a comforting, slow-cooked dish that combines succulent beef with corn, tomatoes, and various fresh herbs. It offers a hearty meal without potatoes or carrots.

Serves: 2

Prep Time: 15 mins

Cook Time: 8 hrs

Ingredients:

- 500g beef chuck, cut into chunks
- 1 cup frozen corn
- 1 large tomato, sliced
- 1 onion, chopped
- 2 tablespoons chopped parsley
- 1 tablespoon chopped dill
- 2 cloves garlic, minced

- ➢ 1 teaspoon salt
- ➢ 1/2 teaspoon black pepper
- ➢ 2 cups beef broth

Instructions:

1. Place the beef chunks at the bottom of the slow cooker.
2. Add the chopped onions and minced garlic over the beef.
3. Scatter the sliced tomatoes and corn around the meat.
4. Sprinkle salt, black pepper, chopped parsley, and dill over the ingredients.
5. Pour the beef broth over everything, ensuring the liquid covers most ingredients.
6. Set the slow cooker to low and cook for 8 hours.
7. Once cooked, gently stir and stir all the flavours.

Nutritional Facts (Per serving):

- ❖ Calories: 410
- ❖ Protein: 35g
- ❖ Fat: 22g
- ❖ Sodium: 870mg
- ❖ Carbohydrates: 18g
- ❖ Fiber: 3g

This simple and nutritious beef stew brings out the ingredients' natural flavours, creating a comforting meal perfect for any day of the week.

08: Irish Stew Made with Beef

Irish stew is traditionally lamb-based, but this variation uses beef with potatoes, carrots, and herbs, simmering to perfection.

Serves: 2

Prep Time: 15 mins

Cook Time: 8 hrs

Ingredients:

- 300g beef chuck, cut into chunks
- 2 large potatoes, peeled and diced
- 2 carrots, peeled and sliced
- 1 onion, chopped
- 2 cloves garlic, minced
- 750ml beef broth (ensure no alcohol content)
- 1 bay leaf
- 1 tsp dried thyme

- ➢ Salt and pepper to taste
- ➢ Chopped parsley for garnish

Instructions:

1. Place the beef, potatoes, carrots, onion, and garlic into the slow cooker.
2. Pour in the beef broth, ensuring it covers the vegetables and meat.
3. Add the bay leaf, thyme, salt, and pepper.
4. Cover and cook on low for 8 hours until the meat is tender and the vegetables are cooked.
5. Adjust seasoning as needed and remove the bay leaf before serving.
6. Garnish with chopped parsley.

Nutritional Facts (Per serving):

- ❖ Calories: 600
- ❖ Protein: 40g
- ❖ Carbohydrates: 50g
- ❖ Fat: 20g
- ❖ Sodium: 870mg
- ❖ Fiber: 6g

This stew is a comforting, hearty meal perfect for a cold day.

09: Cannellini Beans Beef Stew

Cannellini beans and beef blend perfectly in this slow-cooker stew, rooted in hearty, rustic cuisine.

Serves: 2

Prep Time: 15 mins

Cook Time: 8 hrs

Ingredients:

- 300g beef chuck, trimmed and cut into cubes
- 1 can cannellini beans, drained and rinsed
- 2 carrots, peeled and sliced
- 1 onion, chopped
- 2 cloves garlic, minced
- 2 cups beef broth
- 1/2 cup diced tomatoes
- 1 tsp dried rosemary

- ➤ 1 tsp dried thyme
- ➤ Salt and pepper to taste

Instructions:

1. Place the beef chunks at the bottom of the slow cooker.
2. Add the chopped onions, sliced carrots, and minced garlic over the beef.
3. Sprinkle the rosemary, thyme, salt, and pepper evenly over the ingredients.
4. Pour the beef broth and diced tomatoes, ensuring the liquid covers the ingredients.
5. Stir in the cannellini beans until everything is evenly mixed.
6. Set the slow cooker to low and cook for 8 hours, until the beef is tender, and the Flavors are melded together.
7. Adjust seasoning with salt and pepper before serving.

Nutritional Facts (Per serving):

- ❖ Calories: 485
- ❖ Protein: 38g
- ❖ Fat: 15g
- ❖ Carbohydrates: 48g
- ❖ Fiber: 10g
- ❖ Sugar: 5g

This stew offers a nourishing meal that's as simple as it is delicious, perfect for a cozy dinner.

10: Slow Cooked Pot Roast

Pot roast, a classic comfort food, involves slow-cooking beef with vegetables and broth to tender perfection.

Serves: 2

Prep Time: 15 min

Cook Time: 8 hrs

Ingredients:

- 500g beef chuck roast
- 2 carrots, sliced
- 100g green beans, trimmed
- 1 large onion, chopped
- 2 cloves garlic, minced
- 1 cup beef broth (ensure its without alcohol)
- 1 tbsp olive oil
- 1 tsp salt
- 1/2 tsp black pepper
- 1/2 tsp dried thyme
- 2 tbsp all-purpose flour

Instructions:

1. Rub the beef with salt, pepper, and thyme.
2. Heat olive oil over medium heat in a skillet and brown the meat on all sides.
3. Place the browned beef in the slow cooker.
4. In the same skillet, sauté onions and garlic for 2 minutes, then spread over the meat.
5. Arrange carrots and green beans around the meat in the slow cooker.
6. Pour beef broth over the ingredients in the slow cooker.
7. Cover and cook on low for 8 hours.
8. Transfer the beef and vegetables to a plate.
9. Mix flour with 2 tbsp water and stir into the juices in the slow cooker to thicken for gravy.
10. Serve the roast and vegetables with gravy.

Nutritional Facts (Per serving):

- Calories: 560
- Protein: 48g
- Carbohydrates: 15g
- Fat: 34g
- Fiber: 3g
- Sodium: 950mg

This slow-cooked pot roast offers a hearty, nutritious meal, ideal for a comforting dinner.

Chapter 2: Chicken Delights Duo

11: Chicken Cacciatore

Chicken cacciatore is a rustic Italian dish in which chicken is simmered with vegetables and herbs, creating a hearty and flavourful stew.

Serves: 2

Prep Time: 15 min

Cook Time: 4 hrs on high

Ingredients:

- 2 boneless, skinless chicken breasts
- 1 can (14 oz) diced tomatoes
- 1 bell pepper, sliced
- 2 carrots, sliced
- 1 cup sliced mushrooms
- 1 onion, chopped

- 2 garlic cloves, minced
- 1/2 cup chicken broth
- 1 tsp dried oregano
- 1 tsp dried basil
- Salt and pepper, to taste

Instructions:

1. Place the chicken breasts at the bottom of the slow cooker.
2. add the chopped onion, minced garlic, sliced bell pepper, carrots, and mushrooms to the chicken.
3. Pour the diced tomatoes and chicken broth over the vegetables.
4. Season with oregano, basil, salt, and pepper.
5. Cover and cook on high for 4 hours or low for 8 hours until the chicken is tender, and the vegetables are cooked.
6. Adjust seasoning if needed and serve warm.

Nutritional Facts (Per serving):

- Calories: 295
- Protein: 28 g
- Fat: 6 g
- Carbohydrates: 34 g
- Fiber: 5 g
- Sugar: 10 g

This slow-cooker chicken cacciatore is perfect for a cozy meal. It offers a nutritious blend of protein and vegetables flavoured with traditional Italian herbs.

12: Chicken Stroganoff

Chicken Stroganoff is a culinary twist on the traditional Russian beef Stroganoff. It incorporates chicken and a creamy sauce flavoured with mushrooms and thyme.

Serves: 2

Prep Time: 15 min

Cook Time: 4 hrs on low

Ingredients:

- 2 boneless, skinless chicken breasts cut into strips
- 1 cup sliced mushrooms
- 1 small onion, finely chopped
- 2 cloves garlic, minced
- 1 tablespoon fresh thyme, chopped
- 1 tablespoon olive oil
- 1/2 cup chicken broth (no added salt)
- 1 tablespoon Worcestershire sauce
- 1/2 teaspoon ground black pepper
- 1/2 cup sour cream

- ➢ 2 tablespoons all-purpose flour
- ➢ Salt to taste

Instructions:

1. Heat olive oil in a skillet over medium heat. Add onion and garlic, sautéing until translucent.
2. Add mushrooms and thyme, cooking until mushrooms are soft.
3. Transfer the sautéed mixture to a slow cooker. Add chicken strips on top.
4. Mix chicken broth, Worcestershire sauce, flour, and black pepper until smooth. Pour over the chicken.
5. Cover and cook on low for 4 hours in the slow cooker.
6. Stir in sour cream and salt to taste just before serving. Adjust seasoning if necessary.
7. Serve hot, ideally overcooked rice or egg noodles.

Nutritional Facts (Per serving):

- ❖ Calories: 345
- ❖ Protein: 28g
- ❖ Fat: 18g (Saturated: 6g)
- ❖ Carbohydrates: 15g
- ❖ Fiber: 1g
- ❖ Sodium: 390mg
- ❖ Sugar: 5g
- ❖ Cholesterol: 80mg

This slow-cooker chicken stroganoff with creamy brown sauce, enriched with the earthiness of sautéed mushrooms and the aromatic touch of fresh thyme, offers a comforting meal that's easy to prepare. Perfect for a cozy dinner, it combines simplicity with gourmet flavours while keeping the process and ingredients mindful of dietary considerations.

13: Fricassee

Fricassee is a traditional French dish featuring chicken slowly cooked in a creamy sauce with mushrooms. It is perfect for a cozy meal.

Serves: 2

Prep Time: 15 mins

Cook Time: 4 hrs

Ingredients:

- 2 boneless, skinless chicken breasts cut into chunks
- 200g white mushrooms, sliced
- 1 onion, finely chopped
- 2 cloves garlic, minced
- 1 cup chicken broth (ensure no alcohol content)
- 1/2 cup heavy cream
- 2 tbsp all-purpose flour
- 2 tbsp olive oil
- 1 bay leaf
- 1/2 tsp dried thyme
- Salt and pepper, to taste
- Fresh parsley, chopped for garnish

Instructions:

1. Combine flour, salt, and pepper in a small bowl. Toss the chicken pieces in the flour mixture until well coated.
2. Heat olive oil in a skillet over medium heat. Add the floured chicken and brown on all sides, then transfer to the slow cooker.
3. Add the onion and garlic to the same skillet and sautéing until the onion becomes translucent. Add the mushrooms and cook until they start to release their juices.
4. Transfer the sautéed vegetables to the slow cooker. Add chicken broth, bay leaf, and thyme.
5. Cover and cook on low for 4 hours. In the last 30 minutes of cooking, stir in the heavy cream.
6. Adjust seasoning with salt and pepper, and garnish with chopped parsley before serving.

Nutritional Facts (Per serving):

- Calories: 495
- Protein: 35g
- Carbohydrates: 15g
- Fat: 32g
- Cholesterol: 145mg
- Sodium: 870mg

This dish pairs beautifully with steamed vegetables or a light salad for a balanced meal.

14: White Chili Chicken with Beans

White chili chicken transforms a classic comfort dish into a zesty, creamy treat, merging tender chicken with beans and a splash of lime. This variation stands out for its lighter broth and distinct flavour profile.

Serves: 2

Prep Time: 15 mins

Cook Time: 4 hrs on high

Ingredients:

- 2 chicken breasts, boneless and skinless
- 1 can (15 oz) white beans, drained and rinsed
- 1 cup chicken broth
- 1 cup frozen corn
- 1 onion, chopped
- 2 cloves garlic, minced
- 1 green bell pepper, diced
- 1 tsp cumin
- 1/2 tsp oregano
- 1/2 tsp chili powder
- Salt and pepper to taste
- 1 lime, juiced
- Fresh cilantro, chopped (for garnish)

Instructions:

1. Place chicken breasts at the bottom of the slow cooker.
2. Add white beans, corn, onion, garlic, and green bell pepper over the chicken.
3. Season with cumin, oregano, chili powder, salt, and pepper. Pour chicken broth over the mixture.
4. Cover and cook on high for 4 hours until the chicken is tender and fully cooked.
5. Remove the chicken, shred it with two forks, and return it to the slow cooker.
6. Stir in the fresh lime juice and adjust the seasoning if needed.
7. Serve hot, garnished with fresh cilantro.

Nutritional Facts (Per serving):

- Calories: 370
- Protein: 38g
- Carbohydrates: 44g
- Fat: 6g
- Fiber: 10g
- Sodium: 690 mg

This dish is a delightful spin on traditional recipes, offering a comforting yet light meal perfect for cozy evenings.

15: Shredded Chicken Breast Stew with Broccoli

Slow-cooked shredded chicken breast stew is a hearty dish that combines the flavours of tomatoes, red peppers, onions, and broccoli in a delicious tomato sauce. This recipe is a perfect way to enjoy a nutritious meal with minimal effort.

Serves: 2

Prep Time: 15 mins

Cook Time: 4 hrs on high

Ingredients:

- 2 large chicken breasts, boneless and skinless
- 1 can (14.5 oz) diced tomatoes
- 1 red bell pepper, finely chopped
- 1 onion, finely chopped
- 1 cup broccoli florets
- 2 cloves garlic, minced

- 1 teaspoon dried oregano
- 1 teaspoon dried basil
- Salt and pepper to taste
- 1/2 cup chicken broth

Instructions:

1. Place the chicken breasts at the bottom of the slow cooker.
2. Add the diced tomatoes, chopped red bell pepper, onion, and minced garlic over the chicken.
3. Season with dried oregano, basil, salt, and pepper.
4. Pour the chicken broth over the ingredients to ensure they are well-coated.
5. Cover and cook on high for 4 hours.
6. After 4 hours, remove the chicken, shred it using two forks, and return it to the slow cooker.
7. Add the broccoli florets, stir into the stew, and cook on high for 30 minutes.
8. Adjust seasoning, if necessary, before serving.

Nutritional Facts (Per serving):

- Calories: 310
- Protein: 38 g
- Fat: 6 g
- Carbohydrates: 24 g
- Fiber: 5 g
- Sodium: 470 mg

This stew pairs wonderfully with a side of crusty bread or over a bed of cooked rice for a fuller meal. Enjoy the rich flavours and comforting warmth of this slow-cooked delight!

16: Chicken Stew with Vegetables

A chicken stew recipe slow cooked to perfection with vegetables, mushrooms, herbs, and a touch of creamy sauce is a delightful dish that traces its roots back to traditional comfort foods, designed to simmer and develop deep flavours.

Serves: 2

Prep Time: 15 mins

Cook Time: 4 hrs on high or 7 hrs on low

Ingredients:

- 2 boneless, skinless chicken breasts cut into chunks
- 1 cup sliced mushrooms
- 1 medium onion, chopped
- 2 carrots, peeled and sliced
- 2 celery stalks, sliced
- 2 garlic cloves, minced
- 2 potatoes, peeled and cubed

- 1 teaspoon dried thyme
- 1 teaspoon dried rosemary
- 1/2 teaspoon black pepper
- 1/2 teaspoon salt
- 2 cups chicken broth
- 1/2 cup cream
- 2 tablespoons all-purpose flour
- Fresh parsley for garnish

Instructions:

1. Place the chicken, mushrooms, onion, carrots, celery, garlic, and potatoes in the slow cooker.
2. Sprinkle with thyme, rosemary, salt, and pepper.
3. Pour the chicken broth over the ingredients.
4. Cover and cook on high for 4 hours or low for 7 hours.
5. About 30 minutes before serving, mix the cream and flour until smooth, then stir into the stew.
6. Increase the heat to high (if it is low) and cook for 30 minutes or until the stew thickens.
7. Garnish with fresh parsley before serving.

Nutritional Facts (Per serving):

- Calories: 495
- Protein: 38g
- Carbohydrates: 45g
- Fat: 18g
- Sodium: 870mg
- Fiber: 6g

This comforting stew makes a wholesome and satisfying meal, perfect for a chilly evening or a relaxed weekend dinner.

17: Korean Traditional Food Chicken Tang

Chicken Tang, a hearty Korean dish, traces its roots to traditional spicy stews, simmered to deepen flavours.

Serves: 2

Prep Time: 15 mins

Cook Time: 4 hrs (Low)

Ingredients:

- 300g chicken thighs, boneless, skinless, cut into chunks
- 2 cups chicken broth
- 2 potatoes, peeled and cubed
- 1 onion, sliced
- 2 carrots, sliced
- 3 garlic cloves, minced
- 2 tablespoons gochujang (Korean chili paste)
- 1 tablespoon soy sauce

- 1 tablespoon sesame oil
- 1 teaspoon sugar
- 2 green onions, chopped
- 1 teaspoon toasted sesame seeds

Instructions:

1. Place chicken, potatoes, onion, and carrots into the slow cooker.
2. Mix chicken broth, garlic, gochujang, soy sauce, sesame oil, and sugar in a small bowl until well combined.
3. Pour the mixture over the ingredients in the slow cooker.
4. Cover and cook on low for about 4 hours, until the chicken is tender, and the vegetables are cooked.
5. Stir in chopped green onions just before serving.
6. Garnish with toasted sesame seeds.

Nutritional Facts (Per serving):

- Calories: 350
- Protein: 28g
- Carbohydrates: 27g
- Fat: 14g
- Sodium: 850mg
- Fiber: 4g

This recipe offers a delicious exploration into Korean flavours, with a modern slow cooker twist that makes it easy and approachable for any home cook.

18: Moroccan Chicken Tagine with Potatoes

Moroccan chicken tagine is a traditional slow-cooked stew from North Africa, known for its vibrant spices and tender meat.

Serves: 2

Prep Time: 15 min

Cook Time: 4 hrs on low

Ingredients:

- 2 chicken thighs, skinless
- 2 medium potatoes, peeled and cubed
- 1/2 cup green olives, pitted
- 1 large onion, finely chopped
- 2 cloves garlic, minced
- 1/2 teaspoon ground turmeric
- 1/2 teaspoon ground cumin
- 1/2 teaspoon ground ginger
- 1/4 teaspoon ground cinnamon
- Salt and pepper to taste

- 1 cup chicken broth
- 1 tablespoon olive oil
- Fresh cilantro, chopped (for garnish)

Instructions:

1. Heat olive oil in a skillet over medium heat. Add onions and garlic, sautéing until onions are translucent.
2. Place the sautéed onions and garlic in the slow cooker.
3. Add the chicken thighs to the slow cooker.
4. Sprinkle turmeric, cumin, ginger, cinnamon, salt, and pepper over the chicken.
5. Add the potatoes and olives to the slow cooker.
6. Pour chicken broth over the ingredients, ensuring that everything is evenly covered.
7. Cover and cook on low for 4 hours, until the chicken is tender and the potatoes are cooked through.
8. Garnish with chopped cilantro before serving.

Nutritional Facts (Per serving):

- Calories: 310
- Protein: 28 g
- Fat: 15 g
- Carbohydrates: 18 g
- Sodium: 410 mg
- Fiber: 4 g

This slow cooker version of the Moroccan chicken tagine brings a touch of North Africa to your table, perfect for a cozy dinner for two.

19: Thai Green Curry with Chicken

Thai Green Curry with Chicken and Green Peas is a vibrant dish that blends aromatic herbs and spices with tender chicken. It is a specialty of Thai cuisine.

Serves: 2

Prep Time: 15 mins

Cook Time: 4 hrs on low

Ingredients:

- 2 chicken breasts, boneless and skinless, cut into bite-sized pieces
- 200 ml coconut milk
- 2 tbsp Thai green curry paste
- 1 cup green peas, fresh or frozen
- 1 onion, finely chopped
- 2 garlic cloves, minced
- 1 tbsp ginger, grated

- ➢ 1 tbsp fish sauce
- ➢ 1 tsp brown sugar
- ➢ 1/2 lime, juiced
- ➢ 1/2 cup chicken broth
- ➢ Fresh basil leaves for garnish
- ➢ 1 tbsp vegetable oil

Instructions:

1. Heat the vegetable oil in a skillet over medium heat. Add the onion, garlic, ginger, sautéing until the onions become translucent.
2. Add the green curry paste to the skillet and cook for an additional minute until fragrant.
3. Place the sautéed onion mixture, chicken pieces, green peas, coconut milk, chicken broth, fish sauce, and brown sugar into the slow cooker.
4. Stir well to combine all the ingredients.
5. Set the slow cooker to low and cook for 4 hours.
6. Stir in the lime juice just before serving.
7. Serve hot, garnished with fresh basil leaves.

Nutritional Facts (Per serving):

- ❖ Calories: 310
- ❖ Protein: 28 g
- ❖ Fat: 14 g
- ❖ Carbohydrates: 18 g
- ❖ Fiber: 3 g
- ❖ Sugar: 8 g

This dish offers a delicious way to enjoy the tastes of Thailand with the ease of a slow cooker, perfect for a cozy meal for two.

20: British Chicken Thigh Fricassee Stew

A fricassee is a French technique for cooking meat in a white sauce. British cuisine adopted this method because of its comforting texture and rich flavours.

Serves: 2

Prep Time: 15 mins

Cook Time: 4 hrs on high or 7 hrs on low

Ingredients:

- 4 chicken thighs, skinless and boneless
- 1 onion, finely chopped
- 2 cloves garlic, minced
- 2 carrots, sliced
- 1 tomato sliced
- 1 cup frozen peas
- 1/2 cup mushrooms, sliced
- 2 tablespoons flour
- 1 tablespoon olive oil
- 2 cups chicken broth
- 1/2 cup heavy cream
- 1 teaspoon dried thyme
- Salt and pepper, to taste

- ➤ Fresh parsley, chopped for garnish

Instructions:

1. Heat the olive oil in a skillet over medium heat and sauté the onions and garlic until translucent.
2. Add the chicken thighs and brown them slightly on both sides.
3. Transfer the chicken, onions, and garlic into the slow cooker.
4. Sprinkle the flour over the chicken and stir to coat.
5. Add carrots, tomato, mushrooms, chicken broth, thyme, salt, and pepper to the slow cooker. Stir to combine.
6. Cover and cook on high for 4 hours or low for 7 hours.
7. Stir in the heavy cream and peas during the last 30 minutes of cooking.
8. Garnish with fresh parsley before serving.

Nutritional Facts (Per serving):

- ❖ Calories: 590
- ❖ Protein: 36g
- ❖ Carbohydrates: 20g
- ❖ Fat: 40g
- ❖ Cholesterol: 180mg
- ❖ Sodium: 410mg

This creamy, colourful dish pairs well with a side of rice or crusty bread to soak up the delicious sauce.

Chapter 3: Veggie Comforts

21: ESCALIVADA Roasted Eggplant

ESCALIVADA is a Catalan dish featuring roasted eggplant, onions, and bell peppers bathed in olive oil and garlic. It epitomizes Mediterranean simplicity and flavour.

Serves: 2

Prep Time: 15 min

Cook Time: 4 hrs on low

Ingredients:

- 1 large eggplant, sliced into rounds
- 1 large red onion, peeled and cut into wedges
- 2 bell peppers (1 red, one yellow), deseeded and cut into wide strips
- 4 cloves garlic, minced
- 3 tablespoons olive oil

- Salt and black pepper, to taste

Instructions:

1. Layer the eggplant, onion, and bell peppers in the slow cooker.
2. Sprinkle the minced garlic over the vegetables and drizzle with olive oil. Season generously with salt and pepper.
3. Set the slow cooker to low and cook for approximately four hours until the vegetables are tender and flavourful.
4. Once done, gently toss to ensure the vegetables are well coated in the olive oil and garlic mix.
5. Serve warm as a side dish or fabulous as a salad topping.

Nutritional Facts (Per serving):

- Calories: 200
- Protein: 3g
- Fat: 14g
- Carbohydrates: 18g
- Fiber: 6g
- Sugar: 10g

This slow cooker version of ESCALIVADA allows the flavours to meld beautifully over several hours, making it a wonderfully easy and nutritious dish.

22: Stuffed Sweet Peppers

Stuffed sweet peppers with rice, mushrooms, cheese, and herbs blend vibrant flavours and textures inside colourful bell peppers for a comforting meal. This dish has Mediterranean roots and is often enjoyed as a hearty, wholesome staple.

Serves: 2

Prep Time: 15 mins

Cook Time: 4 hrs on low

Ingredients:

- 2 large, sweet bell peppers (one red, one yellow), halved and seeded
- 1/2 cup cooked rice
- 1/2 cup finely chopped mushrooms
- 1/4 cup crumbled feta cheese
- 2 tablespoons chopped fresh herbs (parsley and basil)
- 1 garlic clove, minced
- 1/4 cup diced onion
- 1 tablespoon olive oil
- Salt and black pepper to taste

- 1/4 cup vegetable broth

Instructions:

1. Heat the olive oil in a skillet over medium heat. Add the onions and garlic, sautéing until softened, about 3-4 minutes.

2. Add the chopped mushrooms to the skillet and cook until they're soft and browned, about 5 minutes.

3. Combine the cooked rice, sautéed mushrooms and onions, crumbled feta, and fresh herbs in a bowl—season with salt and pepper to taste.

4. Stuff each pepper half with the rice mixture, packing it tightly.

5. Pour the vegetable broth into the bottom of the slow cooker to help keep the peppers moist and create steam while cooking.

6. Place the stuffed peppers into the slow cooker. Cover and cook on low for about four hours or until the peppers are tender and the filling is heated.

7. Carefully remove the peppers from the slow cooker and serve warm.

Nutritional Facts (Per serving):

- Calories: 265
- Total Fat: 11g
- Saturated Fat: 4g
- Cholesterol: 22mg
- Sodium: 317mg
- Total Carbohydrates: 33g
- Dietary Fiber: 5g
- Sugars: 8g
- Protein: 9g

This delightful stuffed pepper dish is perfect for a cozy, easy-to-prepare, nourishing, and flavourful meal. Enjoy the melding of textures and the burst of fresh Flavors with every bite!

23: Collard Greens

Collard greens are a staple of Southern U.S. cuisine. They are traditionally slow cooked to tender perfection with a hint of smokiness.

Serves: 2

Prep Time: 15 mins

Cook Time: 5 hrs

Ingredients:

- 1 bunch collard greens, stems removed, and leaves chopped
- 2 cups vegetable broth
- 1 onion, chopped
- 2 cloves garlic, minced
- 1 smoked turkey leg (optional for flavour; remove to keep it vegetarian)
- 1 tsp smoked paprika
- 1/2 tsp black pepper

- 1/4 tsp salt
- 1 tbsp apple cider vinegar

Instructions:

1. Rinse the collard greens thoroughly to remove any dirt or grit.
2. Place all ingredients except for the apple cider vinegar in a slow cooker.
3. Cover and cook on low for about five hours or until the greens are tender.
4. Remove the turkey leg (if used), shred some of the meat, and return it to the pot if desired.
5. Stir in the apple cider vinegar, adjust seasoning to taste, and serve warm.

Nutritional Facts (Per serving):

- Calories: 150
- Protein: 10g
- Fat: 1g
- Carbohydrates: 18g
- Fiber: 7g
- Sugar: 2g

This dish pairs beautifully with a simple baked chicken or a hearty grain like quinoa or brown rice for a complete meal.

24: Karnataka curry dish

Sambar is a South Indian stew made with lentils and vegetables from the Karnataka region. This aromatic dish is a staple in Indian cuisine, flavoured with tamarind and a blend of spices.

Serves: 2

Prep Time: 15 mins

Cook Time: 4 hrs (Slow Cooker on Low)

Ingredients:

- 1/2 cup Toor dal (split pigeon peas), rinsed
- 2 cups water
- 1 small carrot, peeled and chopped
- 1 small potato, peeled and diced
- 1/2 cup pumpkin, peeled and chopped
- 1 tomato, chopped
- 1 small onion, sliced
- 3 green chilies, slit
- 1 tsp tamarind paste
- 1/2 tsp turmeric powder
- 1 tsp sambar powder
- Salt to taste

- 1 tbsp cooking oil
- 1/2 tsp mustard seeds
- 1/4 tsp asafoetida (optional)
- 5-6 curry leaves

Instructions:

1. Place the rinsed Toor dal and water in the slow cooker. Cook on low for 2 hours.
2. Add carrot, potato, pumpkin, tomato, onion, green chilies, tamarind paste, turmeric, sambar powder, and salt to the slow cooker. Stir well to combine.
3. Continue cooking on low for another 2 hours until the vegetables and lentils are soft, and the flavours have melded.
4. Heat oil over medium heat in a small pan. Add mustard seeds and let them splutter. Then add asafoetida (if using) and curry leaves, sauté for a few seconds.
5. Pour the tempered spices into the slow cooker. Stir well.
6. Serve the sambar hot with rice or IDLI.

Nutritional Facts (Per serving):

- Calories: 210
- Protein: 9g
- Carbohydrates: 38g
- Fat: 4g
- Fiber: 8g
- Sodium: 400mg

This version of sambar is ideal for those seeking a comforting and nutritious meal that's easy to prepare using a slow cooker.

25: Braised Red Cabbage

Braised red cabbage, a dish with European roots, transforms the humble cabbage into a sweet and tangy delight through slow cooking, enriching its flavours profoundly.

Serves: 2

Prep Time: 15 min

Cook Time: 2 hr 30 min

Ingredients:

- 1/2 head of red cabbage, shredded
- 1 large apple, peeled, cored, and sliced
- 1/2 red onion, thinly sliced
- 2 tablespoons brown sugar
- 1/4 cup apple cider vinegar
- 1/2 teaspoon ground cinnamon
- 1/4 teaspoon ground nutmeg

- ➤ Salt and black pepper, to taste
- ➤ 2 tablespoons olive oil
- ➤ 1/2 cup water

Instructions:

1. Place the olive oil, red onion, and apple slices in the bottom of the slow cooker and sauté until they are slightly softened.
2. Add the shredded red cabbage to the onion and apple mixture.
3. Sprinkle brown sugar, cinnamon, and nutmeg evenly over the cabbage.
4. Pour apple cider vinegar and water over the ingredients.
5. Season with salt and pepper to taste.
6. Cover and cook on low for about 2.5 hours or until the cabbage is tender and the flavours have melded.
7. Stir occasionally during cooking to ensure even flavour distribution.
8. Adjust seasoning if needed before serving.

Nutritional Facts (Per serving):

- ❖ Calories: 210
- ❖ Total Fat: 7g
- ❖ Saturated Fat: 1g
- ❖ Cholesterol: 0mg
- ❖ Sodium: 58mg
- ❖ Total Carbohydrates: 37g
- ❖ Dietary Fiber: 5g
- ❖ Sugars: 28g
- ❖ Protein: 2g

This slow-cooked braised red cabbage is an excellent side dish that pairs beautifully with various main courses. It adds a rich, colourful component to your meal.

26: Cottage Cheese Posto Masala

Paneer Khus Curry, or Cottage Cheese Posto Masala, is a comforting blend of paneer and poppy seeds rooted in Indian culinary traditions.

Serves: 2

Prep Time: 15 min

Cook Time: 4 hrs (Slow Cooker)

Ingredients:

- 200g paneer, cubed
- 3 tablespoons poppy seeds, soaked in water for 2 hours
- 1 large onion, finely chopped
- 2 green chilies, slit
- 1 teaspoon ginger paste
- 1 teaspoon garlic paste
- 1/2 cup tomato puree
- 1/4 teaspoon turmeric powder
- 1/2 teaspoon cumin powder
- 1/2 teaspoon coriander powder
- 1/2 cup coconut milk
- 2 tablespoons vegetable oil

- Salt to taste
- Fresh coriander leaves, for garnish

Instructions:

1. Heat the oil in a skillet over medium heat; sauté onions until translucent.
2. Add ginger, garlic paste, and green chilies, cooking until fragrant.
3. Stir in the tomato puree, turmeric, cumin, and coriander powder. Cook for 2 minutes.
4. Transfer the mixture to a slow cooker. Add the paneer cubes, soaked poppy seeds, and salt.
5. Pour in coconut milk and mix gently.
6. Cover and cook on low for about four hours.
7. Garnish with fresh coriander leaves before serving.

Nutritional Facts (Per serving):

- Calories: 385
- Protein: 18g
- Fat: 27g
- Carbohydrates: 18g
- Fiber: 4g
- Sugar: 6g

Enjoy this rich and aromatic curry with steamed rice or naan for a delightful meal.

27: Dhaba Style Sev Curry

Sev curry is an innovative Indian dish that combines GATHIYA SHEV with a tangy tomato base from roadside eateries called " DHABAS."

Serves: 2

Prep Time: 15 mins

Cook Time: 4 hrs (slow cooker on low)

Ingredients:

- 1 cup GATHIYA SHEV
- 2 large tomatoes, finely chopped
- 1 onion, finely chopped
- 2 cloves garlic, minced
- 1 green chili, finely chopped
- 1 tsp ginger paste
- 1 tsp cumin seeds
- 1/2 tsp turmeric powder
- 1/2 tsp coriander powder
- 1/4 tsp garam masala
- 1/4 tsp red chili powder
- 2 tbsp oil
- Salt to taste
- 2 cups water

- ➤ Fresh cilantro, chopped   (for garnish)

Instructions:

1. Heat oil in the slow cooker on the high setting (if available) or in a pan on the stove. Add cumin seeds and allow them to splutter.
2. Add onions, garlic, green chili, and ginger paste to the cooker until onions are soft.
3. Stir in chopped tomatoes, turmeric, coriander, garam masala, red chili powder, and salt. Mix well until combined.
4. Add water to the mixture and switch the slow cooker to low.
5. Cover and cook for about 4 hours.
6. Just before serving, add GATHIYA SHEV to the slow cooker, mixing gently to combine.
7. Garnish with chopped cilantro and serve warm.

Nutritional Facts (Per serving):

- ❖ Calories: 260
- ❖ Carbohydrates: 28 g
- ❖ Protein: 5 g
- ❖ Fiber: 4 g
- ❖ Fat: 14 g
- ❖ Sugar: 6 g

Enjoy this DHABA-style treat as a delightful, comforting meal, perfect for any cozy night.

28: Baked Potatoes with Mushrooms and Dill

Baked potatoes with mushrooms and dill is a hearty dish that traces its roots to rustic Eastern European cuisine. It combines earthy flavours and simple, wholesome ingredients in a comforting meal.

Serves: 2

Prep Time: 10 mins

Cook Time: 4 hrs on low

Ingredients:

- 4 large potatoes, peeled and sliced
- 1 cup fresh mushrooms, sliced
- 2 tablespoons fresh dill, chopped
- 1 onion, finely chopped
- 2 cloves garlic, minced
- 1 cup vegetable broth
- 2 tablespoons olive oil

- ➤ Salt and pepper, to taste

Instructions:

1. Layer half of the sliced potatoes, mushrooms, onion, and garlic in a slow cooker.
2. Sprinkle with salt, pepper, and half of the chopped dill.
3. Repeat the layering with the remaining potatoes, mushrooms, onion, and garlic, and season again.
4. Drizzle olive oil over the top and pour in the vegetable broth.
5. Cover and cook on low for approximately 4 hours or until the potatoes are tender.
6. Garnish with the remaining dill before serving.

Nutritional Facts (Per serving):

- ❖ Calories: 290
- ❖ Protein: 6g
- ❖ Carbohydrates: 53g
- ❖ Fat: 7g
- ❖ Sodium: 150mg
- ❖ Fiber: 7g

This simple and nutritious dish is perfect for a cozy meal, offering comfort and flavour with every bite.

29: Ratatouille

Ratatouille, a classic French stew, dates to Nice and features summer vegetables slow simmered for deep flavour.

Serves: 2

Prep Time: 15 min

Cook Time: 4 hrs (low in slow cooker)

Ingredients:

- 1 small eggplant, cubed
- 1 zucchini, sliced
- 1 yellow bell pepper, chopped
- 1 red bell pepper, chopped
- 2 tomatoes, diced
- 1 onion, finely chopped
- 2 cloves garlic, minced
- 1/4 cup olive oil
- 1 tsp dried basil
- 1 tsp dried thyme
- 1/2 tsp salt
- 1/4 tsp black pepper
- Fresh parsley, chopped (for garnish)

Instructions:

1. Combine the eggplant, zucchini, bell peppers, tomatoes, onion, and garlic in the slow cooker.
2. Drizzle the olive oil over the vegetables.
3. Sprinkle basil, thyme, salt, and black pepper on top.
4. Stir the ingredients to ensure an even coating of spices and oil.
5. Cover and set the slow cooker to low; let the ratatouille cook for about 4 hours.
6. Stir occasionally, if possible, to help flavours meld together.
7. Garnish with fresh parsley before serving.

Nutritional Facts (Per serving):

- Calories: 280
- Fat: 14g
- Carbohydrates: 35g
- Fiber: 10g
- Protein: 5g
- Sodium: 300mg

This vibrant and healthy dish is perfect for a comforting meal, ensuring a delicious, nutritious, and satisfying experience.

30: Lebanese Vegetarian Eggplant Stew

MAGHMOUR is a Lebanese Moussaka characterized by slow-cooked eggplant in a tomato base, often enriched with chickpeas and spices.

Serves: 2

Prep Time: 15 min

Cook Time: 4 hrs

Ingredients:

- 2 medium eggplants, cubed
- 1 can chickpeas, drained and rinsed
- 2 large tomatoes, diced
- 1 onion, finely chopped
- 3 garlic cloves, minced
- 1/2 cup plain yogurt (for serving)
- 2 tablespoons olive oil
- 1 teaspoon cumin

- 1 teaspoon smoked paprika
- 1/2 teaspoon salt
- 1/4 teaspoon black pepper
- Fresh cilantro or parsley for garnish

Instructions:

1. Combine the olive oil, onions, and garlic in the slow cooker. Set it on high and cook until the onions soften for about 15 minutes.
2. Add the cubed eggplant, chickpeas, tomatoes, cumin, smoked paprika, salt, and pepper to the slow cooker.
3. Stir well to mix all the ingredients. Cover and cook on low for about 4 hours or until the eggplants are tender and the flavours are well blended.
4. Serve the stew warm, topped with a dollop of plain yogurt and a sprinkle of fresh cilantro or parsley.

Nutritional Facts (Per serving):

- Calories: 320
- Protein: 9g
- Fat: 14g
- Carbohydrates: 42g
- Fiber: 12g
- Sugar: 18g

This comforting stew is perfect for a cozy, nourishing meal when served with a side of flatbread or rice.

Chapter 4: Ocean Bites for Pairs

31: Octopus With Vegetables and Sauce

Octopus is a seafood delicacy, cooked here with vegetables in a sauce, a method traced back to Mediterranean cuisines.

Serves: 2

Prep Time: 15 min

Cook Time: 4 hrs

Ingredients:

- 1 small octopus, cleaned and tentacles separated
- 1 cup cherry tomatoes, halved
- 1 bell pepper, sliced
- 1 onion, chopped
- 2 cloves garlic, minced
- 1/2 cup dry white wine

- 2 tablespoons olive oil
- 1 teaspoon dried oregano
- 1 teaspoon dried basil
- Salt and pepper to taste
- 1/2 lemon, juiced

Instructions:

1. Place the octopus in the slow cooker.
2. Add cherry tomatoes, bell pepper, onion, and garlic on top of the octopus.
3. Pour in the white wine and drizzle with olive oil.
4. Sprinkle oregano, basil, salt, and pepper over the ingredients.
5. Cover and cook on low for about 4 hours or until the octopus is tender.
6. Stir in the fresh lemon juice for added zest before serving.

Nutritional Facts (Per serving):

- Calories: 310
- Protein: 25g
- Fat: 14g
- Carbohydrates: 18g
- Fiber: 3g
- Sodium: 460mg

This slow-cooked octopus with vegetables and a hint of lemon makes a flavourful, satisfying meal, perfect for a cozy dinner for two.

32: Slow-Roasted Citrus Salmon

Slow-roasting salmon allows flavours to meld while keeping the fish moist. This method, originating from Mediterranean kitchens, pairs well with vibrant citrus and fresh herbs.

Serves: 2

Prep Time: 10 min

Cook Time: 2 hrs

Ingredients:

- 2 salmon fillets (about 6 oz each)
- 1 orange, thinly sliced
- 1 lemon, thinly sliced
- 2 sprigs of fresh rosemary
- 2 sprigs of fresh thyme
- Salt and pepper, to taste
- 1/4 cup olive oil

- 2 cups mixed fresh herbs (e.g., parsley, dill, cilantro)
- 1/4 red onion, thinly sliced
- 1 tbsp white wine vinegar

Instructions:

1. Arrange the orange and lemon slices at the bottom of the slow cooker.
2. Place the salmon fillets on top of the citrus slices. Sprinkle with rosemary, thyme, salt, and pepper.
3. Drizzle olive oil over the salmon.
4. Cover and cook on low for 2 hours until the salmon is cooked through and flakes quickly.
5. In a bowl, combine the mixed herbs and red onion. Toss with white wine vinegar.
6. Serve the salmon topped with the fresh herb salad.

Nutritional Facts (Per serving):

- Calories: 345
- Protein: 34g
- Fat: 20g (Saturated: 3g, Unsaturated: 17g)
- Carbohydrates: 8g
- Fiber: 2g
- Sodium: 125mg

This slow-roasted citrus salmon with a fresh herb salad is an easy and nutritious meal, perfect for a wholesome dinner.

33: Kerala Fish Curry in Coconut Milk

Kerala fish curry, or Meen Curry, blends regional spices with coconut milk and tangy mangoes, epitomizing southwestern Indian coastal cuisine.

Serves: 2

Prep Time: 15 mins

Cook Time: 4 hrs on low

Ingredients:

- 2 medium fillets of white fish (such as cod or tilapia), cut into chunks
- 1 ripe mango, peeled and cut into cubes
- 1 can (400 ml) coconut milk
- 2 tablespoons coconut oil
- 1 large onion, thinly sliced
- 2 green chilies, slit
- 1 teaspoon mustard seeds
- 1 teaspoon turmeric powder
- 1 teaspoon red chili powder
- 1/2 teaspoon fenugreek seeds

- ➢ 1 tablespoon ginger-garlic paste
- ➢ 1 tomato, chopped
- ➢ Salt, to taste
- ➢ A handful of curry leaves
- ➢ Fresh cilantro for garnish

Instructions:

1. Heat coconut oil in a skillet over medium heat. Add mustard seeds and fenugreek seeds; wait until they begin to pop.
2. Add sliced onions, green chilies, and curry leaves; sauté until onions are soft and golden.
3. Stir in ginger-garlic paste, turmeric powder, and red chili powder; cook for 1-2 minutes until aromatic.
4. Transfer the onion mixture to a slow cooker. Add chopped tomatoes, coconut milk, and mango cubes; mix well.
5. Submerge the fish pieces in the mixture, ensuring they are well coated.
6. Set the slow cooker on low and cook for about 4 hours.
7. Check seasoning, adding salt as required. Garnish with chopped cilantro before serving.

Nutritional Facts (Per serving):

- ❖ Calories: 354
- ❖ Protein: 26g
- ❖ Fat: 18g
- ❖ Carbohydrates: 24g
- ❖ Fiber: 3g
- ❖ Sugar: 14g

This Kerala fish curry recipe offers a delightful mix of mangoes' sweetness and coconut milk's creaminess, making it a comforting meal, especially when served over rice.

34: Slow Cooked Salmon Fillet Steak

Sous-vide salmon fillet steak offers a melt-in-your-mouth texture by slow cooking, preserving its rich flavours and nutrients. This method, which comes from the French term "under vacuum," is ideal for infusing subtle spices.

Serves: 2

Prep Time: 15 min

Cook Time: 2 hr

Ingredients:

- 2 salmon fillets, about 6 oz each
- 1 tablespoon olive oil
- 1/2 teaspoon salt
- 1/4 teaspoon black pepper
- 1 lemon, thinly sliced
- Fresh dill, a few sprigs
- 1 garlic clove, minced

➢ Mixed salad greens for serving

Instructions:

1. Season the salmon fillets with salt and pepper.
2. Place each fillet on a large piece of aluminium foil.
3. Drizzle olive oil and sprinkle minced garlic over the fillets.
4. Top each fillet with lemon slices and a few sprigs of dill.
5. Wrap the foil tightly around the salmon to create a sealed packet.
6. Place the packets into the slow cooker.
7. Cook on low heat for 2 hours or until the salmon is tender and flaky.
8. Serve the salmon on a bed of mixed salad greens.

Nutritional Facts (Per serving):

❖ Calories: 280
❖ Protein: 23 g
❖ Fat: 18 g (Saturated Fat: 3 g)
❖ Carbohydrates: 1 g
❖ Fiber: 0.5 g
❖ Sodium: 390 mg

This recipe ensures a succulent and healthy meal for a wholesome dinner.

35: Delicious Risotto ALLA PESCATORA

Risotto ALLA Pescara is a classic Italian seafood risotto, brimming with the flavours of the ocean.

Serves: 2

Prep Time: 15 min

Cook Time: 2 hrs

Ingredients:

- 1 cup Arborio rice
- 2 cups fish stock
- 1 cup white wine
- 1/2 lb mixed seafood (shrimp, scallops, squid rings)
- 1 small onion, finely chopped
- 2 cloves garlic, minced
- 1/2 cup diced tomatoes
- 1/4 cup fresh parsley, chopped

- 1/4 cup Parmesan cheese, grated
- 2 tbsp olive oil
- Salt and pepper to taste
- Lemon wedges for serving

Instructions:

1. In your slow cooker, heat olive oil and add onion and garlic, cooking until soft.
2. Add the Arborio rice, stirring to coat with oil. Pour in the white wine and allow it to absorb slightly before adding the fish stock.
3. Cover and cook on low for 1.5 hours, stirring occasionally.
4. Stir in the mixed seafood, diced tomatoes, and half of the parsley, and season with salt and pepper.
5. Continue cooking for another 30 minutes or until the seafood and the rice are tender.
6. Mix in the Parmesan cheese and the remaining parsley. Adjust seasoning if necessary.
7. Serve warm with lemon wedges on the side.

Nutritional Facts (Per serving):

- Calories: 560
- Protein: 35g
- Carbohydrates: 70g
- Fat: 16g
- Cholesterol: 120mg
- Sodium: 780mg

Enjoy this delightful, comforting dish that brings a taste of Italian seafood right to your table!

36: MOQUECA BAIANA

MOQUECA BAIANA is a vibrant Brazilian stew made with white fish, bell peppers, lime, tomatoes, and coconut milk. Its roots go back to Bahia.

Serves: 2

Prep Time: 15 min

Cook Time: 4 hrs on low

Ingredients:

- 2 white fish fillets (e.g., tilapia or cod), about 6 oz each
- 1 sweet bell pepper, sliced
- 1 small onion, thinly sliced
- 2 garlic cloves, minced
- 1 medium tomato, chopped
- 1/2 cup coconut milk
- 2 tbsp lime juice
- 2 tbsp olive oil

- ➢ 1/2 tsp paprika
- ➢ Salt and pepper to taste
- ➢ Fresh cilantro, chopped for garnish

Instructions:

1. Arrange the sliced onions, bell pepper, and garlic at the bottom of the slow cooker.
2. Season the fish fillets with salt, pepper, and paprika. Place them on top of the vegetables.
3. Sprinkle the chopped tomatoes evenly over the fish.
4. Mix coconut milk, lime juice, and olive oil in a bowl. Pour this mixture over the ingredients in the slow cooker.
5. Set the slow cooker to low and cook for about 4 hours until the fish is tender and flaky.
6. Garnish with chopped cilantro before serving.

Nutritional Facts (Per serving):

- ❖ Calories: 380
- ❖ Protein: 34g
- ❖ Carbohydrates: 15g
- ❖ Fat: 22g
- ❖ Saturated Fat: 12g
- ❖ Cholesterol: 85mg
- ❖ Sodium: 150mg
- ❖ Fiber: 3g

This simple and flavourful dish brings a taste of Brazilian cuisine right into your kitchen, perfect for a healthy and satisfying meal.

37: Spicy Curry with Shrimp

Curry, a blend of spices with roots in Indian cuisine, enhances dishes like this spicy shrimp creation.

Serves: 2

Prep Time: 15 mins

Cook Time: 4 hrs (Low)

Ingredients:

- 200g shrimp, peeled and deveined
- 1 onion, finely chopped
- 2 cloves garlic, minced
- 1 red bell pepper, sliced
- 2 tbsp curry powder
- 1 tsp red chili flakes
- 400ml coconut milk
- 1 tbsp tomato paste

- 200g diced tomatoes
- 1 tsp ginger, grated
- Salt to taste
- Fresh cilantro, chopped for garnish
- 1 lime, cut into wedges

Instructions:

1. Place the onion, garlic, bell pepper, curry powder, and chili flakes in the slow cooker and mix well.
2. Add the coconut milk, tomato paste, diced tomatoes, and ginger. Stir to combine all the ingredients.
3. Cover and cook on low for 3.5 hours.
4. Add the shrimp to the slow cooker, stir gently, and continue cooking for another 30 minutes until the shrimp are pink and cooked through.
5. Season with salt to taste.
6. Garnish with chopped cilantro and serve with lime wedges.

Nutritional Facts (Per serving):

- Calories: 400
- Protein: 25g
- Carbohydrates: 15g
- Fat: 25g
- Cholesterol: 180mg
- Sodium: 300mg

This slow-cooker shrimp curry has a spicy kick and deep flavours, perfect for a cozy meal for two.

38: Salmon Masala

Salmon masala is a delightful fusion of rich spices and tender salmon, tracing its roots to South Asian culinary traditions.

Serves: 2

Prep Time: 15 mins

Cook Time: 4 hrs

Ingredients:

- 2 salmon fillets (about 6 oz each), skin removed
- 1 tablespoon olive oil
- 1 large onion, finely chopped
- 2 garlic cloves, minced
- 1 tablespoon grated ginger
- 1 teaspoon turmeric
- 1 teaspoon garam masala
- 1 teaspoon ground coriander

- ➢ 1/2 teaspoon chili powder
- ➢ 1 can (14 oz) diced tomatoes
- ➢ 1 can (14 oz) coconut milk
- ➢ Salt to taste
- ➢ Fresh cilantro, chopped for garnish

Instructions:

1. Heat olive oil in a skillet over medium heat. Sauté onion, garlic, and ginger until the onion is translucent.
2. Add turmeric, garam masala, coriander, and chili powder; cook for about 1 minute until fragrant.
3. Transfer the spice mixture to a slow cooker. Add diced tomatoes and coconut milk, stirring to combine.
4. Season the salmon fillets with salt and nestle them into the sauce in the slow cooker.
5. Cover and cook on low for about 4 hours or until the salmon is cooked and flakes easily.
6. Garnish with chopped cilantro before serving.

Nutritional Facts (Per serving):

- ❖ Calories: 485
- ❖ Protein: 35g
- ❖ Fat: 34g (Saturated: 15g)
- ❖ Carbohydrates: 13g
- ❖ Fiber: 3g
- ❖ Sugar: 5g

This spiced salmon masala is flavourful and offers a healthy, satisfying meal perfect for a cozy dinner.

39: Seer Fish Curry

Seer Fish Curry is a flavourful dish from coastal India. It is made with succulent seer fish and aromatic spices simmered to perfection.

Serves: 2

Prep Time: 15 min

Cook Time: 4 hrs

Ingredients:

- 2 seer fish steaks
- 1 onion, finely chopped
- 2 tomatoes, pureed
- 4 cloves garlic, minced
- 1 inch ginger, grated
- 2 green chilies, slit
- 1 tsp turmeric powder
- 1 tsp cumin powder
- 1 tsp coriander powder
- ½ tsp black pepper, ground
- 1 tsp tamarind paste
- 1 cup coconut milk
- 2 tbsp coconut oil
- Salt to taste
- Fresh cilantro, chopped for garnish

Instructions:

1. Heat coconut oil in a skillet over medium heat. Sauté onion, garlic, ginger, and green chilies until the onions become translucent.
2. Add turmeric, cumin, coriander, and black pepper to the skillet, stirring for about a minute until aromatic.
3. Transfer the sautéed spices and vegetables into a slow cooker. Add the pureed tomatoes and tamarind paste and mix well.
4. Place the seer fish steaks on top of the spice and vegetable mixture in the slow cooker.
5. Pour coconut milk over the fish, ensuring the steaks are well-coated with the mixture.
6. Set the slow cooker on low and cook for approximately 4 hours.
7. Once cooked, adjust salt to taste and garnish with fresh cilantro before serving.

Nutritional Facts (Per serving):

- Calories: 350
- Protein: 25g
- Carbohydrates: 15g
- Fat: 22g
- Saturated Fat: 18g
- Cholesterol: 60mg
- Sodium: 150mg
- Fiber: 3g

This dish pairs beautifully with basmati rice or naan bread for a comforting meal.

40: Thai Curry Orange with Prawn

Thai curry orange with prawn and asparagus is a delightful slow cooker recipe that infuses the vibrant zest of oranges into traditional Thai cuisine. Originating from Thailand's rich culinary landscapes, this dish adapts beautifully to slow cooking, allowing the flavours to meld perfectly.

Serves: 2

Prep Time: 15 mins

Cook Time: 4 hrs on low

Ingredients:

- 200g prawns, peeled and deveined
- 1 bunch of asparagus, trimmed and cut into pieces
- 1 small orange, zest and juice
- 1 can (400 ml) coconut milk
- 2 tbsp Thai red curry paste
- 1 tbsp fish sauce
- 1 tsp sugar
- 1 red bell pepper, thinly sliced
- 1 small onion, sliced
- 2 garlic cloves, minced

- ➢ 1 tbsp ginger, grated
- ➢ Fresh basil leaves for garnish
- ➢ Salt, to taste

Instructions:

1. Place the onion, bell pepper, garlic, and ginger in the slow cooker and stir in the red curry paste.
2. Add the coconut milk, orange zest, orange juice, fish sauce, and sugar. Stir to combine thoroughly.
3. Cover and cook on low for 3 hours.
4. Add the prawns and asparagus to the slow cooker. Stir gently to mix them with the sauce.
5. Cover and cook for 1 hour or until the prawns are pink and fully cooked.
6. Taste and add salt, if needed.
7. Garnish with fresh basil leaves before serving.

Nutritional Facts (Per serving):

- ❖ Calories: 300
- ❖ Protein: 25g
- ❖ Carbohydrates: 20g
- ❖ Fat: 15g
- ❖ Fiber: 3g
- ❖ Sugar: 10g

This slow-cooked Thai curry orange with prawns and asparagus is not only flavourful but also nutritious and easy to prepare, perfect for a cozy dinner for two.

Chapter 5: Cozy Soups Together

41: Turkey Soup with Vegetables

Turkey soup with vegetables is a hearty, slow-cooked dish that originated as a way to use leftover turkey. It is often served during the colder months.

Serves: 2

Prep Time: 15 mins

Cook Time: 4 hrs

Ingredients:

- 2 cups cooked turkey, shredded
- 4 cups low-sodium chicken broth
- 1 cup carrots, diced
- 1 cup celery, diced
- 1/2 cup onions, chopped
- 2 garlic cloves, minced

- 1/2 tsp dried thyme
- 1/2 tsp dried rosemary
- Salt and pepper, to taste
- 1 bay leaf
- 1/2 cup frozen peas
- 1/4 cup fresh parsley, chopped

Instructions:

1. Place the shredded turkey, carrots, celery, onions, garlic, thyme, rosemary, salt, pepper, and bay leaf in the slow cooker.
2. Pour the chicken broth over the ingredients, fully submerging them.
3. Cover and cook on low for about 4 hours.
4. Thirty minutes before serving, remove the bay leaf and add the frozen peas.
5. Adjust seasoning if necessary and add the chopped parsley just before serving for freshness.

Nutritional Facts (Per serving):

- Calories: 300
- Protein: 28 g
- Fat: 12 g
- Carbohydrates: 18 g
- Fiber: 4 g
- Sodium: 450 mg

This nutritious turkey soup is perfect for a comforting meal, easy to prepare, and flavourful.

42: Slow Cooker Corned Beef and Cabbage Soup

Corned beef and cabbage soup is a hearty dish with Irish roots, combining salt-cured brisket with cabbage.

Serves: 2

Prep Time: 15 min

Cook Time: 8 hrs

Ingredients:

- 200g corned beef brisket, trimmed of fat and cubed
- 1/2 head of cabbage, chopped
- 1 large carrot, peeled and sliced
- 2 medium potatoes, peeled and cubed
- 1 onion, chopped
- 2 cloves garlic, minced
- 1 bay leaf

- 1/2 teaspoon dried thyme
- 1/2 teaspoon black pepper
- 4 cups beef broth
- 2 cups water
- Chopped parsley for garnish

Instructions:

1. Place the corned beef, cabbage, carrot, potatoes, onion, and garlic into the slow cooker.
2. Add the bay leaf, thyme, and black pepper.
3. Pour the beef broth and water, ensuring the ingredients are well covered.
4. Cover and set the slow cooker on low for 8 hours.
5. Once cooked, discard the bay leaf and adjust the seasoning if necessary.
6. Serve hot, garnished with chopped parsley.

Nutritional Facts (Per serving):

- Calories: 310
- Protein: 25g
- Carbohydrates: 33g
- Fat: 9g
- Sodium: 950mg
- Fiber: 6g

This soup offers a filling meal with all the traditional flavours of corned beef and cabbage in a simple, slow-cooked soup form.

43: Chicken Soup

Chicken soup, a comfort food staple, has roots in ancient cultures as a remedy and nourishing dish, often linked to healing.

Serves: 2

Prep Time: 15 min

Cook Time: 4 hrs

Ingredients:

- 2 large chicken breasts, skinless and boneless
- 4 cups chicken broth (low sodium)
- 1 medium onion, chopped
- 2 carrots, peeled and sliced
- 2 celery stalks, sliced
- 3 garlic cloves, minced
- 1/2 teaspoon dried thyme
- 1/2 teaspoon dried parsley

- Salt and pepper, to taste
- 1/2 cup whole wheat noodles

Instructions:

1. Place the chicken breasts at the bottom of the slow cooker.
2. Add the chopped onion, sliced carrots, celery, and minced garlic.
3. Pour the chicken broth and sprinkle with dried thyme, parsley, salt, and pepper.
4. Cover and cook on low for about four hours or until the chicken is tender and fully cooked.
5. Remove the chicken from the slow cooker, shred it using two forks, and return it to the pot.
6. Add the whole wheat noodles to the slow cooker, cover, and cook for 20 minutes or until tender.
7. Adjust seasoning with salt and pepper, if needed, before serving.

Nutritional Facts (Per serving):

- Calories: 295
- Protein: 28g
- Carbohydrates: 24g
- Fat: 8g
- Sodium: 410mg
- Fiber: 3g

This wholesome slow-cooker chicken soup is easy to prepare and offers a comforting meal that warms the soul and body.

44: Norwegian Soup with Cream and Salmon

A delightful blend of fresh salmon and cream, this Norwegian soup captures the essence of Norway's culinary heritage, using the abundant local seafood.

Serves: 2

Prep Time: 15 mins

Cook Time: 4 hrs

Ingredients:

- 200g fresh salmon fillet, skin removed and cubed
- 1 cup heavy cream
- 2 cups fish or vegetable stock
- 1 leek, thinly sliced
- 1 carrot, diced
- 1 celery stalk, diced
- 2 potatoes, peeled and cubed
- 1 tsp dried dill

- ➢ Salt and pepper to taste
- ➢ Fresh dill for garnish

Instructions:

1. Place the salmon, leek, carrot, celery, potatoes, and dried dill in the slow cooker.
2. Pour in the stock, ensuring that the ingredients are fully submerged.
3. Cover and cook on low for 3.5 hours.
4. Stir in the heavy cream and season with salt and pepper.
5. Cover and cook for 30 minutes on low or until everything is tender.
6. Ladle the soup into bowls and garnish with fresh dill.

Nutritional Facts (Per serving):

- ❖ Calories: 480
- ❖ Protein: 25g
- ❖ Carbohydrates: 38g
- ❖ Fat: 28g
- ❖ Cholesterol: 130mg
- ❖ Sodium: 710mg

Enjoy the rich and comforting flavours of this slow-cooked Norwegian salmon soup, perfect for a cozy meal.

45: Chickpea Soup with Pumpkin

Chickpea soup with pumpkin and spinach blends hearty legumes and vibrant vegetables. It originates from Mediterranean roots and is adaptable to slow cooker methods for ease and flavour.

Serves: 2

Prep Time: 10 min

Cook Time: 4 hrs

Ingredients:

- 1 cup dried chickpeas, soaked overnight
- 2 cups pumpkin, peeled and cubed
- 1 cup fresh spinach, roughly chopped
- 1 onion, finely chopped
- 2 cloves garlic, minced
- 1 teaspoon ground cumin
- 1/2 teaspoon ground coriander

- ➢ 1/4 teaspoon ground turmeric
- ➢ 4 cups vegetable broth
- ➢ Salt and pepper, to taste
- ➢ Fresh coriander, for garnish
- ➢ 1 tablespoon olive oil (for sautéing)

Instructions:

1. Drain and rinse the soaked chickpeas.
2. Heat the olive oil in a skillet over medium heat. Sauté the onion and garlic until translucent.
3. Transfer the sautéed onion and garlic to the slow cooker.
4. Add the soaked chickpeas, cubed pumpkin, spices, and vegetable broth to the slow cooker.
5. Set the slow cooker to low and cook for 4 hours.
6. Add the chopped spinach in the last 30 minutes of cooking.
7. Season with salt and pepper to taste.
8. Serve hot, garnished with fresh coriander.

Nutritional Facts (Per serving):

- ❖ Calories: 295
- ❖ Carbohydrates: 47 g
- ❖ Protein: 14 g
- ❖ Fiber: 13 g
- ❖ Fat: 7 g
- ❖ Sugar: 9 g

This delicious soup is a nourishing and complete meal, perfect for chilly evenings or as a wholesome lunch option.

46: Indonesian Chicken Soup

Soto is a flavourful Indonesian chicken soup rooted in traditional Indonesian cuisine. It is accented with hard-boiled eggs, tomatoes, bean sprouts, lemon, and cayenne pepper.

Serves: 2

Prep Time: 15 min

Cook Time: 6 hrs (Slow Cooker)

Ingredients:

- 2 chicken breasts, skinless and boneless
- 4 cups chicken stock
- 2 hard-boiled eggs, peeled and halved
- 1 large tomato, chopped
- 1 cup bean sprouts
- 1 lemon, quartered
- 1/2 teaspoon cayenne pepper

- ➢ 2 garlic cloves, minced
- ➢ 1 small onion, thinly sliced
- ➢ 2 teaspoons turmeric powder
- ➢ 2 tablespoons soy sauce
- ➢ Salt to taste
- ➢ Fresh cilantro, chopped (for garnish)

Instructions:

1. Place the chicken breasts in the slow cooker.
2. Add chicken stock, garlic, onion, turmeric, soy sauce, and a pinch of salt.
3. Cook on low for 6 hours.
4. After 6 hours, remove the chicken, shred it, and return it to the slow cooker.
5. Add the chopped tomato, bean sprouts, and cayenne pepper to the slow cooker. Stir well and cook on high for an additional 15 minutes.
6. Serve the soup in bowls, topped with two halves of a hard-boiled egg, lemon quarters, and fresh cilantro.

Nutritional Facts (Per serving):

- ❖ Calories: 290
- ❖ Protein: 36g
- ❖ Fat: 8g
- ❖ Carbohydrates: 18g
- ❖ Fiber: 3g
- ❖ Sugar: 5g

This slow cooker version of Soto ensures a deeply infused flavour, making it a comforting and hearty dish.

47: Slow Cooker Vegetable and Beans Soup

A slow cooker vegetable and bean soup is a hearty dish blending various vegetables and beans simmered to perfection. It originated from the need for a nutritious meal with minimal preparation and is a staple for busy or chilly days.

Serves: 2

Prep Time: 10 min

Cook Time: 6 hrs

Ingredients:

- 1 carrot, peeled and diced
- 2 celery stalks, diced
- 1 small onion, chopped
- 2 garlic cloves, minced
- 1 cup diced tomatoes
- 1 cup cauliflower
- 1/2 cup green beans, trimmed and cut into 1-inch pieces

- 1/2 cup kidney beans, drained and rinsed
- 1/2 cup chickpeas, drained and rinsed
- 4 cups vegetable broth
- 1 teaspoon dried thyme
- 1 teaspoon dried basil
- Salt and pepper to taste

Instructions:

1. Place all chopped vegetables, beans, and garlic into the slow cooker.
2. Add the diced tomatoes, vegetable broth, thyme, and basil.
3. Stir to mix all ingredients well.
4. Set the slow cooker to low and cook for 6 hours.
5. Season with salt and pepper according to taste.
6. Serve hot, garnished with fresh herbs if desired.

Nutritional Facts (Per serving):

- Calories: 210
- Protein: 12g
- Carbohydrates: 39g
- Fat: 2g
- Fiber: 11g
- Sodium: 300mg

This simple and nutritious soup is perfect for a cozy dinner or a healthy lunch, offering warmth and wellness in every spoonful.

48: Creamy Garlic Carrot Mushroom

Creamy garlic carrot mushroom pasta sauce blends traditional flavours into a modern dish, drawing from European techniques to enrich pasta with vegetables and herbs.

Serves: 2

Prep Time: 10 min

Cook Time: 3 hrs (Slow Cooker)

Ingredients:

- 1 cup carrots, diced
- 1 cup mushrooms, sliced
- 4 cloves garlic, minced
- 1 cup heavy cream
- 1/2 cup vegetable broth
- 1/4 cup grated Parmesan cheese
- 1 tablespoon olive oil

- ➢ 1 teaspoon dried thyme
- ➢ Salt and pepper to taste

Instructions:

1. Place the carrots, mushrooms, and garlic into the slow cooker.
2. Pour the heavy cream and vegetable broth, ensuring the vegetables are well-covered.
3. Stir in olive oil, thyme, salt, and pepper.
4. Cover and cook on low for 3 hours.
5. Once the vegetables are tender, blend the mixture until smooth using an immersion blender.
6. Stir in the grated Parmesan cheese until melted and well incorporated.
7. Serve over your choice of cooked pasta.

Nutritional Facts (Per serving):

- ❖ Calories: 485
- ❖ Total Fat: 42g
- ❖ Saturated Fat: 25g
- ❖ Cholesterol: 137mg
- ❖ Sodium: 390mg
- ❖ Total Carbohydrates: 17g
- ❖ Dietary Fiber: 3g
- ❖ Sugars: 8g
- ❖ Protein: 10g

This rich and flavourful sauce is perfect for a cozy dinner. It provides a hearty and nutritious meal that's easy to prepare in your slow cooker.

49: CALDO de Gallina Chicken Noodle Soup

CALDO de Gallina is a comforting South American chicken noodle soup from Peru. It is often enriched with a boiled egg and fresh herbs.

Serves: 2

Prep Time: 15 mins

Cook Time: 4 hrs (Slow Cooker on Low)

Ingredients:

- 1 large chicken breast, boneless and skinless
- 4 cups chicken broth
- 1 medium onion, chopped
- 2 cloves garlic, minced
- 2 medium carrots, sliced
- 1 stalk celery, sliced
- 1/2 teaspoon cumin
- Salt and pepper to taste

- 100g egg noodles
- 2 eggs, hard-boiled
- 2 tablespoons fresh cilantro, chopped
- 1 tablespoon fresh parsley, chopped

Instructions:

1. Place the chicken breast in the slow cooker.
2. Add the chicken broth, onion, garlic, carrots, celery, cumin, salt, and pepper.
3. Cover and cook on low for about 4 hours or until the chicken is tender and fully cooked.
4. About 30 minutes before serving, remove the chicken breast, shred it with two forks, and return it to the slow cooker.
5. Add the egg noodles to the slow cooker, cover, and cook for 20 minutes or until tender.
6. Adjust seasoning if necessary.
7. Ladle the soup into bowls, ensuring each serving gets equal noodles and vegetables.
8. Top each serving with a hard-boiled egg and sprinkle with chopped cilantro and parsley.

Nutritional Facts (Per serving):

- Calories: 330
- Protein: 28g
- Carbohydrates: 32g
- Fat: 10g
- Sodium: 820mg
- Fiber: 3g

This recipe offers a wholesome and nourishing meal that is simple to prepare and full of flavour, embodying the spirit of South American home cooking.

50: Minestrone Soup

Minestrone is a hearty Italian staple that combines vegetables, pasta, and broth. It has evolved from a simple peasant dish to a beloved global classic.

Serves: 2

Prep Time: 15 mins

Cook Time: 6 hrs (slow cooker on low)

Ingredients:

- 1 carrot, diced
- 1 celery stalk, diced
- 1 small onion, chopped
- 2 cloves garlic, minced
- 400g can diced tomatoes
- 400g can kidney beans, rinsed and drained
- 500ml vegetable broth
- 1 tsp dried basil

- 1 tsp dried oregano
- 50g small pasta shapes
- 1 small zucchini, diced
- Salt and pepper, to taste
- Fresh parsley, chopped (for garnish)
- Grated Parmesan cheese (optional for serving)

Instructions:

1. Place the carrot, celery, onion, and garlic into the slow cooker.
2. Add the canned tomatoes, kidney beans, and vegetable broth.
3. Stir in the basil and oregano.
4. Cover and cook on low for 5 hours.
5. Add the pasta and zucchini to the slow cooker. Stir well.
6. Continue cooking for another 1 hour or until the pasta is tender.
7. Season with salt and pepper. Serve hot, garnished with fresh parsley and grated Parmesan cheese if desired.

Nutritional Facts (Per serving):

- Calories: 330
- Protein: 16g
- Carbohydrates: 60g
- Fat: 3g
- Fiber: 12g
- Sodium: 690mg

This slow cooker minestrone is perfect for a nourishing, effortless meal brimming with flavour and healthy ingredients.

Conclusion

Congratulations on completing your journey through the *Easy Slow Cooker Recipes Cookbook for Two: Effortless & Delicious Meals Perfect for Couples with Pictures*! By now, you've discovered how simple and rewarding it can be to create flavorful, wholesome meals for two using your slow cooker. Whether you've tried a comforting stew, a zesty pasta dish, or a sweet treat, I hope these recipes have brought joy to your kitchen and made mealtime a little easier.

Cooking together is more than just preparing food, it's an opportunity to connect, share, and create lasting memories. With your slow cook as your trusted companion, you've unlocked the secret to effortless cooking that fits seamlessly into your busy lives. No more stressing over-complicated recipes or spending hours in the kitchen. Instead, you can focus on what truly matters: enjoying delicious meals and each other's company.

As you explore new recipes and make them your own, remember that cooking is as much about the process as it is about the result. Don't be afraid to experiment, swap ingredients, or adjust flavors to suit your tastes. The beauty of these recipes lies in their versatility and simplicity, making them perfect for any occasion.

Thank you for allowing this cookbook to be a part of your culinary adventures. It has inspired you to try new dishes, share more meals, and embrace the joy of slow cooking. Here's to many more delicious moments and the love that brings you together around the table.

Happy cooking, and may your slow cooker always be filled with warmth and flavor!

Made in the USA
Monee, IL
17 April 2025